Rendezvous at Kamakura Inn

Also by Marshall Browne

The Eye of the Abyss
Inspector Anders and the Ship of Fools
The Wooden Leg of Inspector Anders

Rendezvous
at Kamakura Inn

MARSHALL BROWNE

Thomas Dunne Books
St. Martin's Minotaur ✖ *New York*

THOMAS DUNNE BOOKS.
An imprint of St. Martin's Press.

www.minotaurbooks.com

Library of Congress Cataloging-in-Publication Data

Browne, Marshall.
    Rendezvous at Kamakura Inn / Marshall Browne.— 1st ed.
        p. cm.
    ISBN 0-312-31158-3
    EAN 978-0-312-31158-2
    1. Police—Japan—Fiction. 2. Missing persons—Fiction. 3. Resorts—
Fiction. 4. Storms—Fiction. 5. Japan—Fiction. I. Title.

PR9619.3.B7594R46 2005
823'.914—dc22

                                                                2005049382

First Edition: November 2005

10 9 8 7 6 5 4 3 2 1

For Merell, beloved wife, friend

If you meet a Buddha, kill him.
If you meet a patriarch of the law, kill him.

—ZEN MOTTO

Rendezvous at Kamakura Inn

Chapter One

AOKI'S BRAIN REGISTERED THE MUZZLE *flash as the bullet went* bzzzz *past his head. His pistol was thrust forward two-handed as he fired a fast bracket at where he'd seen the flash. Ten yards into the alley a figure detached itself from the darkness and Aoki fired again. The figure toppled backward and thumped on concrete. Aoki, breathing hard, sweat drenching his armpits, edged forward. Saburi, weapon extended, moved past him and the prone figure, going deeper into the alley.*

Nothing more. No one else. Only the muffled sound of traffic, the rattling of air conditioners, and water spitting down. In Aoki's flashlight the wide-open eyes of the dead yakuza shone like glass buttons.

Today, gazing down into the street from his window at the incoming tide of salarymen and women, the flashback from two years ago had come as a momentary distraction to Aoki. In the here and now his stomach was queasy, as if he'd had a meal of bad food. He sucked softly at his lower lip.

The terse brevity of Superintendent Watanabe, when he'd reported to him on the interoffice phone five minutes ago, had been a wake-up call, but more than that, it was the general atmosphere he was taking in. After twenty years in the Tokyo police, the beeping of the excrement detector in his brain was a definite warning that shit was coming down the freeway.

Turning away from the window he told himself, "Overnight, something's changed." At 10:00 P.M. everything seemed on schedule.

Aoki was a man of medium height, broad-shouldered, with a wide, dark-complexioned face that had a prominent mole on its left cheek. He stood in his glass cubicle and, eyes narrowed, watched the seven detectives of his team emerge from the elevator. Initially there'd been ten, but three had cracked under the strain and departed. Assistant Inspectors Nishi and Sagamoto, who were to accompany him and the superintendent to the director general's office at 8:15 A.M., led the way, each with an armful of files.

It was just after 8:00 A.M. on a Thursday in August. In the modern air-conditioned building that housed several divisions of the Tokyo Metropolitan Police Department's Criminal Investigation Bureau, computer screens were flashing on, and phones beginning to ring.

Aoki lit a cigarette and stared through the glass at his men assembling outside his door. He looked solid, seasoned, and tough, and all of that was true.

Just possibly, his imagination was acting up, though he wasn't strong on imagination. He muttered, "We'll just go in and do it." He butted the cigarette in an ashtray, turned, put on his suit coat, and stepped outside.

The waiting detectives bowed as one, and he gave a perfunctory response. Their eyes were on his face. Two years before, he'd broken a big insurance fraud case that had hit the headlines, and three big-time businessmen, despite the intervention of local politicians, had gone to prison. Relentlessly, Aoki had flushed them out from behind a complex corporate structure, together with the crooked appraiser who inflated the building's valuation before they set it alight. The same year, Aoki had taken over a stalled double-murder investigation in Shinjuku, unearthing a new set of witnesses and solving the case. His team members might sometimes curse him behind his back, but they respected his record, as did his superiors.

Now, possibly, this major case was about to break, bringing them all promotions.

"Okay, let's go," he said to Nishi and Sagamoto.

"Good luck, Aoki-san," Sergeant Saburi said, with a thumbs-up. They took the elevator to the top floor.

Superintendent Watanabe was waiting in the director general's anteroom, his thin lips skeptical, wearing one of his yellow silk ties. He was an ambivalent supporter of the case, as Aoki'd known for a long time, though Watanabe's agenda was always hard to precisely determine.

Something *was* wrong. Aoki knew that as soon as the female secretary, all bows, ushered them in. The only person in the room was Director General Omori, and he was standing, his hands locked behind him, gazing at a wall map of the central business district. Every other time Aoki had entered this room the DG had been seated at his desk, and he'd reported here the last Friday of each of the past seventeen months, to brief the CIB chief.

The director general was a sawn-off heap of muscle, thick-necked, with a bull-like torso and a sparse hatch of spiky hair. His face was molded by impatience and pressure, as were his movements, but this morning, gazing at the map, he was as inert as a squat stone statue.

The long conference table wasn't set up for a meeting, and the district prosecutor and his aides weren't there. Aoki took this in.

In unison, the four detectives bowed to the DG's back, and the secretary withdrew, closing the door. Watanabe cleared his throat, the DG turned around, and right then, Aoki knew what was coming.

Omori nodded at Superintendent Watanabe, then peered at Aoki. "The case won't be proceeding," he growled. "There's to be no prosecution. The decision's come down from the top. The investigation's to be closed off, the work records sealed." He took a step forward, and peered harder at Aoki's face. "This is bad news for you, after all your good work."

Aoki watched the DG's lips move, heard the words spoken in the harsh, irritated voice, and his brain was analyzing them—yet was it someone else's brain?

Omori said, "Do you understand? There's nothing more to be done. There'll be no discussion. *That* man is now off-limits."

In the silence, Aoki heard the distant hum of the traffic below. "Yes, Director General," the superintendent said for the silent Aoki. "That is understood, by everyone."

"Very well." The DG had eyes only for Aoki.

Aoki's mind was in a turmoil now, but his face was blank. Overnight, it appeared, even the ex-governor's *name* had become unmentionable; it was the fact his brain had seized on to be amazed at. He'd had so much to say, so much careful and watertight evidence to present. He felt his face begin to redden.

Abruptly, restored to full energy, the DG turned his back on his officers and headed for his desk. They bowed and filed out.

In the anteroom, Watanabe took Aoki aside. "Politicians give and they take away. That's the world you and I live in, Inspector." His all-seeing, cynical eyes studied Aoki. "You and your team will receive new assignments tomorrow. Today, there'll be some cleaning up to do."

That was the moment when Aoki realized that this was no surprise to the superintendent.

In the elevator, Watanabe said into Aoki's ear, "At least you'll get your life back."

In his glass cubicle, his team standing in a half-circle, Aoki told them precisely what had been said, nothing less, nothing more. He absorbed the shock on the younger cops' faces. Sergeant Saburi was red-faced and squinting. Aoki knew almost nothing about his team's private lives, but he did know the case had cost Saburi his marriage. Assistant Inspectors Nishi and Sagamoto, who were about Aoki's age, had not spoken a word since leaving the DG's office.

Through the glass wall he could see that five men in plain clothes had arrived. Two of them he recognized: senior officers from the internal affairs unit. They were wheeling a cart piled with flattened cardboard boxes.

At 2:30 P.M. Aoki led the team out of the building, across the road, and into a narrow Ginza street lined with bars and overhung with racketing air conditioners. The air felt heavy and liquid. Even at this hour, rock music beat bruises on the brain. Aoki's wet brow was deep set in a frown. *Where does this leave me? Where in the fuck does it leave me?* He pushed through the entrance of a bar and ordered beer for all.

His men drank in silence, some of them glancing at the inspector. Among themselves, they'd nicknamed him De Niro after the American film actor he resembled, especially because of the mole. Gradually the shock loosened its grip as they drank the beer. They'd all had to hand in their notebooks and computer disks on the case and, supervised by the internal affairs officers, clean the files from their computers. All of them, in varying degrees, had found it a demeaning experience.

Slamming his pile of notebooks into one of the boxes, Aoki had felt deeply dishonored. The internal affairs inspector had shot him a look, but Aoki had tightened his lips and kept silent: His men were all taking their cue from him.

He fumbled for a cigarette and lit up. The internal affairs men had been impersonal, but Aoki had seen the senior man observing him closely, doubtless under instructions. He'd have to watch himself. Already, in walking out with his team like this, he'd made a wrong move.

His ex-team. He'd driven them hard: fourteen-hour days, six-day weeks, no vacation for seventeen months, each guy sworn to secrecy. It was a wonder the casualty rate hadn't been higher. Occasionally, usually after a breakthrough, he'd taken them out for beer, his only concession to a note of relaxation.

They were drinking Kirin. Assistant Inspector Nishi, who had a cousin who was an executive with the brewer, drank that beer out of family solidarity and encouraged colleagues to follow suit. All of them were smoking.

Chin in hand, Aoki gazed at a huge colored photograph of Mount Fuji on the bar's wall. The great snow-capped dome gleamed against an azure sky, captured on one of the few days in the year when smog and the weather permitted it to reveal itself in its full glory. Mostly its presence was as elusive as the shape of the case they'd been working on.

Aoki took a sudden long pull at his beer. The case was etched on his brain like a steel engraving, from the first day till this one: corruption, and other crimes, at top level in the government; specifically, ex-governor Yukio Tamaki, known in the ruling party's circles, even nationwide, as the Fatman. The case had been assigned to Aoki in extraordinary secrecy, with a personal briefing by the director general, Superintendent Watanabe, at his most enigmatic, sitting in.

That ex-governor Tamaki had connections to the yakuza had been no surprise to Aoki. Cynical gossip had enfolded the man over a long political career; every post he'd held—in his prefecture, in the national government, on parliamentary committees—had been a pipeline for the gangsters. Massive apartment developments that had bypassed planning rules were nicknamed Fatman's Towers, or Gardens, or some such. Even a large bridge that had only been necessary in the eyes of the developers and certain officials was unofficially named for him. The yakuza had been deep in these projects.

Aoki glanced along the bar. Sergeant Saburi appeared to be in a daze. Poor bastard. Aoki stubbed out his cigarette and stuck a fresh one in his lips.

The only surprise was that politicians in Tamaki's own party, albeit from a different faction, had decided to destroy him. Naturally, this wasn't mentioned at the briefing, but it had soon become clear enough. Aoki had handpicked his ten detectives, and they'd begun to identify committees Tamaki had been on and suspicious projects in the wide spectrum of the ex-governor's affairs. Then they'd gone after witnesses. For a man with so many enemies, the Fatman was careless in protecting his back. Painstakingly, they'd assembled the evidence, persuading a dozen witnesses to testify.

In this, Aoki had been as forceful as he needed to be. Using blackmail and intimidation didn't worry him, and he cut corners where he judged he could get away with it. His attitude: The ends justified the means. It was *all* knife-edge stuff anyway. Of those in his team who'd fallen by the wayside, one had developed an ulcer, another'd had a nervous breakdown, and the third had resigned from the force.

"Do it all as softly as a spring breeze in bamboo," the director general had said. "Keep it quiet, keep it low-key, for now."

Some hope! They were forbidden to interview Tamaki; his factional opponents didn't want the Fatman forewarned of his impending fall. But Aoki had never fooled himself that word wouldn't soon wing back to the politician, who had eyes and ears planted in the nation's interlocking political and business structures. People who owed him.

Doubtless, he'd found out. When he'd sprung into the spotlight again as an alternative prime minister, the opposing faction had decided to back off. Sitting in the lazy afternoon, in the dim coolness of this bar, Aoki read it that way. Seventeen months! He stared again through the cigarette smoke at Mount Fuji. The Fatman! It was said that he gloried in that name, and he'd slipped through yet another net.

Deeply dishonored. Aoki turned his eyes to the survivors.

The younger guys, even Sagamoto, were getting boisterous. Assistant Inspector Nishi, silent, stared into space. Saburi played with his glass. It was 5:00 P.M., and he should send them home. Tomorrow, he'd have Watanabe on his back about this. Departmental discipline and the strictly hierarchical nature of the Tokyo Metropolitan Police didn't countenance such actions; the walkout and the drinking session would be taken as an act of dissent, though he guessed his yellow-tied boss would try to keep it quiet. He wouldn't want the undermining of his authority publicized.

A patrolman from the nearby police kiosk put his head in the door, attracted by the unusual volume of noise at this hour. Two of the detectives fumbled out ID, and he nodded companionably and went on his way.

Time to go. Aoki's wife and father would be startled by his return home at this early hour—unprecedented.

"Is it really all over?" Nishi muttered the question out of the corner of his mouth as they left.

Aoki gave him a terse nod. "We took too long. The climate's changed."

Smelling ripe with beer, they bowed to him. Tomorrow they'd be far-flung on new assignments.

Inspector Aoki didn't go home. A little drunk, but not showing it, he took the subway to Roppongi. From Roppongi station he walked ten minutes to the building where Tamaki had his apartment. Moisture from air conditioners flicked onto his head. The city and its citizens were suffering and enduring. "Everyone dies a little faster in a Tokyo summer"—his father's words. Down a stairway leading to a jazz club, a band was warming up, and Aoki turned toward the sound, but tonight it just didn't mean a thing.

The building was a prestigious high-rise, with expensive potted plants in the lobby and a uniformed doorman. The adjoining narrow streets were jam-packed with bars, restaurants, and human commotion. Soaked with perspiration, Aoki gazed up at the fourth-floor windows. How many times had he, or his men, watched this apartment, recording the comings and goings? The windows were dark. Tamaki was out and about, reveling in his multifarious activities and connections, scheming to get his fat ass into the prime minister's chair; scheming in a hundred fucking directions.

Aoki had penetrated the murky channels of much of the Fatman's world, but there was a lot more they hadn't uncovered. Now a steel door had crashed down, and here he was, saying good-bye to it, like a mourner at a funeral. This was going to take some getting used to.

Aoki took the train back to Central and walked through to the platform for Kamakura. The homeward commute was at its most virulent, and he had to stand for most of the one-hour journey. A wind of hot air hit Aoki in the face when the doors opened to disgorge people. He ignored the red-faced salarymen, coats slung over their arms. The bare-armed women looked cooler. He gazed at them, thinking that his wife, Tokie, had pressed his best suit for him last night—for the big day.

At Kamakura, Aoki entered a bar and ordered a bottle of Heineken. He sat down, drank, ate nuts. The air-conditioning froze the perspiration on his body; he ordered a second bottle. For sure, shit had been coming down the freeway, and it'd buried him.

At seven o'clock he got himself up and went home. He was less steady on his feet now, and both men and women walked around him in the street.

Aoki and his wife lived with his widowed father on the ground floor of a small building on one of Kamakura's many low hills, near a temple. A grove of slender bamboo stood beside the path that led to his door; tonight it was dead still, no breeze from the sea. A few electrified ground lanterns lit the way.

Aoki couldn't find his door key. Trying to locate it, he knocked over a couple of small bonsai in pots Tokie had on a ledge beside the door, and swore. In the end, he leaned against the doorjamb and rang the bell.

Tokie's eyes widened as she took in his condition. Behind her, his father, his face alert, held a newspaper. On this day to forget, though Aoki never would, these were the last images that the inspector's brain registered.

Chapter Two

SUPERINTENDENT WATANABE HAD ON AN orange tie. Aoki had read somewhere that men who wore yellow ties couldn't be trusted, so what did a change to orange mean? Watanabe hissed through his teeth. He hadn't brought up the obvious dissenting body language Aoki had used with the internal affairs cops, the walkout, or the half-day's sojourn at the bar. Instead, he'd let a long silence and a hard stare do the job.

Now he ceased his hissing and tapped on the desktop with his fingernails. "Here is your new assignment," he said.

Aoki was assigned to a homicide case being run by an inspector whom he knew slightly.

On the third floor the desks of his former team were unoccupied; his men had been scattered far and wide to other divisions and offices across Tokyo. For the moment Aoki kept his cubicle, but he spent much of the day in another being briefed by his new colleague and reading up on his new assignment: the murder of a moneylender by a businessman. He'd been slotted back into a case about as routine as they came.

The inspector running the case, Natsumi, looked at Aoki with a certain sympathy. Over seventeen months, it would've taken a miracle to keep the existence of the Fatman investigation totally under wraps. Of course, stuff had leaked out, and yesterday's disbanding of the team had been a crystal-clear message to inside observers.

Throughout the day Aoki was on automatic pilot, going through the motions, doing it by memory—all the defensive clichés of the experienced detective who'd been terminated from a case that he'd been deeply committed to. Hazily, he'd remembered his wife, assisted by his father, showering him and putting him to bed last night; their quiet, speculative voices as he'd finally faded out. He'd left without breakfast. His father had already gone out on his early morning walk, and Tokie said nothing about his drunken homecoming; naturally, they knew something had happened.

After going off duty, Aokie went to the same bar in the Ginza and gazed again at Mount Fuji. In the early days of his marriage, he'd told Tokie that one day they'd climb the mountain together, to see the sunrise. Somehow, the hope and intimacy of those days had slipped through Aoki's fingers.

There was no one in the bar he recognized. He curtly dismissed a hostess who offered her company, then sat on a barstool, drank beer, and smoked, surrounded by noise and vivacity that, for him, could've been on another planet.

It hit him like a spasm of pain. *He had lost his face.* After the seventeen months of massive effort, of driving his men to, and beyond, their limits, the case's abandonment had made him look ridiculous—in his eyes, at least. Kicks in the face from the system came with the job, but he'd never had to deal with anything like this.

Did the Fatman know what a narrow escape he'd had? He *would* know—though did "narrow escape" accurately describe the situation? Aoki's face muscles felt as tight as braided steel. He'd become so immersed in the case that he'd forgotten its sponsors were a breed who always kept their options open.

He shook his shoulders, stubbed out the cigarette, and looked at his watch. Tokie and his father would be sitting down to dinner, a meal he was rarely home for. His wife prepared delicious meals: simple, refined, and traditional, much appreciated by his father, who valued all things traditional. Ten years ago the old man, an associate professor of literature at Tokyo University, had retired. These days he lived his life by a kind of cultural calendar. Right now, it was the Kabuki theater season, and tonight he and Tokie had tickets for a play.

Aoki never accompanied them. It wasn't to his taste, and he didn't have the time, nor was it his world. He had gone straight from college into the metropolitan police and, in due course, had been stamped out of its mold. Clearly he didn't take after his father—more after his earthy, pragmatic mother. Three years since she'd died. The last month she'd been in a nursing home, and every night he could get off, Aoki went out to spoon-feed the old lady mushed-up delicacies from Tokie, the tiny amount of food his mother wanted. In the lengthy periods between spoonfuls, she told him things about her rice-farmer parents, whom he'd never known, talking softly, laughing quietly at the memories of the long-ago, lost life, wanting him to know them. On the other side of the bed his father sat in silence, already grieving. Yet in forty-two years of marriage, in Aoki's experience, the two had never seemed to communicate except on day-to-day household matters. She died leaning forward to take a spoonful of soup from Aoki.

Tokie's father, a classmate of the senior Aoki, had also been a professor—of arts, at Kyoto University. Tokie had been a high school art teacher. The two old professors got together, a match was made, and Aoki, at age thirty, and Tokie, at twenty-five, were married. Each of them had been amenable to it. Several years later it had occurred to Aoki that his father had been choosing a daughter-in-law as much as a wife for his son. Tokie's father had died five years ago.

Aoki squinted his eyes against the drifting cigarette smoke in the bar. He hadn't had time to think about his marriage in the past seventeen months.

Would his wife and father go to the Kabuki tonight? In view of his unexplained behavior last night, they might not. He hoped they would.

At nine o'clock he took the train to Kamakura. A young man sitting opposite caught his eye and bowed in his seat. "Aoki-san," he said.

The inspector looked at him blankly, then recognized the young fellow, who had hair down to his shoulders. Two years ago, he'd been in a karate class that Aoki and one of his colleagues had given at a club for youngsters from poor families. "Shimazu-san?" The young man nodded. "How's it going?"

The young man stood up to get out at the next station. "I've got my black belt, thanks to you."

"Congratulations."

The young man bowed low and left the train.

At Kamakura, taking his jacket off, Aoki walked home. Compared to the previous night, he was sober. The bonsai trees had been set back in place. Tokie must've just watered them, and the velvety moss around the miniature roots was damp, the tiny foliage sprinkled with moisture. One was missing. Killed in action.

His family wasn't home. He took a shower, then sat in the kitchen, an icy can of beer in hand, remembering the midmorning call from Assistant Inspector Nishi, who was also having difficulty letting the case go. Aoki couldn't offer Nishi any consolation.

Tokie had left him a meal on the usual shelf in the fridge, but he ignored it and took out another can of beer.

Soon Aoki went to bed and fell into a deep sleep, the air conditioner humming in his ears. In his dream, the case files were before him, and he was looking at them, one by one, each a documented brief for the district prosecutor. The Fatman was standing in the bedroom, watching him; then the ex-governor turned and walked out, his broad back shaking with silent laughter.

Aoki jerked awake and listened to Tokie's quiet breathing beside him. Home from Kabuki.

The next day Aoki and a sergeant, nearly sixty and close to retirement, went by train to Yokohama to talk to a witness and take a statement in the moneylender case. The witness lived in an old part of town, and they called at the local police kiosk to pick up a uniformed officer to guide them to the address.

Two more days went past. Aoki was now working regular shifts: from 8:30 A.M. to 5:15 P.M. the first shift day, then a twenty-four shift from 8:30 A.M. to 8:30 A.M. the following morning, followed by a day off. Still, he continued to come home at erratic hours. He didn't see Superintendent Watanabe.

Each night that week his father and Tokie went to another play with their prebooked tickets. On Thursday morning Tokie said, faint hope in her voice, "Won't you come with us tonight, Hideo? Probably we can buy an extra ticket."

"Yes, please do," his father added.

Aoki shook his head.

On Friday night, he and Tokie made love for the first time in a month. Friday night was their usual night for lovemaking, but he hadn't been home the previous three. By tacit agreement, on Friday nights, his father usually went to a nearby hall to play Go, coming home at 11:00 P.M. His delicacy and the thin walls of the small flat made it a convenient arrangement.

Afterward, lying there in the dark, Aoki spoke at last. "The case is over. The high-ups have decided it's not to go ahead." His voice was flat. His wife put her hand on his arm but didn't ask this taciturn husband why. She had ten years' experience at the edge of his world, and of him, but he knew that she'd think about it, and probably discuss it with his father.

On Saturday he had a day off and read the newspaper, feeling restless and unemployed.

Ah. He turned a page and there was a big picture of Tamaki, smiling benignly at the public. The article said that the ruling party's power broker had reemerged as a candidate for the prime ministership, with the new support of several factions. Grimly, Aoki stared at the photograph. Yeah, the Fatman had played an unexpected card, upstaged the faction that had been gunning for him. Not an avid newspaper reader, Aoki read every word of the article. "Fatman" was not used once by the journalist in the piece. Nor was there a hint of the case against him having been dropped, which was quite understandable, as there'd been nothing in the press about a case in the first place.

Laying the paper down, Aoki saw that his father was watching him over the top of his own paper. "I've read that article," the old man said. His father was a gentleman of the old school, and the comment was the maximum extent of his intrusion into his son's affairs, but the way he said things gave them a wealth of meaning. Clearly Tokie had told him what had happened.

That afternoon, Aoki, dressed in casual clothes, walked down the street, passing the temple. His father walked for an hour each morning, then took a shorter walk in the late afternoon; the temple was one of his short ones. The old fellow was familiar with every hill, temple, and narrow street in Kamakura.

Aoki went to a bar, ordered a Heineken, and sat watching a baseball game on television—except he wasn't watching it, he was seeing Tamaki's photographed face.

Aoki was a pragmatist, like his mother. What came to him—in his police life, in his sparse life beyond that—he accepted. He took orders and worked hard and efficiently. Whatever way something finished, he went on to the next task, the next stage, but this time was different. He was beginning to realize just *how* different. He frowned at the TV screen. Deep in the heart of the Tamaki investigation, he'd been alert, as fine-tuned as he'd ever been. Frequently he'd been exhausted, but even amid the frustration and setbacks they'd encountered he'd felt totally involved—elevated to a higher level.

Now he felt dazed, and drained.

He went home to dinner. Saturday night. Tokie had made special dishes, but he barely touched each, despite her gentle prompting. She and his father discussed one of the plays they'd seen during the week.

After a restless night, Aoki slept in on Sunday. Rising at ten o'clock, he padded across the cool tatami mats to where Tokie had left a breakfast tray waiting for him. She was in an alcove off the living room, seated on a cushion, making broad inky strokes with a brush on large sheets of white paper. Several sheets were scattered beside her. He stood watching for a moment, and she turned and smiled at him, the brush poised. He noticed that she had on a blue kimono, which she often wore on Sunday mornings to do this work. He smiled back at her.

This morning there was a breeze from the sea, and the humidity had temporarily dissipated. His father was still out, possibly sitting in the park after finishing his walk, gazing at trees, at nature, in the careful, absorbed way that puzzled Aoki.

Aoki had woken again in the night, just as he'd opened a file on a Yokohama apartment project where two witnesses had provided sworn statements that Tamaki's secretary had negotiated a substantial "commission" for the Fatman in return for his influencing a planning approval. It was one of the twenty-three documented charges that he'd been ready to brief the prosecutor on. The secretary, a sharklike guy of about forty, had been investigated by Nishi. Over the last year and a half, the fellow had been especially active in dirtying his hands: the Fatman's shadow and bagman.

Seventeen months. Eating his breakfast, Aoki brooded on this. His wife worked on in silence. The brushstrokes made a soft whisper, if you listened hard, though what Aoki heard this morning was a kind of buzzing in the air, as if something more were coming down on him.

On Monday morning he accompanied Inspector Natsumi on a re-visit to the scene of the moneylender's murder. Aoki had suggested to his colleague that some details needed checking. The crime scene was still sealed, and a smart young constable from the local police kiosk saluted them on their arrival and departure.

Back in his office, looking up and across the heads and desks, he saw Superintendent Watanabe standing in front of the elevator staring at him. Abruptly, the superintendent turned away.

It hit Aoki that he was under observation. Frowning, he sat back in his chair and lit a cigarette. Someone must be worried about him, nervous about what he might do next. His brief display of temper and the aberrant walkout and drinking session: That impromptu and singular dissent and defiance had made them look at him in a new light. An alarm bell had rung—probably in Watanabe's mind. Could a minor thing like that change your life? He knew that it could; in the world of the metropolitan police, something like that was not minor.

He rang Nishi, who'd been reassigned to the Fourth Criminal Investigation Division. He hesitated before speaking, then said, "Pass the word. Everyone should keep their heads down and their mouths zipped. The brass are nervous, watching for a false move. Don't ask me why. What could, or would, any one of us do?"

The plainest thing about it was that ex-governor Tamaki had obviously swept back into favor with a vengeance.

Again Aoki heard that buzzing in his brain. He wondered if he was becoming unwell, if it was a kind of delayed nervous shock. Certainly his energy was failing him, and he was back to smoking thirty cigarettes a day.

That night, as he sat at the dining table, the distant buzzing in his brain without warning became a crescendo. Something happened to his face. It was rigid. The muscles in the side of his neck locked in a painful spasm, and he gripped his neck. Tokie and his father, chopsticks frozen in midair, eyes wide, were staring at him.

The spasm was passing, as though something in him were unblocking, and a violent gasp burst forth. *"They're letting Tamaki off. Before, they wanted to get him. Now they see him as prime minister. One of the greatest crooks I've ever heard of. Up to his neck in corruption, even in murder. A partner with the yakuza. And we had him cold!"*

Aoki was staring blindly past their shocked faces at the small thicket of bamboo framed in the window. He was shouting now, unaware of his violent gestures; a bowl of pickles went flying across the table. *"The director general is corrupt. My boss is corrupt. Everyone who stopped it is corrupt. My team is dishonored. The politicians, the cunts have screwed us . . ."*

It was like spasmodic vomiting that couldn't be stopped, and his wife and father, faces stricken, were gazing at a new person, into another world. A man who never discussed his work was graphically laying it out for his family, these gentle, cultivated souls, ripping open his mind for them, spilling the guts of the Fatman case, voiding his own of the misery and humiliation. Finally, he plunged his face into his arms on the low table and sobbed like a child.

Tokie rushed to him and put her arm around his shoulders. Tears were streaming down her face. His father came to his side and laid a hand on his arm.

The sobs shaking his shoulders quickly subsided. Aoki lifted his head and rubbed with a handkerchief at his face, instantly red with shame. Here was a man who'd never shed a tear in adulthood, weeping like a schoolgirl. *Another disgrace.*

The next morning, riding the train into town, Aoki saw the scene afresh, and it seemed unbelievable. He knew the case had gone down deep in him, but it had gone down to bedrock. He shook his head in his embarrassed disbelief. Even so, he was sure that in the past he would've surmounted such a defeat. Why not now? Aoki tired hard to understand the point he'd reached—in the police, in his life—but he couldn't, and it made him deeply uneasy. He had been too ashamed to look his wife and father in the eye as he left.

Glancing at the salarymen's faces in the carriage, he realized that ex-governor Tamaki was in his brain like a tumor, and there was no treatment that he could think of.

That day he and Inspector Natsumi finished off the brief for the prosecutor on the moneylender case, and Aoki bowed to his colleague and went back to his cubicle. An hour later, he reported to Superintendent Watanabe.

"This is tragic," Watanabe said, as the inspector entered the room. Aoki looked at his boss without comprehension. "*Ah,* you haven't heard. Sergeant Saburi took his own life—thirty minutes ago. Shot himself in the park outside his apartment building." Aoki blinked, and his head went back. "Tragic, and most unfortunate in its timing. Of course, it has nothing to do with the case. He was having great marital difficulties. It is to be treated as an accident while cleaning his pistol."

Cleaning it in the park? Aoki stood there, rigid. Twelve months into the Fatman's case, Saburi's wife had left him, taking their two children, and refused all attempts at reconciliation. She'd been pleading with him to transfer to the uniformed branch. Aoki had observed the sergeant more closely, but his demeanor and his efficiency hadn't seemed affected.

"Please represent me at the service."

Aoki nodded. Then he received his new assignment. He was to report to an inspector in the Second Division who was working on a drug case in the Shibuya district.

Aoki left without a word. Was this to be his fate—to play second fiddle to another inspector? Perhaps it was temporary; whatever, it would be useless to ask Watanabe.

In the corridor he pulled up short. Sergeant Saburi dead! How much responsibility for that lay on his shoulders? Aoki's jaw tightened. He needed a space of time to think about that.

Three nights later, alone in a Ginza bar, Aoki confronted Saburi's suicide. It was the case that had killed the sergeant, the relentless pressure Aoki had put on him. The dead man's wife and children had been at the shrine in the temple, and all of his old team had been present. There were flowers from the department.

Ex-governor Tamaki's photograph was in the papers that day. He was opening a new section of expressway in his home prefecture.

Aoki stared at himself in the bar mirror. He realized he'd become even more reticent during the course of the week, and at home Tokie and his father were watching him as though he were recuperating from an illness. At work he was under similar observation, from observers not as precisely identifiable. He worked on the drug case. They'd raided premises in Shibuya, but the perpetrators, obviously, had been tipped off. There was no one there and no incriminating evidence. They needed their own tip-off, and Aoki had begun working through contacts he had in that district.

Aoki thought more about his marriage. It was another case to solve, an even more difficult one. He and Tokie lived in different worlds: art and culture, crime and, maybe, punishment. He couldn't see how that could change. In whatever direction he looked, the future appeared bleak.

The faint buzzing had come into his head again, or was it his ears? Aoki finished his beer and walked out to the Ginza street, entering a stream of close-packed bodies moving wearily in the humidity. A jungle of neon signs imprinted blazing patterns and characters on the night. The motor traffic crawled along as if it were heat-exhausted, too. Everything in his city was suffering from summer. He draped his jacket over his arm and headed for the station, instantly bathed in perspiration.

Of course, whatever was said, and despite his guilt at the pressure he'd put on Saburi, it was the Fatman who'd killed the sergeant.

Chapter Three

ONE MORNING, A WEEK LATER, an unseen hand laid the time bomb on Inspector Aoki's desk.

The newspaper was folded open to display the article, and the block of print seemed to lift off the page as though it had been suddenly magnified. Unconsciously, Aoki drew in his breath.

Police Abandon Investigation into
Diet Member's Business Connections
By Eichi Kimura

A long-running investigation into allegations of corruption and yakuza links surrounding prominent Liberal Democrat Party Diet member Yukio Tamaki has been abandoned by the police. Reportedly the links involved yakuza connections with certain unnamed banks, allegedly sponsored by former governor Tamaki. Reliable sources advise that the high-powered investigation team has been disbanded. Senior police would not comment on the case, and no reason for its terminaton is available. In 1991, allegations of corruption surfaced against Tamaki when the Judicial Commission looked into development approvals in Osaka in the late 1980s, but these fizzled out, as did the commission. In the 1970s, when he was governor of _____ prefecture, similar allegations went unanswered. It appears that yet again the Fatman is fireproof against worrying allegations, and that public interest has again been put aside.

Aoki sat there, stunned—at the article and at the Eichi Kimura connection. The fellow was the husband of his wife's best friend! Perspiration had broken out on Aoki's forehead and hands. What in the hell! How did Kimura get the story? He sank back in his chair, and sickeningly the suspicion came down on him.

He was fumbling for a cigarette when his phone rang, making him jump. He was summoned to the director general's office! Aoki put on his coat, dried off his hands, and went up in the elevator. His throat had tightened so that it ached.

The bowing secretary conducted him into the room. The DG was seated behind his desk, staring fixedly ahead. Then his eyes shot to Aoki. Superintendent Watanabe stood to one side, his eyes hooded. A hostile silence drenched the room.

The DG drew in his breath. "How did the paper get this?" He lifted it up and thrust the article in Aoki's direction. The newspaper was shaking in his hairy hands. Aoki was expressionless. With an effort, he was keeping his composure, waiting to see which way things would go, still in the dark like them. The DG's authoritarian but hitherto reasonably polite manner had vanished. Here was a man of fractured nerves, exuding the pressure pouring down on him from above.

Watanabe appeared calm.

"I don't know, sir," Aoki replied.

The director general's face turned red. He bit at his lips, glaring at the detective with heavy suspicion, and said, "If you have anything to tell me about it, do so now."

Aoki got the message—later would be too late—but he had nothing to say.

"Very well, Inspector. We will be looking into this." He dismissed Aoki with a curt nod.

Aoki left. Superintendent Watanabe did not go with him.

Back in his cubicle, Aoki sat at his desk and gazed out over the thirty or so detectives seated at their desks and computers. His hand found the mole on his cheek and fingered it. He had nothing urgent to do; his inspector colleague on the drug case was off duty, and he was waiting on calls from his own contacts.

Minutes ago, Watanabe's attitude had been enigmatic, normal for him. During the Fatman investigation, Aoki had been reporting directly to the DG, but the superintendent had been hovering around its edges. Once he'd stopped Aoki in a corridor and said, "How's it going?" Aoki was surprised: The superintendent had been present at the last weekly briefing of the DG. Watanabe had examined him with shrewd eyes. "I mean, how's it really going?" Aoki had shrugged, hiding his anger. It had been the day before the investigation was shut down.

Eichi Kimura was a feature writer and crime reporter on the *Tokyo Shimbun*. Aoki hardly knew the fellow, despite the closeness of their wives.

Aoki picked up the phone to call Tokie, then put it down and gazed afresh out of his glass cubicle. He guessed Watanabe would be calling him soon, but no call came.

Inspector Aoki signed off at 5:30 P.M. and went home. Strung tight with tension, he rode the train out to Kamakura, tonight having to stand all the way. His stomach was upset, sour with lack of food and uncertainty—the suspicion that kept rising up in his mind, and that he kept rejecting. It was unbelievable, *inconceivable,* that his wife could be involved *in any way whatsoever.* He'd folded the newspaper into his pocket.

At Kamakura he stopped in a bar and ordered a Heineken. A compulsion was on him to get home and clear up the matter; nonetheless, he needed a breathing space to put himself in order for it. Hopefully, it would all be dismissed by his wife in a few incredulous words. But if not? He knew it was a bad sign that he couldn't force himself to phone her.

Aoki wasn't an ambitious man; the case was the biggest assignment he'd had. Despite his successes, it totally outgunned his rank, and at the outset he'd been amazed, then deeply doubtful, about that fact. However, as they'd delved deeper and deeper the doubts had vanished. He'd become as one with a world that in the past had been off-limits to him—or any other inspector of the TMPD. Slowly he shook his head, then drank up the beer, squared his shoulders, and left the bar.

Fifteen minutes later, Aoki entered the peaceful enclave that was their home: a minuscule clearing in the vast urban jungle that was Tokyo, yet the place where he was least comfortable. Tight with tension, he let himself in and stepped into the living room. His father held a book open in his hands, but Aoki could tell that he wasn't reading it. Tokie came forward with a bow and took his suit coat. His shirt was stuck to his back with perspiration. She gave him her usual quiet and pleasant welcome. He needed to be very calm about this. He was still embarrassed about the emotional scene, and the humiliation hadn't abated. He would take a shower and further prepare himself.

Today Tokie and his father had been to an art exhibition at a Kamakura gallery, and they'd had tea in a garden next to one of the tranquil temples. Pouring him beer, Tokie told him this.

They ate their dinner. Her manner seemed strained and earnest. The folded newspaper was still in Aoki's pocket. In the ascetic face with its mottled brown age marks, his father's eyes were worried. Down what tributary were the old man's thoughts moving? Aoki wondered, his heart beating faster.

Tokie took away the plates, brought in a platter of fruit, and resumed her seat.

Aoki forced himself to reach for the newspaper in his pocket and, fumbling, unfolded it to display the article. Wordlessly, he laid it before them. They stared at it.

Tokie raised her eyes first, and Aoki knew.

"What have you done?" he said quietly.

She shook her head vehemently, but her eyes had become clouded. His father was staring down at his small hands.

Aoki felt wretched, and he knew his face had darkened. He compressed his lips, as if to stop any further utterance. How could he ever have foreseen such a thing? His gentle, artistic wife? This scholarly old man who was his father? He shook his head slowly. Far beyond his knowledge or his idea of her, was his wife some kind of activist? Aoki grappled with these thoughts. *Stay calm,* he told himself in the midst of them. His hands somehow had become clasped together.

"*Why* didn't you come to me first?" Aoki heard his voice say. His control was slipping.

Quietly, his father said, "Your wife feels very deeply the great indignity you've suffered, the injustice. She sees what it has done to you, what it is doing to you. She went to Kimura-san's wife, then him, in strict confidence."

Tokie leaned forward, earnest, desperate. "I told him that you could not, would not, speak about it. He promised me anonymity."

Aoki shook his head in bewilderment. Strict confidence! In a case like ex-governor Tamaki's! Their naive idea of security, the anonymity that could be expected, rendered him speechless. The real world would throw out the source like an animal spitting out poisonous food!

The great chasm between their worlds, their lives, had brought this on. He groaned—could not stop it. Then he questioned her in detail. Without his knowing it, his voice had turned rough, terse in his disbelief that behind his back she'd done what she'd done.

Throughout the interrogation she stared fixedly at the platter of sliced fruit, the dessert they wouldn't eat.

He had the story from her quiet answers, and gradually their voices faded away into the summer night. Tears had flooded his wife's eyes, but she made no sound.

Aoki rose from the table, found his shoes, and left the apartment. He needed a bar, and solitude. Everything ahead was now very clearly mapped out for him, he thought, stiff with anger and despair, but that was not the case at all.

First thing the next morning, Aoki was again summoned to the director general's office. He entered a doom-laden atmosphere. Early this morning they'd questioned Kimura. Aoki believed that the journalist would've tried to protect his source, his wife's friends, but even he would not have had the full measure of what he was up against. The Fatman's power, always formidable, had been revitalized, and, anyway, there were ways to break down even the most obstinate if the stakes were high enough.

"What in hell was your wife thinking?" the director general demanded, emphasizing each word. "Did *you* put her up to it?" He jumped up and paced the room, unable to control his agitation, but not taking his eyes off Aoki. Superintendent Watanabe sat like the Sphinx.

Aoki remained speechless. He couldn't explain what had happened. They knew more than he did! And he couldn't blame his wife before these men.

Ten minutes later, Aoki was expelled from the DG's office. *Suspended from duty.* He surrendered his badge and his gun, and Watanabe escorted him off the premises. Aoki shook his head in disbelief. He was a first-class shot, and they were taking away his gun. The illogical thought gave way; now he was stiff and silent with anger.

"Stay cool and it'll probably blow over," his boss said, giving him a critical look. "Do anything rash and you'll be in *deep* shit. Treat it as a vacation. You're still on full pay."

Before noon, Assistant Inspector Nishi called him on his cell phone, finding him in a Ginza bar, and passed on the regrets of some of his team members. *It's gone down deep with us all,* Aoki thought. The news hadn't taken long to get out.

He wasn't drunk when he arrived home at about 9:00 P.M.

His father was in the kitchen making tea. They regarded each other. "I've been suspended until further notice," Aoki said.

The old man nodded as if to himself. "The only disgrace lies with your superiors," he said quietly.

Tokie had come from their bedroom to hover in the background, a pale witness to this exchange between father and son. She seemed in a daze.

At 10:00 P.M. Aoki was standing at the kitchen sink looking out the small window, drinking beer from the bottle, when his father came in. The old man said in his soft voice, "It grieved me to hear you talk like that to Tokie last night. What was done came from loyalty, and a fine woman's horror at the unjust treatment of the man she cares for most."

Aoki made a gesture of helplessness with the bottle and muttered an apology. Fatalistically, he thought, *He's right. I've got to cool it, cool everything, swallow it down.* What did it matter anyway? His suspension was just to placate the shadowy figures on the DG's back. If he was lucky he'd even keep his rank, and after a few weeks he'd be recalled and thrust into the thick of something else— so long as it didn't concern politicians!

At 10:00 A.M. that first morning of his suspension, Aoki walked to a coffee shop near home and had two cups of Colombian coffee. Then he went to the park and, from a bench, watched the aged and the women and children, a new world to him. At lunchtime, he walked to the bar next to the coffee shop and drank two small bottles of Heineken, then read a newspaper and snacked on cocktail nuts. Unconsciously, he was laying down a pattern, and in the following days, he was to decide that he'd stepped into a slow-motion world.

A man came into the bar and went to a corner table. He ordered a beer and picked up a newspaper. Aoki, immersed in his thoughts and his new regimen, hardly noticed him.

A few minutes later, he did. Bitterly, he smiled to himself. What in hell did they think he'd do? Someone was really worried for ex-governor Tamaki! And that worry was being poured onto the backs of the director general and Superintendent Watanabe—by some high-up bastard.

From that first day of his suspension, Aoki was under surveillance.

Chapter Four

IT WAS A WEEK AFTER the day of Aoki's suspension when the phone's shrilling ruptured the apartment's early-morning peace. Aoki was lying in bed, half asleep, a cool sea breeze blowing on his face. He raised himself on his elbow, listening as Tokie padded softly to answer it. There was a pause. Were they calling him back in?

The scream sliced through the flat. Aoki sprang up and ran out to the living room, but his father was ahead of him.

Both of them pulled up, gazing at Tokie, who was slumped on the floor, her loose hair fallen over her face, her torso bowed like a broken flower. Absolutely still. The scream was an echo in their heads. The phone receiver dangled from its cord. His father went forward and kneeled down beside her, put his arm around her shoulders, and spoke to her in a gentle voice. She murmured a few words to the old man that Aoki couldn't hear.

Aoki took up the phone and listened. The line was dead. He heard only the radio playing softly in the kitchen. He replaced the receiver. What in hell's name? He stared at the tears running down his wife's face.

The old man straightened up, his face grave. He turned to Aoki and took him aside. "Kimura, the journalist, has been killed. This morning. Murdered on the stairs of his building."

Aoki stared at his father as if not understanding the words spoken. The old man reached out, took his arm, and shook him slightly. Then Aoki was looking at his wife, who hadn't moved; her eyes were staring at the tatami mat.

At 10:00 A.M. the broad pattern of it was all very clear to Aoki; the details—or some of them—would come later. He sat in the coffee shop, a cup of the Colombian brew untasted and cold in front of him.

Tokie had gone to Madam Kimura, accompanied by his father. At the door, Aoki had touched her hand, but she'd given him only a fleeting look. At that moment, the closeness between his wife and his father had never been more evident to him, and he'd felt like a bystander.

He brooded on the coffee shop and its few occupants. The waitress looked at him, removed the cold cup, and replaced it with a fresh one. The cop was in the corner, behind the paper. Aoki shook his head slowly. Kimura, the poor bastard. That article, it had to be. *Tokie.* It was so cruel. But it was Tamaki that his thoughts settled on. The Fatman's past was layered with corrupt deals; however, they'd found two cases where people within his ambit had been murdered, and several others where persons had just disappeared— in Osaka, Yokohama, and Kobe. It had been impossible to obtain evidence linking him to those cases. Where they had him was in those twenty-odd cases of corruption. As Assistant Inspector Nishi had commented, that was the deep shit they'd caught him standing in; witnesses to the bloodstained stuff were unavailable.

The journalist, in taking up the case, had plunged into the pool of corruption; maybe the one of the blood was to have been next. Possibly Kimura knew what the Fatman was capable of. If so, the crusade he'd begun was even more courageous—and Aoki's personal situation just a way station on a longer journey.

Aoki sighed heavily. His wife had really upset an applecart. He got out his cell phone and called Nishi and asked for details of the murder. The assistant inspector said he would find out and call him back.

Aoki sipped the coffee this time. He pictured Tokie and his father calling on the new widow. A tragic scene.

Twenty minutes later his phone rang and Nishi's voice was giving him the information. Kimura had been strangled at about 6:45 A.M. *Worse than that*—his wife had found him minutes later on their landing, his eyeballs dragged out on his cheeks, his tongue partly severed, and his ears sliced off and tossed on the floor. Already the police had found out he'd been working on a follow-up story to the first. A yakuza killing, they were saying at this point. That was all Nishi could get at the moment. Inspector Yoshikawa of the Second Division had the case.

Aoki pondered what he'd heard. His throat muscles had tightened. The killing was especially nasty. How much detail had Tokie been told on the phone? His heart went cold for his wife. She was going to feel very responsible for the murder of her best friend's husband, and there was not a thing he could do about that.

The savage nature of the killing was a graphic message: a terrible lesson in *not* seeing, hearing, or telling. The yakuza's sinister shadow lay over it like an oil slick in Tokyo Bay, and for Aoki, superimposed over that was the obese shadow of the Fatman.

Automatically, Aoki pictured the routines Inspector Yoshikawa's team would be engaged in. They'd be checking Kimura's latest phone calls and appointments. But this crime was *top-level* yakuza. The investigation wouldn't move fast and eventually would run into a dead end. Aoki could foresee that.

What he couldn't foresee was what other disasters were still coming down the freeway.

Four days later, Tokie and her father-in-law attended Kimura's funeral service while Aoki sat in the park watching the pigeons being fed by the young and by the old and infirm. At one point, he'd considered going to see Kimura's widow to try to find out more, but his suspension, and the shadow on his tail, made it a hopeless move. The brass would read it as another breach of discipline, and probably the DG would decide that this inspector was just too much trouble to keep on the force.

In the nights between the murder and the funeral, Aoki had started awake, listening for his wife's breathing. On each occasion, he'd been unable to hear it above the humming of the air conditioner and had wondered if she was lying awake. Or a worse thing. Each time, she'd stirred slightly, as though aware of his vigil, as if giving him a signal that she was still with him. One night he got up and stared from the window at their small garden. For an hour he stood there, hearing the hum of the mosquitoes outside the wire screen, trying to make sense of what was happening in their lives.

In those few days she prepared their meals, moving through the apartment, a pale ghost of her former self, and Aoki and his father began to attend to small chores around the house that were new to them. Each morning now, his father took a basket on his walk and visited the market for their food.

After the funeral, Tokie packed a bag to go and stay with

Madam Kimura and her elderly mother, leaving Aoki and his father to look after themselves. Five days later she came home, and Aoki was jolted by the change in her. In a distracted way, she spoke of her friend. She was more talkative than he'd ever known her to be, except half the time she didn't finish a sentence before beginning another. A kind of semicrazy vivacity. "Dear daughter-in-law," his father said. The old man talked to her gently; Aoki spoke his condolences stiffly, feeling ashamed of the way he'd questioned her the night of the day Kimura's article had come out. The next day, the old man took her to a garden he knew. "It is famous for its tranquility," he told Aoki. "There, your spirit becomes as still as a forest pool."

The murder and investigation were featured daily in Kimura's paper, and on the weekend it printed an obituary. Aoki read about the significant things in Kimura's thirty-eight years. The man he hadn't known had won several important prizes for his journalism.

It was plain that Tokie could not talk about the tragedy itself, and Aoki wondered how she had been able to help her friend. Everything was strange in the household. Aoki spent most of his time in the park, the coffee shop, or the local bars. He phoned Nishi once more, but there'd been no breakthrough that his colleague knew of.

On the Friday night, his father, in the middle of a calm and scholarly talk on the Silver Pavilion in Kyoto, his concerned eyes on Tokie, slumped on the table, scattering the dishes, and was dead within seconds.

In the following days, it was very clear to Aoki that ex-governor Tamaki had reached into his and his family's existence with a malignancy that transcended the poisonous layers of corruption the detective had unearthed. Aoki was certain that worry—about his son's situation, about the terrible blow that had fallen on his daughter-in-law with Kimura's death—had brought on his father's death. Up against such tragedy, Aoki felt totally helpless, and now concern for his wife gnawed in his belly. He tried to imagine the depth of the despair that must be in her heart, though she spoke not a single word of it.

On a humid morning, several old professors and other colleagues, a scattering of former students, and a few friends made up the twenty or so persons who attended the ceremony for his father's spirit, at a shrine in the temple at the end of the street. At the start, Tokie slumped against him, and Aoki put his arm around her to hold her up.

Aoki, his head full of incense, oblivious to the chanting of the Buddhist priest, was hearing the last words his father had said to him of a personal nature. "The only disgrace lies with your superiors."

Grimly, turning his head to look around, he imagined that the Fatman was there, somewhere in the temple precincts, watching the ceremony from concealment. Of course, it was a ridiculous notion: He would know nothing of the old professor of literature; probably wouldn't have known much about Aoki, and certainly would've forgotten him by now. To the Fatman, the investigation would be history, as he pointed himself toward the political horizon where his sun was rising.

Later, Aoki told himself that his father's years of twice-daily walks over this hilly suburb could well be responsible for his death. After all, he was seventy-eight. But he didn't believe that; out of professional habit he was just assembling all the evidence. Sergeant Saburi, Kimura, and now his father. The Fatman's crimes were relentlessly accumulating. It was a coldhearted thought in the midst of this sadness.

Tokie was sobbing quietly against his shoulder. Now there was just the two of them.

The next morning, Aoki sat forward when Tamaki's face flashed onto the television news. He was making a speech at a business-men's conference in Kobe. A powerful sincerity oozed from him.

A hard knot of pain came into Aoki's stomach. The government was caught up in one of its innumerable crises, not that it was in any danger of defeat. The Liberal Democrat Party's hold on power was unshakable, and the opposition parties were hardly more effective than the shadow play of puppets. The strife that most often oc-curred was between the ruling party's own factions. Tamaki was playing peacemaker.

Aoki turned off the television. The apartment seemed as quiet as a tomb.

At breakfast, Aoki did not know what to say to Tokie. He didn't know how she would fill the gap in her life. Not looking at her, he said, "I will come to the rest of the plays with you, if you wish."

She gave him her sad shy smile. It was the first time he'd seen her smile since Kimura had been killed.

The day was humid and rainy. In midafternoon, gusts of wind came from the sea, blowing away the rain clouds. Tokie had gone into the alcove where she did her calligraphy and was staring down at blank white paper. When she began to work, Aoki went out and took his father's short walk to the temple.

He checked his back. No one. It seemed the surveillance had been withdrawn.

After the rain, it was hot and even more humid, and Aoki bought an icy aluminum can of soda from a vending machine. He rolled it back and forth across his forehead, sighing with relief. It was September, but the summer heat was fighting a rear-guard action.

After his walk, Aoki went to the coffee shop, drank coffee, and read the paper. Especially he looked at the latest batch of crime reports, reading between the lines with his experienced eye. Today, Kimura's case wasn't mentioned.

Aoki frowned, concentrating. Had Tamaki initiated Kimura's murder, or had his yakuza associates just stepped in to take care of it, protecting themselves from more of Kimura's fact-finding, crusading articles on the Fatman and his shadowy associates? Inspector Yoshikawa of the Second Criminal Investigation Division would be thinking identical thoughts, which wouldn't take him anywhere, either.

Aoki reconsidered whether he might attempt to interview Madam Kimura, in particular to find out what her husband had been doing in his last days; try to do some work behind the official investigation. Grimly, he realized that it would be useless. The cop might or might not be on his tail today, but Watanabe would be keeping in touch with what was going on. Aoki would have zero room to move, and it'd just bring them down on him like a sledgehammer.

At 5:30 P.M. Aoki transferred to the bar down the street. He lit a cigarette and drank a beer. He was just filling in time, waiting to go home to dinner.

Something dark and heavy came down on Aoki as he fumbled for his key, brushing against the bonsai in their pots on the small porch—something like a weighty traditional cloak thrown over his shoulders. One winter, his father had spread such a cloak over the teenaged Hideo's back.

The apartment was in total darkness, and a new tightness gripped his throat. He switched on the light in the hall. The kitchen door was closed, which was unusual. He opened it, and the electric light flooded into the small room.

His wife's lifeless kimonoed body was suspended from the light fixture by a cord.

Chapter Five

ONE MONTH AND THREE DAYS after his wife's suicide, Inspector Aoki reentered the world: He was seeing and hearing what was going on about him; was aware of his body, his thoughts, where he was. It was as though he'd been shot up into air and light from the depths of a dark pool.

The reentry point, he believed at that moment, was the bar facing the municipal park. However, the past month remained substantially a mystery. Fragments were progressively to come back—coming into view like debris flowing down a storm-water channel—such as the uncle who'd appeared from nowhere and taken care of all the arrangements; of him.

His sole memory of Tokie's funeral ceremony was of incense. That odor was all that he retained. The rest of it was lost in a dense fog.

He'd been in this clinic. There'd been injections. Bits and pieces of that were reassembling: a man who talked on and on, with many questions. A single utterance from the fellow jumped in Aoki's mind, like a fish feeding in a stream: "Sometimes it's the individual who is *most* familiar with trauma and disaster who crashes hardest."

❖

Another fragment that emerged was the face of Superintendent Watanabe, leaning over him, saying something, but about any of that time, nothing was one hundred percent certain.

He'd realized he was not in the bar at all but in a white, stainless-steel-fitted room, with a picture on the wall of a mountain covered with autumn-tinted woods. In reality, *that* was the reentry point. The next day, the police psychiatrist discharged him. He was to return each week for further treatment. Without fail, he was to take the prescribed medication.

The hot, sultry summer had vanished. Now the days were cooler, and he began to take walks. Probably, some of them overlapped with his father's, but he only knew for sure about the short one to the temple. He felt stronger each day, part of which he spent in the coffee shop and the bar, again reading the papers. He had lost weight in the clinic.

He brought himself up to date on the Kimura case; it had faded to brief reports in the middle pages. According to the paper, the police had no leads, just as he'd expected. Soon it would fade away altogether, almost as though it had never happened. He didn't contact anyone on the force, and no one contacted him; he'd fallen out of the loop.

One night he took the train into Shinjuku and visited a jazz cellar. He listened to a scratch group and drank beer and smoked, speaking to no one. They'd played old stuff like "My Melancholy Baby." It had made him so sad that he'd left after three-quarters of an hour. He'd been there a score of times in the past, but Tokie had never known.

At his weekly appointments with the psychiatrist, he was withdrawn and uncommunicative.

Daily now, he was looking for news of ex-governor Tamaki in the papers. The Fatman had stepped back into focus, out of that month of fog; the fellow had been lying low while he'd been battling with other demons. Inspector Aoki especially didn't mention this to the shrink. There had to be a way to deal with Tamaki, a way to expose the bastard and bring him to justice, a way to penetrate the system. He had some hard thinking to do—when he was fit to do it.

He had blocked out that night. The leap forward to support her weight, the savage slashes at the cord with the kitchen knife, his desperate cries, the laying on the kitchen table of her drooping figure in the blue kimono, her sensitive fingers now limp, stained with ink from the calligraphy.

She'd been gone for hours while he'd been sitting in the park, the coffee shop, or the bar. *That* was something he'd never get over. The police shrink had wanted to talk about it, but he hadn't, and couldn't.

The first day after his discharge from the clinic, he spotted the police watcher, across the coffee shop, tucked behind a paper. They were at it again. Aoki stared, then almost got up to go and speak to the detective, but he restrained himself. *Play it cool,* an inner voice said.

The earlier surveillance, after his suspension, had only lasted a few days. He saw Watanabe's hand behind that, and behind this. Starting with his flare-up of anger at the internal affairs cops when they'd been sealing up the case records, and the walkout with his team, doubts about him—his reliability—had obviously accumulated in certain minds. Now, after Tokie's suicide and his breakdown, they'd been renewed. He might be a dangerous man!

That afternoon he took the train into Central and then to Roppongi. At Central he took evasive action, automatically using the tricks of criminals to lose his police shadow. "Unless the cop's well above the average, it'll do the trick," he told himself.

Early in the evening, he stood across the Roppongi street gazing up at the Fatman's apartment. No lights. Then he remembered it was Friday.

Aoki caught a train back to Central, bought another ticket, and went downstairs to the platform that was used by the trains going to Hakone. He had five minutes to wait, and he fed coins into a gleaming machine, extracted a chocolate bar, and ate half of it.

Forty-five minutes later, he alighted in a leafy district. Outside the station he paused for a moment, checking his memory. The lighted police kiosk was a hundred yards away to his left, and he turned and started off in the opposite direction. This was a circuitous way to the house, but it took him only ten minutes to get there.

The street was overhung by large trees, which obliterated the meager illumination from the streetlights. The house, narrow-fronted, was partly screened behind a small thicket of slender bamboo. Two stone lanterns were unlit. Dimly, Aoki made out the stepping-stones, set in moss that went to the front door. It had warmed up again, and everything was drenched in humidity and stillness.

Another dark residence. Where was the bastard tonight? Aoki stared at the silent house. He'd come here to this obscure place without any intention or plan, knowing only that it was one of the Fatman's destinations, and in his mind, the politician had become a destination himself.

One night early in the investigation, they'd followed Tamaki's car here, about an hour's drive from central Tokyo. Nishi had dropped Aoki close to the house and then gone around the corner to park. Tamaki's car and driver, and his bodyguard, had disappeared into the night, presumably back to Tokyo. "What's this all about?" Aoki had asked himself. This semirural property was a strong contrast to the politician's luxury apartment in Roppongi, and he had a vacation house on Oshima Island. This one appeared to be an old wooden house of the type traditional to the area. Some kind of assignation?

Alert and curious, he'd taken a position in the narrow lane among tree trunks and watched. There'd been no movement except for the breeze in the bamboo and the trees. The house, following the usual pattern, would run back a long way in a succession of rooms to a garden at the rear. Aoki had wondered what place in the Fatman's convoluted life it had. The ex–prefectural governor, ex–minister of finance, and ex-chairman of several Diet committees was ex a lot of things. Was this house ex-something or currently in play?

It had been a sterile hour that had yielded no answer. Aoki and Nishi drove back to Tokyo, and the next day he found out that the house had belonged to Tamaki's deceased parents; on many Friday nights he went into retreat there. Years before, he'd told a journalist, "I go there to commune with my revered parents." It almost made him seem human, doubtless the point of the remark.

Now, Aoki stood in the night air, slapping at buzzing mosquitoes. There was movement in his brain, but he did not know where it was headed, nor even the possibilities of where it might go. After a while, he turned to go back to the station.

Down the street, the policeman, who was a smart operator, straining his eyes to keep the inspector's figure detached from the shadowy background, began to follow.

Back at his apartment, Aoki opened a beer and prepared a bowl of noodles. He had nothing to add to them, not even pickles. All

Tokie's fine meals, which he'd so often been absent from, were lost to the past. "In time, the real appreciation of certain lost things comes to most of us," his father had said once. "It is often accompanied by great sadness." The old man's voice resonated in his head—or was it in the apartment?

Aoki held the beer can against his cheek and felt the chill go right through into his teeth. On the bureau at one side of the living room were neat stacks of papers, which the departed uncle must have left for him. On top was a bunch of news clippings. Aoki took up the first and read it.

Police Inspector's Wife Commits Suicide

TOKYO. Madam Tokie Aoki was found hanged on Wednesday evening. She was discovered by her husband, Inspector Hideo Aoki of the Third Criminal Investigation Division, Metropolitan Police, when he returned to their Kamakura flat. According to police there are no suspicious circumstances. Sources advise that Aoki was under suspension from duty for several weeks, on "disciplinary grounds."

Aoki stared at this. Then he flicked through the others. His photograph and Tokie's and Kimura's ran side by side in several follow-up articles, with rehashes of the dead journalist's scoop on the abandoned investigation and Aoki's role in it. The Fatman, or his associates, had thought Kimura's death would kill that business, but Tokie had made sure that it hadn't. There was no doubt in his mind that Tamaki and his yakuza friends were responsible for Kimura's savage murder.

Lying on the futon, listening to the air conditioner, hearing faintly the waves from the beach, Aoki wondered what he could do with his life. The misery in him was as hard and cold as a steel ingot, and the silence in his home seemed absolute.

When Aoki opened his door in response to the bell the next morning, Superintendent Watanabe was standing next to the bonsai pots. Immediately, Aoki guessed that he hadn't shaken off yesterday's surveillance: His visit to the Fatman's residences had gone into the records. The shadowing cop had been better than competent.

Watanabe studied him for a moment. "Ah, Aoki-san," he said in a tone that expressed both greeting and censure. "Let's go for a walk." He grimaced. "There seem to be plenty of retired fellows around here doing just that, knocking their hearts around on these hills."

Aoki put on a suit coat and fetched his wallet, and they walked to the bar that was becoming Aoki's home away from home. It was not yet eight-thirty, but he ordered a Heineken, and a mineral water for his visitor. They had the bar to themselves. The bartender was watching the replay of a sumo contest, the sound turned down.

Aoki nibbled nuts, his breakfast, and waited.

Watanabe was deep in thought. He inspected the bar, then looked out to the depopulated park, where almost overnight the trees had turned autumn colours, hissing softly all the while through his teeth. It was a habit Aoki had observed for years. Another yellow tie, but with a different pattern, Aoki noted. It stood out against the hand-stitched navy blue suit. Except for that unreliable sighting of his face during the fog-shrouded month, Aoki hadn't seen or spoken to his boss since the day of his suspension. He noted also Watanabe's disparaging glance at his creased suit.

Tokie was no longer here to take it to the cleaners; usually, she'd taken his clothes on rainy days to get the discount.

Anyway, he thought, *I go into darker and dirtier places than you. Used to,* he corrected, *when I wasn't suspended.*

Watanabe ceased the soft hissing sound. "The shrink says you've got a long way to go. *He's* still preying on your mind."

Aoki looked at his boss, then shrugged.

A new cop was on duty, a tall, thin man who followed them into the bar and sat down in a corner. This morning Aoki hardly spared him a glance, and Watanabe appeared unaware of his arrival. Aoki was surprised at the tension in his boss; usually he was inscrutable.

Watanabe's hair covered his head in tiny black curls. What kind of genetic kick-in gave a compatriot hair like that, Aoki wondered—not for the first time.

The superintendent turned on Aoki. His lips twisted angrily. "Haven't you learned anything in your twenty years on the force? When the brass say it's over, it's over. It can't be changed, because that's the message that's coming down from *their* brass."

Aoki rinsed nuts down with a mouthful of beer.

Watanabe was frowning hard now, as if at an intractable problem. "Who are you? A fellow who thinks he can do what he likes? That's not how things work for the likes of you—or me, Inspector. We take orders." The fingertips of his right hand were tapping on the table. "Well, what about it?"

Aoki half-turned away, then swung back, taking a deep breath. "First it was one thing, then another. A journalist I knew is dead, his wife is a sad widow, and I know who's behind it. Why should I forget?" To himself, his voice sounded calm but depressed.

The superintendent's face hardened. "You *think* you know. Journalists like that make a *lot* of enemies."

I know, Aoki thought. He said, "Not to mention my wife."

Watanabe shook his head forcefully. "We've got to get on with our lives, and psycho thoughts won't help."

Aoki looked away at the park. He grunted. Psycho thoughts! And how did his boss's life come into it? With a quick gesture he scooped up more nuts.

"What's happened to you is tough, and people are concerned for you." Watanabe flexed the fingers of each hand in turn, as though about to grab hold of something. "I agree with the medico, you're not ready to return to duty yet." Aoki thought he read in the voice doubt that he ever would be.

Watanabe leaned forward and stared into Aoki's eyes. "Stay away from the governor. Get him out of your mind. Don't step any deeper into the shit, Inspector."

Without another word, he got up and left the bar. Aoki watched him go. He'd never seen his boss stirred up like this before.

Aoki moved in the new routine of his life. Every morning, he watered the bonsai plants, as Tokie had done. He guessed his uncle had attended to it while he was in the clinic—must have; they were still alive. She'd been a great believer in talking to plants, and he pictured her watering, snipping the tiny leaves and branches, speaking to them. He had assumed the responsibility for these orphans.

He had one conversation with Assistant Inspector Nishi. His ex–team member had sounded slightly embarrassed. Aoki's admittance to the clinic was doubtless well known among his colleagues, and Nishi was wondering how "with it" he was. Nishi had nothing to report on the Kimura case.

At 6:45 A.M. on the third morning following the superintendent's visit, he was in the coffee shop, stirring his Colombian brew, when a shadow fell over the table. He looked up—into Watanabe's dark-eyed appraisal.

Aoki blinked his surprise. He was slipping, had gone rusty, if his boss could come up on him like that—and another visit! At this hour! The superintendent must have a clear desk to take the trip out here again.

Watanabe nodded, moved forward, and pulled out a chair. In the past few days it had turned cold. He was wearing yellow kid gloves and his camel overcoat. His face, as ever, showed a calculating look, as though his mind were already in new territory, which he might or might not bring you into. Efficiently he stripped off his gloves.

"You're taking a trip today, Inspector, to Hokkaido."

Aoki blinked again. An envelope had appeared and lay on the table between the superintendent's now-bare, lean hands.

"You're going to a ryokan in the mountains, where they'll feed you more than cocktail nuts and potato chips, where you'll have a change of scene and a chance to think through your future."

Watanabe thrust his head forward, as though to stare into Aoki's brain. "You've got to get away from here, out of your apartment, if you're ever going to make it back."

Frowning, Aoki studied his boss. A ryokan? He was only vaguely familiar with such establishments; when he traveled, he stayed at basic, low-cost modern hotels, not these ultratraditional, pricey inns where every room had its own maid. *Everything in my life is changing.*

"*You're going,* Inspector. Last time, I told you what the shrink said. He's not happy with your lack of cooperation, and the DG's getting impatient. You're too good a man to throw on the scrap heap, but don't worry, they'll do it, unless you get it together." The superintendent's austere eyes regarded his subordinate. "I've gone out on a limb for you."

"Out on a limb," Aoki murmured, and resumed stirring his coffee.

Watanabe hissed softly through his teeth. "Here's a reserved ticket on the 8:45 A.M. bullet train to Morioka, and tickets for the two connecting trains. I've written down directions for getting to the ryokan. A reservation's been made for four nights, but stay a week, eat the food, take the hot-spring baths. They don't know anything about you." He added succinctly, "Get moving. You should look on this as a last chance." He was flexing his hands into the gloves.

Aoki sat like a statue and watched him go. His boss walked in a quick, determined way; an ambitious walk, though it was well known that his promotion had stalled. The superintendent disliked him but somehow was intrigued by him, by the way he operated, the successes he'd had. Watanabe's calculating mind-set saw value in Aoki's methods and contrasting personality—years ago Aoki had decided this. "It must be why he's taking this trouble," he told himself. Yet, right now, the superintendent seemed to have more on his mind than that.

Through the plate-glass window, Aoki watched Watanabe talk to the cop who sprang up from a bench when the impeccably dressed senior officer beckoned him. Probably, he was to ensure Aoki caught that train, and maybe be his shadow to Hokkaido. The shadow of a damaged and dangerous man!

Aoki did not know yet how dangerous he was, or might become. To him that prospect lay in a future even foggier than his recent past.

Chapter Six

"IS THIS WHAT I EXPECTED?" Inspector Aoki asked himself. In the best part of a day, he'd traveled almost the length of Japan. During the journey, he'd hardly spared the physical nature of his destination a thought. The taxi he'd engaged at the station was descending into a valley. The road was narrow and potholed, and the dark blue asphalt coiled down through the trees in tight **S**-bends.

At this season, and this hour, strangers to the district might have sensed an atmosphere of menace in the road, but Aoki merely found it wretched, though he had realized something on the train: His destination, the ryokan at this road's end, had figured in a case seven years ago, a notorious, unsolved case about a missing woman. In his reserved seat, in a smoking car (Superintendent Watanabe had thought of that), speeding north through alternating urban and rural scenes, this had come back to him in a stab of memory.

He took out his battered wallet; something else had also come back to him. At first he couldn't find it in the numerous paper- and card-stuffed recesses, then he did. From 1993, yellowed, folded into deep creases, appearing as dead as the seven-year-old story it told. This had been his first big case as a junior detective; that was why he'd kept the clipping.

Missing Wife of Bank Chairman
Feared Murdered

The bloodstained women's clothing found in a luggage locker at Tokyo Central station has been identified as belonging to Misako Ito, wife of a prominent banker. Madam Ito was reported missing to police a week ago. Grave fears are held for her safety. Reportedly, the blood group on the clothing matches the missing woman's. A large police team headed by Superintendent Kuga Watanabe has been detailed to the investigation. Her husband, Hiroshi Ito, chairman of Tokyo Citizens Bank, who reported her disappearance, is appealing for information to assist police with their inquiries. Superintendent Watanabe said Madam Ito was last seen leaving an address in Shimbashi by taxi, at approximately 11:00 P.M. on October 24 . . .

Ah, yes! Watanabe's case! Reportedly the one that had stalled his promotion. Aoki had studied the photograph of the attractive middle-aged woman who was smiling enigmatically at the camera. Shaking his head in wonderment, he'd carefully replaced the clipping in his wallet. How remarkable that he'd been carrying it around all these years; it was as if it had been traveling with him, in waiting for this moment.

Aoki frowned. Had Watanabe chosen this ryokan for his rest cure based on his recollection of it from the case, or was it a coincidence?

Beside him the taxi driver downshifted and pumped the brakes. He said, "Sir, I fear your timing isn't right. The colors are nearly finished, and last week we had a fall of snow, which didn't help, though it was gone the next day. Now the weather bureau's forecasting a storm."

It was true. The mountain slopes, which a week or so earlier must have been ablaze with color, were now merely speckled with scarlet. The man assumed that Aoki was here to observe autumn leaves; probably that was the only kind of visitor that came at this time of the year.

The inspector said, "A storm? If that happens, how will I get down the mountain?"

The driver grunted, twisting the steering wheel. "Don't worry, they'll clear the road. Only with the big snows in late November will it become impassable for the winter, and by then the ryokan's closed."

Aoki nodded and looked ahead. Like a slide flashed on a screen the ryokan appeared far below, cut into fragments by the intervening trees: a straggling timber building descending the mountainside on terraces.

This morning in Tokyo, the superintendent, with a meaningful look, had emphasized the ryokan's peaceful isolation, as though that were the tonic needed. It certainly looked peaceful enough. *Kamakura Inn.* Why was it called that? It was a hell of a long way from Kamakura. The taxi continued its descent, plunging deeper into evening shadows.

Abruptly, Aoki felt annoyed with himself that he'd come. Traveling north, increasingly, the trip hadn't felt right. Why had it been sprung on him at such short notice, and why Watanabe's air of impatience, even agitation? Aoki fumbled for cigarettes. Probably, his unease was due to his distrust of most of Watanabe's motives; however, the way his senior officer had put it, he'd had no choice. Even in the warmth of the car the cold seemed to be pouring depression and doubt into his soul, as if there weren't enough of it there already! They coasted down a final section of road, and the ryokan was now plainly revealed.

Climbing out of the taxi, Aoki was shocked by the temperature. He stood there in his overcoat, bareheaded, his short, sparse hair ruffled from the long journey. His hand brushed at the mole. His throat had tightened with nerves, and his heart had begun to hammer in his chest. Deliberately he hardened himself and felt the spasm passing. He lit the cigarette he'd taken out in the taxi.

He turned to face the wooden building. Overhanging eaves were supported by rough-hewn log pillars. Two, three hundred years old? Aoki didn't know or care; he was examining it from his habit of accumulating information and to get his brain back into the present.

The driver had stopped the taxi at the door and now opened the trunk by pulling a lever. A middle-aged woman appeared, bowed to Aoki, and lifted out first his suitcase, then the cardboard box into which he'd jabbed airholes. She waited while he paid the driver.

The Tokyo policeman pinched out the cigarette and entered the ryokan, ducking through a doorway decorated with welcoming maple branches. In the entranceway, he removed his shoes and slid his feet into the waiting slippers. Then he entered the hall that served as the inn's lobby.

The inspector had stepped into a gloomy space smelling of floor wax and enclosed by dark-stained timber—into claustrophobia. A ceiling strutted with chunky beams seemed a head hazard; involuntarily, he lowered his. The maid was following with his baggage.

Another woman was waiting for him behind a counter. A younger one, thirty, Aoki judged. A coiffure as black and shiny as lacquer was presented to him as she bowed a greeting. Responding,

Aoki looked at her curiously as she lifted her head. Her face had the healthy flush of the mountains; beneath her eyes were large freckles, and the eyes were assessing him in a polite and practiced way. As she presented the register for signing, Aoki stared at the thin white wrists revealed by the kimono sleeves.

"You're with us four nights, sir, I believe. We're offering you the Camellia Room." She smiled faintly. Her voice was husky and pleasant, the accent new to Aoki. He nodded and lowered his eyes.

She said, "The radio is forecasting a snowstorm, I'm afraid." In a slight change the smile had become rueful.

Aoki thought, *Doubtless it'll cut short the ryokan's fall season.* "Are there other guests?" he asked. Automatically, he wanted to know.

"A gentleman from Osaka will arrive shortly. Two other gentlemen came this afternoon from Tokyo." Her eyes seemed to be studying him afresh. Watanabe had said he hadn't revealed Aoki's occupation when he made the reservation, but if she read the newspapers she might remember him from his photograph.

Politely, the woman regarded her guest. Her name was Kazu Hatano; she was thirty-five and one of the ryokan's two proprietors. What she was seeing was a man not yet forty, of medium height, with a broad, brown face. Very tense. She thought, *That affair! A* good *resemblance to the photo in the paper. Does that mole worry him, the way he touches it?* She dropped her eyes. Thousands of ryokans in Japan; why pick this remote one? The day was turning out to be one of surprises, and the two men from Tokyo had been a big one.

Aoki thought, *She knows.* He nodded and followed the maid. They went down a staircase, then along dim corridors whose dark wooden boards glowed with a dull shine, and came to a door that had a timeworn painting of a flower on it. The Camellia Room, she'd said. The fusuma door slid open as quietly as a sigh, and he stepped into the room.

The maid brought in his suitcase and the cardboard box. There was a dining room, but did he want his evening meal served in his room? No, Aoki said, he would go to the dining room. He asked for directions to the bath; she told him and withdrew. Faintly, he heard the taxi departing. He had to duck his head to see out the window. The mountain peaks were glowing red now with the last of the sunset, and there was a deeper chill to the landscape.

Six forty-five this morning . . . Superintendent Watanabe. Did his boss really think a week's rest cure at the other end of Japan, in such a forlorn establishment, was going to make a difference and get a subordinate useful to him back on track? In the circumstances, that would be stupid thinking, and Watanabe was as smart, as calculating, as anyone Aoki had come up against. So what had happened at headquarters to make him take this trouble? Did Aoki's being dispatched here connect with the old case? Was the health cure just a pretext?

The volume of new questions shooting through his head must mean he wasn't brain-dead!

Aoki sighed and turned to the box. One by one, he took out Tokie's five bonsai plants, then laid the plastic sheet from the bottom of the box atop a chest and set the mini plants in their ceramic containers on it. The orphans. They needed daily watering, and there was no one to do that at the apartment.

Then he undressed, took the lightweight cotton yukata from the cupboard and put it on, and went to look for the bath. Following the maid's directions, he descended another staircase, walked the length of a corridor, and found it. He noted that the toilet was next door. He washed himself with soap and a cloth under an ancient shower and then stepped into the stone bath. He lowered himself into the steaming water and lay there, soaking away this day of travel and doubt. He got out twice to throw containers of cold water over his head and body.

Aoki's body was glowing and relaxed when he returned to his room. He hadn't had such a bath for years. He didn't see anyone. His bed had been made up on the floor, a kimono laid out on top. He moved it aside, lay down, and slept.

He awoke in darkness. Groggy with sleep, he switched on the bedside lamp. Shards of a dream, shards of the past, hovered in his mind. He was gazing at the blurry-white painting in the alcove, another camellia. In his stomach, the nerves were back.

Rest cure! He threw back the quilt and stood up, his arms rigid at his sides. Ex-governor Tamaki in all his grossness had come looping out of the darkness, into his head. A chill ran through his body. Today, various aspects of the past were on the march in his mind. With a conscious effort, he snapped out of it and began to pace the small room. He lit a cigarette. "It's set in concrete. It's over, Inspector." He heard Watanabe's voice, as clearly as if he'd just spoken. His heart began to thump in his chest as he relived the shock that had hit him that unforgettable morning they'd killed the investigation. He'd been as shocked as a schoolkid who'd failed an exam! After all, *anything* had been possible given that politicians were involved, though what had followed had been the real nightmare.

It was 7:20 P.M., and the ryokan's atmosphere seemed to be shrilling in Aoki's ears—mysteriously significant, different from the hollow echoes of his apartment, which now were like deep boomings in a dry, abandoned well. He stubbed out his cigarette and, ignoring the kimono, dressed again in his suit. He took a couple of deep breaths, then left the room.

A man in a gray suit sat on a bench in the hall. A man with plainly nowhere to go and *on duty*—Aoki had that instantly. The guy was built like a miniature sumo wrestler; his torso seemed about to burst from his coat with muscle power. Stubble covered a conical skull upon which was a bright red birthmark. His eyes flicked to Aoki as he rose to his feet and bowed.

Bodyguard, the policeman identified him. For whom, in this end-of-the-line place? Frowning, he turned away and went looking for the dining room. In its anteroom, a fire burned in a stone-flagged hearth, and its light flickered on the dusky ceiling beams—and over a Go board and its opposing ranks of white and black stones.

Strangely, Aoki saw that an instant before he saw the man sitting behind the board: a man in his fifties, whose eyes had lifted to regard the newcomer; a big man with luxuriant hair, glossy in the light, and a formidable, overhanging brow.

Aoki bowed. Here, he supposed, was the man from Osaka.

From his seated position, the man responded. Then he stood up, and they exchanged name cards, studied them, and bowed a second time. The man wore a dark kimono. His demeanor, the hairstyle, and the long, patrician face gave him an ascetic air, but what Aoki most absorbed was an undercurrent of power. It was likely that this man was bodyguard material. Printed on the card was OGATA SAITO and an Osaka address. No company name, no professional identification, but Aoki's card gave no such information, either. The man's dark-colored kimono made him an indistinct figure in the room's half-light; it was the reason Aoki hadn't seen him immediately.

"Are you a Go-player, Mr. Aoki?" The voice was deep.

Aoki was not, and said so. His father had played Go all his life, and when Aoki was much younger had tried to get him interested. The game was ancient, invented thousands of years ago; its origins were lost in obscurity, though traditionally its invention was ascribed to one of the earliest Chinese emperors. That information rose in Aoki's mind. He frowned. It was startling how bits and pieces of knowledge his father had imparted to him kept emerging from his brain. Planted there, like sleepers?

With the trace of a smile the man said, "I hoped to view the autumn leaves, but I've misjudged the season, and I fear I'm too late."

Aoki nodded. A maid slid open the door to the dining room, speaking in the lilting dialect to someone behind her. The two other guests were already at dinner, seated at a low table in a corner. The men from Tokyo. Aoki glanced through the open door.

Inspector Aoki froze. His glance had become a rigid stare. He knew them both. Hiroshi Ito, chairman of the Tokyo Citizens Bank, and Haruki Yamazaki, a senior official of the Ministry of Finance. These prominent figures of the Tokyo financial world—here! He rubbed his jaw. *But more than that*—both had been major players in the unsolved case he'd recalled on the bullet train: Ito, the husband of the missing woman, and Yamazaki, her lover. This was amazing—

Aoki tore his gaze away. At a stroke, his surprise and mystification at Watanabe's sending him here had soared to another level. These two men, deep in that case, were also strongly connected to this ryokan! Aoki lowered his eyes to the Go table. What in hell was going on?

Aoki looked up. The bodyguard in the hall—it clicked into place. He'd be looking after the prominent banker, not this Go-player.

Aoki's eyes met the Go-player's. A stone held between thumb and forefinger poised in midair, the big man was watching the policeman like a hawk.

Aoki gave him a terse, preoccupied nod and turned toward the dining room. The maid showed him to a place distant from the others. They turned their heads, obviously recognizing him, and polite bows were exchanged across the room. He imagined they were as surprised as he was, though their familiarity with him would have nothing to do with the missing-woman case.

The maid poured his beer as he gazed at the menu card. The old unsolved case had fairly leaped into his mind as he set eyes on the two men—stronger and sharper than his earlier recollection on the train of the ryokan's link with it.

He ordered the simplest meal on the menu. His head down, Aoki ate his fish, had his miso soup and rice, drank his beer. In contrast, the high-powered pair were having a banquet, talking quietly as a sucession of trays of lacquered and porcelain bowls came and went. Clearly they knew the specialities of the ryokan. That figured! Madam Ito had been a divorcée named Hatano and the owner of the ryokan when she met Ito. The banker had courted her, taken her off to Tokyo, and married her.

The two men were drinking sake, and the scent of the warmed alcohol wafted faintly to him.

Aoki's daze had cleared, and his mind was following old tracks. *A murder never solved. The body never discovered.* Had there even been a murder? His superiors had made no progress; the investigation had floundered. The case had been supervised by the then–director general of the CIB. *Top level.* The sensation had fizzled out in the media, and the case had been retired from high-priority status. He'd been one of about fifty detectives who worked on it, though Ito and Yamazaki couldn't know of his low-level involvement; their knowledge of him would relate to the Fatman's case. Everyone was interested in the ex-governor, and Aoki's face had been on the front pages after Kimura's article and Tokie's suicide.

And Superintendent Watanabe headed the Ito investigation! Watanabe hadn't been Aoki's boss in those days. Aoki smoothed his hand over his cheekbone. Watanabe's assessing look in the coffee shop this morning was stark in his mind. But could it be that the situation he'd walked in on *was* a strange coincidence? *No.* His jaw tightened. Watanabe was up to something. He glanced across to the table in the corner where the two men were toasting each other in sake, which seemed about as strange as anything else.

Aoki's mind was clicking over in the old way, as if he'd punched a panic button. He turned his eyes down, as though analyzing each morsel of food. In reality he was assessing each image from the past moving in his brain. He finished eating, rose from the cushions, and walked out. Behind him the quiet hum of talk ceased.

In the anteroom, the man from Osaka might not've moved a muscle. Big hands joined under his chin, he meditated on the game. "Please join me," he said, smiling up at the detective with an air that suggested he'd decided to get to know him better. He tinkled a small handbell, and a maid appeared at once. "A scotch and water, please. Cutty Sark. What will you have?" The dense eyebrows lifted slightly.

"A scotch, too." Aoki almost asked for a double, but he was settling down. He sighed to himself.

The man turned his eyes back to the board. Frowning, Aoki stared at it, too. He was surprised that he hadn't given the case more than a passing thought in the intervening years. His first criminal case. Watanabe never spoke of it.

He looked up at his surroundings. It had come to him that today he'd entered a zone where time might be meaningless. It was an unusual thought for Aoki, but a notion his father and his wife would've understood.

A log in the fireplace cracked, expelling sparks. His head drooped, and his eyes closed. He'd had a long day of travel and surprises, and he was convinced now that this journey had nothing to do with his rehabilitation—so what kind of hand had his boss dealt him this morning?

Chapter Seven

"IS THERE BLOOD ON THEIR hands?" the Go-player said.

Aoki's head jerked up. He'd drifted off only momentarily. The words spoken were clear in his head—said so casually, in that Osaka dialect, but the guy had put his finger on it. Yet another surprise! The Osaka man spoke as though he had a deep knowledge of the missing-woman case.

Saito immediately lowered his eyes and was again concentrating on the board. He picked up a black stone. "Anyway, quite a scandal, wasn't it?"

Frowning, Aoki waited.

"I wonder if they're talking about it right now." The big man placed the stone. "The woman's body never found, just her blood-stained clothes turning up in that Tokyo Central station locker, and those two"—he inclined his head toward the dining room—"unable to assist the police much, though each had been with her at different times the night she vanished."

His tone sounded half-amused, at what appeared to have been a tragedy.

Aoki's brow remained creased. Yeah. Blood without a corpse.

Suspects without an arrest. Stalemated, month after month, the investigator's nightmare. This man had read the papers of the day and had a good memory. That must be it—it'd come back to him in a rush when the two public figures arrived, or maybe, like Aoki, he'd remembered it en route to the ryokan, which had been so publicly tied in with the case. Or maybe he'd come here knowing it, which was something to think about. However, it was his superintendent's purposeful intensity this morning, as he'd sent Aoki on this last-chance health cure, that was stuck in his mind like a fishbone in the throat.

Into a lengthening silence, Aoki said, "You know a lot about it."

The Go-player shrugged as if to say, *Who doesn't?* In a new tone, he said, "This is the classic game of 1938, between Master Shusai and the challenger, Mr. Kitani Minoru of the seventh rank. The state of play at the end of the second Hakone session on July 16, a match financed by Osaka and Tokyo newspapers."

Aoki stared at him. This man appeared to have his father's mind-set in matters of culture, but the similarity to the old professor finished there. This one was tough and sharp; that was as plain as the black and white stones placed on the board in their battle formations.

Saito smiled. "I replay this same match every autumn. I find an old, remote ryokan to do it, such as this one. It's a spiritual discipline I impose on myself. Last autumn, I went to a ryokan on the Noto Peninsula."

Aoki nodded tersely. He'd never heard of the famous match, and it was of no interest to him. Spiritual discipline? That sounded like some kind of bunk.

The Osaka man straightened his torso and studied the detective. "I'm also a student of famous criminal cases, those I find interesting.

About this case, much was written, and I've read most of it. *So!* which one of them murdered her, or did they conspire in it? Or was neither responsible?"

Aoki, increasingly wary, stared harder. Again that mordantly humorous tone. He'd come out of the bemused state he'd been in in the dining room; now he felt alert, intrigued by this Saito's comments and by the man's assumption that he'd also remember the case. He said, "What's *your* theory?"

The other showed yellowed teeth in a grimace. "Theory? Ito, her husband, a cuckold! Yamazaki, her lover, her seducer! For two years that'd been common knowledge in certain circles in Tokyo. Like the burst of a firework, it was revealed to the nation. My theory? Was there a murder at all?"

Aoki's eyes were held by the Go board. The confronting formations of black and white stones glittered alike. Yeah, for a while, the police had gone down that line. He ran his hand through his sparse hair. "The bloodstained clothing, which matched her rare blood type?" he queried concisely. How far could this stranger take it?

The maid brought in a bottle of Cutty Sark, disinterred from some distant storage cabinet, glasses, and a jug of water and placed them on a side table. Saito drew back, and his hand made the whiskey bottle seem half-size. "So? Such things can be arranged. I don't dispute she'd become an embarrassment to each, and they contemptible to her. The newspaper reports brought that out, but the police couldn't prove there'd been a murder—as you well know." He poured the whiskey into the glasses.

Aoki nodded slowly, considering "as you well know." This man knew who he was! As did the woman on the front desk, as did the two men in the dining room. *What had he walked into?* He took up his glass and said, "A missing person for seven years? And why those clothes in that locker, identified as hers?"

Saito's fleshy lips pouted. "Did you know this match lasted for nearly half a year, was reported by the novelist Kawabata for the newspapers?"

Aoki's eyes narrowed. The man's mind was running on twin tracks. He didn't know this—after all, 1938. He'd heard of Kawabata but never read anyone's novels. He guessed his father had read them. He drank half the whiskey at a gulp and impatiently glanced through the open door to the dining room. The two men from Tokyo were still deep in food and conversation.

Saito said, "What is especially interesting is that they've turned up *here*, of all places." The dark eyes were set back deeply under the projecting brows. "What does that mean?"

Aoki didn't reply. *Yeah,* he thought. *But why is this man so deep into it?* If he *was* one of those busybodies who avidly followed lurid crimes, what a bonanza to find yourself under the same roof as two key figures in a famous case.

"Perhaps you'll play chess with me tomorrow. I trust you aren't planning to leave for several days. Heavy snow will fall tonight."

Eyeing the other, Aoki downed his drink and rose to his feet. He wished to get away and think about the situation. He bowed a good night and went out into the dim, breezy corridor hung with ancient calligraphy scrolls, which scraped and whispered against the wall, as if reciting their messages. The electric light in the whole ryokan was feeble.

In the hall, fallen maple leaves lay on the floorboards. Aoki noticed how they flared bright red in the dusk, like the flames in the heart of the fire. He realized he was seeing some things with fresh eyes. Mountain air? New surroundings? His nervous state? His father had once told him that the brain functioned better in cold weather. "Winter's the best time for calligraphy," he'd said.

Aoki sighed. The weariness he'd felt earlier had returned, like a drug. Maybe he'd sleep better tonight.

The squat, sumo-like man had disappeared.

The woman who had greeted him came out of her office, and Aoki saw that she'd changed into a dark blue kimono flecked with white. She said, "A kotatsu has been put in your room, sir. I do hope you'll be warm enough. It's always colder before a snowfall." The same lilting mountain accent the taxi driver had. Her face, with only a trace of lipstick when he'd arrived, had been made up for the evening. The freckles under the eyes had vanished beneath white pancake makeup; the red-painted lips were vivid and precise. But she'd retired deeper into herself, if that was possible—into old traditions. "*Ah,* except the eyes," Aoki told himself. They were cool, assessing, on guard, and very human.

Tokie had had much of this, but beneath it she had been modern in many ways.

Another fragment of the old case had emerged from his memory—the part that connected to the ryokan. Was this woman one of the missing Madam Ito's twin daughters, possibly the inheritor, with her sister, of the ryokan? If she was, what did she think of them being there: the banker Ito, her mother's reportedly complaisant second husband, and Yamazaki, Madam Ito's seducer, who'd been extensively questioned by the police about her disappearance? He'd find out her name. Tonight, there was a lot more in the air than an approaching snowstorm.

Her attitude modest and attentive, she was waiting on his pleasure. In a flash, he decided that she had the essence of this remote mountainous region, for him—yet another unusual thought. Was he turning into a poet?

He said, "The man sitting here earlier, who is he?"

"Shoba-san, Mr. Ito's man."

In a rush of air, as if he'd been cued in, steady on his feet, though his round face was red from alcohol, Ito entered the hall. He went to the woman and inquired about an outside line for his room phone. She responded. He turned and peered at Aoki for a long moment, then bowed. "My condolences on the tragic loss of your wife."

Aoki's face tightened in amazement. Then he blinked at the change in the woman, subtle, yet to his trained eye distinct. Her body had stiffened as she gazed with a deep intensity on the banker's flushed face. Under her gaze Ito dropped his eyes and turned away to descend the stairs.

Lighting a cigarette, Aoki walked the shadowy corridors to his room. Hatred, subtle but malicious, had been in that look, hardly a thing for a ryokan proprietor to show a customer! But then, if his guess was right, he was also her stepfather.

He shook his head. suddenly the old case seemed to be hemming him in from all sides, minute by minute, to be flaring into life.

Inspector Aoki reached his room and paused, hand on the door, again amazed that he and Ito had simultaneously arrived at this dot in the mountains, each with his particular knowledge of the other.

There was a slight movement farther along the dim corridor. Aoki peered in that direction and was surprised to make out a cat sitting there, watching him. Abruptly it came forward. Aoki didn't know much about cats but had nothing against them. He lowered his hand, and tentatively the cat sniffed it.

"What are you doing?" he said. *Hunting time,* he thought. This place would be a paradise for mice, and cats. He stroked it briefly and then slid open the door, with its aged painted camellia.

A padded kimono had replaced the other on the futon. The charcoal brazier to warm his feet and hands glowed in the electric light. The temperature was dropping, all right. He'd drunk the large whiskey quickly, and it had affected him. His bed had been re-made. He butted the cigarette in an ashtray, sat on a cushion, and gazed into the alcove at the other dusky camellia.

This ryokan was steeped in tradition, foreign territory to him. Tokie and his father, the traditionalists, would've been at home here. His loved ones, and all they stood for, had slipped through his fingers, seemingly in an eyeblink. Aoki stood up in the small room and held out his hands, confirming that they were shaking. His misery, his defeat, came crowding up on him. *Ex-governor Tamaki.* He turned away from the alcove, but whichever way he turned, the Fat-man's face was over his shoulder, hard and contemptuous, an untouchable, a winner.

Aoki took a deep breath. He needed another Cutty Sark, but he fumbled in his bag and found one of the six chocolate bars he'd extracted from a vending machine at Tokyo Central station. He peeled off the silver wrapper and bit into the candy. On the wooden chest, the five orphans looked forlorn. He touched the moss around their tiny roots. Barely damp. He trickled water from a glass onto each; he'd have to remember to do this daily.

Aoki heard a sudden rush of wind and lifted his head as it whined past the eaves. It had come from nowhere, and even as he listened it grew in force. The charcoal fire in the kotatsu shifted in an uneasy sound. The faint smell of ash was in the room. He glanced at his watch: 11:15 P.M. One whiskey and his head felt fuzzy. The altitude? No, fatigue. He undressed and put on the yukata to sleep in.

The wind was howling around the ryokan now like a predator who'd cornered prey. Aoki, a stranger to mountain country, had never heard anything like it. He lay down on the padded mattress, and his mind looped back to Watanabe. Had the head of the investigation seven years ago been keeping his eye on the chief suspects, Ito and Yamazaki, all the while? Had the superintendent known that the two men were coming here and thrown Aoki back into the case for his own purposes? But if so, why hadn't his boss filled him in?

Frowning, he thought back to what he'd known of the superintendent's involvement in the case that, reportedly, had permanently stalled his promotion. Plenty of cops had unsolved cases on their records, even high-profile ones, but they still got promoted. The case had run into a dead end, and Watanabe had turned his focus onto her ex-husband, Hatano, a chef in Osaka. So far as Watanabe had been concerned, the man, a violent type who'd been sent packing years before by his ex-wife, had been furious at her marriage to the rich banker. Watanabe had become obsessed with the idea that the woman was the victim of her ex's jealousy. Hatano had made a few drunken threats, but Watanabe's terrific efforts had found no hard evidence to support a prosecution, especially without a corpse. Even so, he'd relentlessly kept on down that track, despite mounting criticism from his superiors. Finally, he'd become convinced that the twin daughters, who would inherit the ryokan, had conspired with their father in a murder. At that point, he'd been taken off the case.

Aoki shook his head. Even the smartest operators sometimes

ran off the rails. Feeling baffled and remote from civilization, he reached across to switch off the light. Saito's long, sardonic face emerged in his mind. He wondered if the man from Osaka's interest in the case went beyond the voyeur's. He clucked his tongue; perhaps he was getting carried away with it all.

He thought of something else and switched the light back on and reached out for his wallet and took the news clipping from it again. For the second time that day, he squinted at the faded newsprint. He confirmed what had entered his mind: Madam Ito had disappeared on the evening of October 24, 1993. Today was October 22, 2000. The day after tomorrow would be the seventh anniversary of the night she'd gone missing.

He switched the light off and lay back under the quilt. Moment by moment, the creaks from the antique timbers were increasing in tempo; the scroll was banging against the alcove wall, the window glass was rattling in the frame, and torn paper panels in the fusuma door were flapping. Aoki sat up as the whole wooden structure shuddered in a fiercer blast, seeming to shift sideways. He felt like a man on a storm-tossed ship that was about to go down without a trace.

Chapter Eight

AOKI STARTED AWAKE INTO A darkness that was as dense as crude oil. His neck was running with moisture, his heart bounding from the cruel nightmare that came too often. Lying back, he surmised that one night it would kill him with a chest-wrenching heart attack. As long as it was quick.

Nothing in his past had prepared him for what he'd found in the kitchen that night: not the mayhem that had come his way as a homicide detective, or earlier, as a traffic cop; not the surrealistic scenes in the Tokyo subway the day of the gas attack by the Aum Shinrikyo cult. *Nothing.* Not even his father plunging forward on the dinner table, his face contorted in his death agony.

The lifeless fingers of her right hand, slightly inky from the last brushstrokes of her calligraphy . . .

That horror—deep-set in him, the police psychiatrist said—was a significant part of his problem. "Turn your mind to the future," the shrink advised. But he'd never get over it.

Using the bedside flashlight, he peered at his watch: three minutes to three. Outside the covers, the air was freezing on his arm as he reached for a towel and mopped his neck and chest. The charcoal in the kotatsu had turned to ash.

With a stab of surprise, he realized that the wooden building's shuddering and the wind's banshee wailing had ceased. Beyond the walls, in the wake of the departed storm, the absolute silence seemed a roar in his ears.

Aoki got up and put on his overcoat, slid back the door, and stepped out of the Camellia Room. With the aid of the flashlight, he set out along the corridors. Faint snoring came from a door he passed, the only hint of humanity except for his quiet footfalls, which brought a subtle creaking from the floorboards. He ascended the staircase, went through the dark hall and along the corridor, and entered the anteroom.

His breath hissed out; his arm came up automatically, as if to shield his face. The room was awash with dazzling white light. Framed in the large window was a dense white curtain of falling snow. On the Go board, the black stones were sharp and lethal, the white ones almost invisible. Shivering, he went to the window and gazed out. Before the nightmare had woken him, the old case had been in an earlier dream, and now it returned like a figure in white walking through these dark and rambling rooms.

It must have been about sixteen years ago when Ito had met the divorced Madam Hatano. She'd inherited the ryokan from her father. After her disappearance, the papers claimed Ito had wooed her for a year, coming and going from Tokyo. A fresh mountain beauty, they wrote, though the photograph in his wallet was of the more mature woman, fine-featured and delicate. Yet a strong character did show in her face, and a sophistication that went beyond "fresh mountain beauty." The Mona Lisa smile the photographer had caught heightened the enigma.

As he watched the snow fall on the deeply silent mountain, swinging his arms for warmth, more and more of the case was coming back to Aoki. It was said that she'd also had an air of the demi-monde, later; probably that was what had attracted Yamazaki, given his reputation with women. At any rate, the Ministry of Finance official had made his move—"seduced this leading banker's wife, the owner of a mountain ryokan," reported one paper, sprinkling spice for the salarymen and their wives. Throughout the case there'd been a shortage of facts, but avidly the media had embroidered what they had. It came out that the affair with Yamazaki had lasted about two years, accepted by her "complaisant" husband. Both men had had several mistresses during the period, and much about that had come out, too. Each was then in his early forties, the libido in its second flowering. It was strange how the raw publicity hadn't harmed either man's career.

Aoki rubbed his hands vigorously; the aching cold was penetrating his bones. For Superintendent Watanabe, the case had been *his* nightmare. Aoki was realizing, more and more, how it must have been festering in his boss's mind all these years.

He should go back to the room before he froze to death, but the partially reconstructed though still essentially mysterious night in October 1993 was relentlessly seeping into his consciousness. Ito and Yamazaki had told the police their stories of that night, as had others, but it all led nowhere. When Ito had reported her as a missing person, given his influence, the police had responded diligently. Then the bloodstained clothes had turned up, and their interest had sparked. It appeared they had a murder investigation on their hands—and Superintendent Watanabe had been up and running.

Aoki stood like a statue in the snow's light. If anything, the snowfall was becoming heavier. *Crack!* Startled, he peered under the eaves into the snowy world. *Crack! Crack!* The weight of the snow was snapping branches off the trees. It had terminated his thinking, and he was shivering violently now as though he'd caught a chill. He left to find his way back to his room, hurrying toward warmth.

In the room he warmed his hands in the kotatsu, then found his cigarettes. The lighter flared. He drew in tobacco smoke and immediately felt warmer and more lucid in his thinking. One paper, seeking readership, had speculated that she'd been dismembered and minced up for pig food. It was hard to see the bankerly Ito or the urbane Yamazaki having a hand in such a demise! Yet each had been shown up as ruthless in his profession, and what calculations and fantasies went on behind any person's professional facade?

He butted the half-smoked cigarette and returned to bed, keeping the overcoat on.

When Aoki awoke for the second time, he didn't know where he was. Then he lifted his head and made out the blurred flower in the alcove. The sound of the stream, like the gale, had died away, leaving an out-of-the-world silence, a pregnant one. He sat up, now alert. In the space of twelve hours his brain had gone from the moribund to the hyperactive. For months, his mind had been dormant except for the gathering stone-hard hatred for Tamaki. It was working again—yet, he felt, not quite reliable. He flung the covers back and walked to the bath. Thirty minutes later he returned, red-faced and glowing. The cat was sitting outside his door, and he bent down to stroke it. Its yellow eyes turned up to his, assessing him. Another assessor.

He was dressed when a female voice came from outside the door. It slid open, and the middle-aged maid who'd carried in his luggage was there, on her knees, head lowered in a bow. A lacquered tray with a steaming tea bowl was on the floor in front of her.

She got to her feet and put the tray beside the bonsai pots, giving them a curious look.

"What is your name?" Aoki asked. Clearly she was to be his room maid.

"Mori, sir."

"Well, Mori-san, who does that cat belong to?"

Surprised, she turned to look at the cat sitting in the doorway. "No one, sir, it is the house cat."

"What's its name?"

"Cat, sir."

Aoki smiled, and she bowed and withdrew.

At 8:30 A.M. he went to the main hall. The mini sumo look-alike was back, seated against the wall, same gray suit, same vacant stare from the tiny dark eyes. The policeman observed him narrowly. A punch from those muscular arms could smash bones. Aoki had his black belt in karate, but he hadn't practiced since pressure of work had forced him to give up instructing at the boys' club a year ago.

A large charcoal brazier was burning brightly. The remaining maple leaves had fallen from the display branches. *As if the snow's told them the show's over,* he thought. The situation he'd stepped into might be reactivating his investigator's brain, but was this mountain ryokan changing his thinking in this other way? He grunted.

The woman appeared from her office, businesslike, briskly confronting the premature termination of the fall season. The daughter! He felt certain of it. If so, one of the sisters who, according to Watanabe, had conspired with their father in their mother's "disappearance."

"I'm afraid we're snowed in, sir. Nearly six feet have fallen."
Aoki nodded. The weather forecasters, the taxi driver, the man
from Osaka, the proprietor—each had foretold the situation accurately. "It's the earliest big fall for many years. And the telephone
line is down somewhere."

Aoki was surprised at this. He doubted cell phones would oper-
ate here, not that he'd brought his own; there was no one he'd want
to call. Through the glass doors he could see how deep the snow lay;
six feet would become ten if it kept up like this. He'd put on a heavy
cable-stitch pullover that his wife had knitted two years before.

He gazed at the woman. She wore a padded black kimono
streaked with red and had reddened her lips with lipstick.

Shoba sprang to his feet, bowing. Ito had hurried in. The bank
chairman sharply inclined his head to acknowledge his fellow guest.
"What is wrong with the phone?" he said to the woman. "I need to
contact my office in Tokyo. It's most urgent."

"I am afraid the line is down."

"*What!*" He hissed through his teeth. "*For how long?*"

She hesitated. "A day or so."

Ito stared at her, consternation on his round face, his breathing
audible. The air was rank with his overnight digestion. He recol-
lected himself, gave a cursory bow, and turned on his heel to leave.
She watched him go. For an instant her eyes met Aoki's; then, with
a bow, she returned to her office.

The bodyguard sat down again, boss gone, energy deflated.

Walking past the scrolls of calligraphy to breakfast, Aoki had a
feeling that something significant was going to happen. As though a
switch had been flicked on, it seemed that his pragmatic street cop's
sixth sense had been reactivated, and everything in him was jerking
back into action.

He'd found in an alcove what he'd been looking for: the framed business registration certificate with the managing proprietor's name, Kazu Hatano. He stroked his chin thoughtfully. The proprietor-manager of the ryokan was, indeed, the daughter of the missing woman and thus this big-time banker's stepdaughter.

Chapter Nine

AOKI BREAKFASTED ALONE. WHEN HE came out to the anteroom, there was no one to be seen, not even a maid, and the fire was crackling away. He returned to his room, rubbing his hands against the cold, though the temperature had risen from the overnight freeze. He unpacked his Sony shortwave radio and placed it on the low table. In his old life, he'd sometimes surfed the international airwaves looking for jazz.

He went to the window. The glass was opaque, the snow ridged against it a mere shadow line, and he reached out with his fingertips. They stuck to the glass: Everything here was as cold as his thoughts.

Never could he have anticipated what Tokie had done. Criminal minds he knew about, but he'd been ambushed by an honest one bent on a mission springing from a naive notion of justice and, above all, from love. Had she found her inspiration in the melodrama and convoluted plots of the Kabuki plays?

Aoki sneezed. He turned from the window and looked at the padded kimono but put on a tweed jacket that felt tight over the sweater. One of the bonsai plants looked sick, and he peered at its tiny root system. Not enough moisture, or too much? He supposed the maid would relight the kotatsu. He glanced at his watch, switched on the radio, and tuned the dial through fields of static to NHK.

This morning shock waves hit the nation when the giant Tokyo Citizens Bank failed to open for business. Overnight government regulators moved into the bank. The head of the Diet Committee for Banking Industry Reconstruction, Yukio Tamaki, said the bank's ability to meet its obligations had deteriorated dramatically in the past two days, and the government had no choice but to step in. On the news, the Nikkei index fell 8 percent in early trading. In an intriguing development, the bank's chairman, Hiroshi Ito, has not been seen since Sunday afternoon, and all efforts to contact him have failed.

The first words struck Aoki like a punch in the chest. Normally he would have passed over such news with a shrug. Not now! He switched off the radio, lit a cigarette, and inhaled deeply. No wonder Ito had been agitated; he must've heard an earlier broadcast.

The Fatman, head of the Diet banking committee! Another pie the ex-governor had gotten his fingers into. And the bank's chairman and a key MOF official locked away in the mountains at the other end of the nation!

Aoki paced the room, drawing on the cigarette. He pulled up and shook his head in amazement. It must've hit those two like a sledgehammer—but the catastrophe had to've been in the wind. They must've been walking a tightrope, so why in hell had they taken the terrific risk of absenting themselves from the center of power? Unbelievable—that no one in Tokyo knew their whereabouts. "What is going on?" he asked himself.

What he'd read in the newspaper clipping came back. Perhaps they'd planned to be away only a few nights—for the seventh anniversary. Whatever, with Tamaki heading that committee, they'd been playing with fire, because, for sure, the Fatman would have an agenda. With the bank's chairman incommunicado for whatever reason, Tamaki had grabbed the opportunity. Time and time again, he'd shown himself to be a fast mover when it suited his interests. It was the kind of scenario that fit the Fatman like a glove.

Aoki, his brow creased, was wearing out the tatami mat. He stubbed out his cigarette, left his room, slid the door shut, and walked the breezy corridors. Yeah, alert like the old days, yet cut off, powerless, and trapped in this missing-woman mystery—and in Watanabe's hidden agenda.

However, as if granted to him as compensation, his personal misery and despair had receded in his mind.

In the anteroom, a maid had just fed extra logs onto the fire, and it burned with new energy. Saito was gazing down at the Go board. Aoki cleared his throat. "Your weather forecast was accurate."

The big man looked up sharply. "I've an instinct for weather. Also a shortwave radio."

His dark face, the color of mahogany, showed cynical amusement. A bit more evident than yesterday's, Aoki decided. Despite his age, his shoulders were powerful. He wore a dark blue suit, with hand-stitched lapels, and a luxurious silk tie. The change of clothing puzzled Aoki—overdressed for the mountains and underdressed for the weather. There wasn't anywhere the man could go, but what was going on in his head? What was his game apart from this boring Go?

Saito's large, brown-mottled hand motioned Aoki to sit down. "Even our powerful co-guests are locked in with us, away from their power bases. Their cell phones aren't effective here." He nodded at the board. "And *this* game is also at a crucial stage. The Master's health was bad, and it was making the conduct of the match difficult." He grimaced. "On July 31, the challenger, Minoru, deliberated for an hour and forty-eight minutes on a move—Black 83."

Aoki stared at the board. Saito had heard the broadcast. The policeman turned his head toward the window. The snow was up to the sill, and, silent and thick, still it fell. With a rustle of kimono another maid passed through the anteroom, and the rough Osaka voice cut in. "They're not men who have a true feeling for the Japanese spirit. They make a point of going to view cherry blossoms, colored leaves in fall, to hear the New Year bells in Kyoto, but it's not in their souls."

The Go-player sat back and fixed his gaze on Aoki. He'd spoken with a tough formality, yet again Aoki detected the mocking humor. Against them—or him? Frowning, he stared back. What gave the fellow this special insight into the psyche of the Tokyo finance leaders?

Saito said, "Their *true* feeling is for the yen, the dollar, political intrigue, for high office, power, and for expensive possessions. Madam Ito was of that nature to Ito. She was beautiful, and her mountain background added something special."

He interlaced his big hands and cracked his knuckles, startling Aoki. "But even with the yen and the dollar, their touch has been stupendously incompetent! The chaotic condition of the Citizens Bank bears this out." A log exploded, spitting cinders. "Have you heard *that* news?" Aoki gave a terse nod. The man's eyes were boring into him. "You have your own special experience of such men."

That hit home, but Aoki remained silent. Most of what Saito had said about the old case could've been gleaned from the papers, but had it been? And this man from Osaka knew who he was— again the papers! What was his profession? He talked about the business world like a damned television guru, but none of it seemed on the level. A tricky joker? After its hibernation, Aoki's brain wouldn't stop working.

Saito weighed a white stone in his right hand. "Their talk last night? What's your deduction—a reconciliation? A reconstruction of her disappearance, seeking the truth, or did they discuss only the bank's situation?"

Ah! Aoki ran his tongue over his teeth. While the dishes of last night's banquet had come and gone, they'd certainly been absorbed in their talk. Did Saito know that tomorrow night was the anniversary of Madam Ito's disappearance?

Saito frowned and murmured, "You don't answer." He placed Black 89 and looked up. "My guess is that each believes the other murdered her, each seeks to know the truth. It's like a fine splinter of steel in their brains, and they're going over it, sparring with each other, trying to fill in the blanks of that fatal night."

Aoki nodded slowly. "That's an interesting theory. It implies—"

"That *neither* murdered her, perhaps that she wasn't murdered at all. As I said."

Aoki's finger found the mole.

Saito gave a faint smile. "This was the Master's retirement match." Aoki frowned. The conversation about Ito and Yamazaki was a parallel shadow game to the Go match—though which game was the shadow, which the substance? Crazy thinking. Succinctly, he said, "It seems the Citizens Bank's troubles have been well hidden until now."

Saito laughed roughly. "Doubtless there's been a conspiracy with the government to keep it under wraps, but suddenly—crisis point. Chairman Ito must be driven half mad, a prisoner here, while his enemies cut loose, his world implodes! Well, he shouldn't have rushed off, should he? A general lost on the battlefield is no good to anyone except the enemy. Yamazaki will have his worries, too. Will it come out he's been covering up the bank's desperate situation at the ministry?"

This man was releasing his startling surmises into the dark old ryokan, the way the fishermen sent their cormorants diving into the Nagara River's night waters. Startling, but with a certain logic. The last one was a note to depart on. Brusquely, Aoki excused himself.

In the hall, Ito and Yamazaki, heads close, voices confidential, paced back and forth. From his bench, Shoba was watching them as if following a rally in a tennis match. The banker appeared even more rotund in a padded kimono, Aoki thought, and his soft body trembled as he walked, though his brain was certainly not soft. The heavy-lidded eyes gave him a somnolent appearance, a mask for his ruthless spirit.

Yet Ito must've been asleep during the years when his vast city bank had embarked on its reckless lending spree, the years when Yamazaki had swept his wife off to their passionate trysts. A well-fed gentleman, but not rancid fat, perfumed fat. "Quiet and fast as a cobra," a journalist had written, using the banker's nickname: Buddha.

Yamazaki, tall, less voluble, wore his bureaucratic power with a kind of sinister urbanity.

Unnoticed, Aoki passed behind them, unable to glean anything from their lowered voices. A moment later he came upon Mori in the corridor and asked her to bring tea to his room. The kotatsu was alight again, and he warmed his hands, wondering if Saito made mistakes as he replayed that match from memory. Fellows like him, committed to a way of life involving annual repetitions of pieces of traditional culture, weren't that rare in Japan. Take his father. Both were a light-year away from Aoki's mind-set.

His father had occasionally stayed at a ryokan. Aoki remembered one in Kyoto that the old man had regarded going to as a pilgrimage. He screwed up his eyes, trying to remember more. The old man had chosen moments to impart information on matters that interested him. A scrap surfaced . . . In the early seventeenth century, five highways had been built linking the provinces with Edo, the old name for Tokyo. Road travelers had needed places to stay overnight . . . Such places were linked to the top brass of the day. The shogun had forced the feudal lords—daimyos—to travel these roads and spend alternate years at Edo, under his watchful eye.

But this ryokan was on no highway.

Aoki tried to remember more . . . no use. He switched on the radio and found dance music in a former republic of the USSR. Thinking of the sound traveling across the Siberian wastes to this snowbound ryokan high in these mountains made him feel more alone.

When the maid brought his tea, he asked if there were any women available for companionship. Averting her eyes, she said there was one. Men's business, which she gave a helping hand to. Would he like her to come this evening?

Aoki nodded his assent. The woman must already be under the roof. He'd heard that these places usually had a local geisha on call, or one or two complaisant maids available for male guests. Like many of his colleagues, most of his adult life Aoki had engaged in casual sex—sometimes when he was nervous or morose, or when he was drunk. He had only done it a few times since his marriage, times when he'd felt an even greater distance from Tokie than usual. He'd felt bad about it afterward. Now he was at the greatest distance of all.

After lunch, Aoki slept. When he awoke he took a walk through the corridors and dusky rooms, trying to fit the plan of the place into his head. Ito and Yamazaki hadn't reappeared, nor was Saito at the Go table. At four, when he went to take a bath, it was still snowing. Outside, the mountains had frozen over; inside, it felt as cloistered as a monastery, and as bone-chilling. To get out of the building they'd have to dig a tunnel from the front door, but where could one go to? Snowplows wouldn't be operating on the road yet, they said.

The ryokan had two baths, each of a size adequate to take several people, each fed by water from a hot spring. One was hollowed out of stone, the other made of fragrant old cypress wood. Up to his neck in the cypress one, he lay in the water and slowly soaked in the heat, just over a hundred degrees, he estimated. For him, this kind of bathing was a luxury. His mind drifted . . .

On the night she disappeared, Ito had dined with his wife at a restaurant in the Ginza. At nine, after putting her in a taxi to return home, the banker had gone to a well-known businessmen's club. He'd left the club at ten-thirty and arrived home after eleven. She had not returned. In fact, she'd gone to see Yamazaki. The MOF official had met her at nine-thirty at an apartment he kept in Shimbashi. He'd filed a sworn statement that she left by taxi before eleven, to go home. Though his wife wasn't back yet, in the circumstances of his marriage, Ito had gone to bed. The next morning he'd phoned Yamazaki—doubtless an interesting conversation—then, after some deliberation, a high police official whom he knew. The police had found the taxi driver who'd brought Ito home, and also the driver who'd taken Madam Ito to Yamazaki's apartment, but not the one who'd taken her from there. For a while, the investigation centered on Yamazaki, but he was unshakable in his story. The police, aided by the media, had scoured the city for other witnesses. They'd found none.

That October night, Madam Ito had vanished from the face of the earth. Then, a week later, her bloodstained clothes had been discovered at Central station and identified by both men. After that, apart from matching the blood on the clothing with the missing woman's rare group, and a few minor details, the investigation had stalled. Months passed. Aoki and his fifty colleagues had been reassigned to a new batch of crimes. By that time Superintendent Watanabe was off the case. Aoki had only known him by sight in those days.

His face steaming with heat and moisture, frowning with the effort to remember more details, Aoki found himself wishing he had the case dossier.

A man came into the bathhouse. Aoki peered through the rising steam and saw Yamazaki. The Ministry of Finance man completed his wash and rinse, then stepped into the bath, moving back to rest his head in a corner angle and floating his legs out—long, thin, well-shaped legs, absolutely hairless. He closed his eyes, ignoring Aoki's presence. His face was saturnine, his chin prominent, yet the overall impression was harmonious. He was in good shape for a man in his middle fifties, his stomach flat and muscled.

Aoki climbed from the bath and reached for a towel. Out of the steam, the official's voice came, thick and nasal. "Sincere condolences on your wife's passing. A sad and regrettable situation."

Aoki gazed into the steamy bath at the indistinct figure. Last night, Ito had spoken similar words. What a strange place, a bizarre moment, to make such a remark.

Aoki wrapped the towel around his waist, put on his yukata and slippers, bowed briefly at the recumbent form, and left the bathhouse.

In the Camellia Room, he considered who'd be paying for Yamazaki's mountain interlude. Yamazaki wouldn't have put his hand in his pocket for innumerable costly banquets, golf dates, and trips like this one; Ito and his executives would've been the free-spenders. The monolithic government ministries were ripe with such practices—*and* the political scene. The power brokers who'd fucked him!

His anger cooled. Yamazaki would be immune, like ex-governor Tamaki, to any qualms of conscience; it was the system, their home ground. However, the affair with the chairman's wife was on another plane. A thought struck Aoki: Might it have been part of a bargain with Ito? Far from being a weak and feckless cuckold, had Ito coolly traded his beautiful wife to the sensual Yamazaki to protect himself as the bank weakened? Had that possibility occurred to the senior police investigators on the case?

He'd surprised himself with the thought.

Put on the padded kimono. I'm worried about you. Your clothes are not adequate here. It was Tokie's voice in his brain.

Yes, I also recommend it, his father said.

Stock-still, Aoki stared at the picture of the camellia as the voices faded in his head. A month after his wife's death, he'd begun talking to them both. Walking around the silent apartment, sitting in the coffee shop or the bar, he'd say, "What do you think of this?" Or "Do you remember that day?" This was the first time *they'd* spoken.

He removed his Western clothing and put on the kimono. Immediately he felt warmer, and hungry. From a drawer he took a chocolate bar and broke it in half.

It was seven days after his article appeared that Eichi Kimura had been murdered. Assistant Inspector Nishi had told him that the reporter had been working on a follow-up story, calling on contacts, doing his own research this time. Kimura's poor wife, finding *that* body.

The old-fashioned phone jangled. Aoki's head snapped up, out of the past, away from a vision of burst-out eyeballs, a half-severed tongue, and sliced-off ears.

Chapter Ten

SAITO'S ROUGH VOICE WAS IN Aoki's ear. "I would like to continue our conversation and drink whiskey with you. I'll be at the Go board from five thirty."

Aoki hesitated, then agreed to meet at six thirty and hung up. For a moment he'd thought the line to outside had been restored. Conversation! It had been mainly one-way traffic, though that was partly Aoki's choice. What else did the guy have to say? Again, the feeling that something significant was about to happen came down on him.

At 6:15 P.M. the electricity failed. Aoki, about to go to the anteroom, fumbled for the flashlight. Its beam stabbed out, transfixing a bonsai like a searchlight. He stood, listening. During the previous night the stream had gone silent; it was iced over, submerged by snow.

He lit his way along the corridors. Under electric light the ryokan had seemed barely in the present; under oil lamps and candles, which had been rapidly put in place, it had regressed to the past. Aoki grunted, smelling the odor of molten candle wax. Flexing his shoulders in the warmth of the kimono, he paused in a small hall. On an impulse, he entered a corridor new to him.

❖

The voice, low but fierce in tone, was coming from behind a door on which a white azalea was painted. Aoki stopped beside it, trying to make out the words. Another voice, calmer, responded. Then the fierce one again. *Who called the dogs off the bastard? And why—"*

Ito's!

Beneath Aoki, a floorboard creaked. The angry voice cut off. Quickly the policeman moved on, eyes on the flashlight beam flickering ahead of his slippers. Behind him the azalea door slid open. He glanced back. In the lamplight from the room, Ito was peering along the corridor. To the banker, Aoki would just be a shadowy figure.

He went on. Was Yamazaki the other party in the room? Hitherto, things had seemed equable between the two. Perhaps it was the bodyguard, Shoba. At the foot of the stairs, Aoki pulled up. The Fatman! Ito must've been referring to the investigation. The situation that had plunged Aoki into the abyss. *Who called the dogs off the bastard?* . . . Aoki drew in air. Freezer-cold air. He ascended the stairs to the hall.

Kazu Hatano was there, dressed tonight in a white kimono, speckled with an indeterminable color, and an obi, with a design of flying dragons. She finished giving instructions to a maid, who hurried away with a secretive, sliding sound, and turned to him with her official smile. "I'm so sorry, sir, the electricity line's gone down, somewhere on the mountain." She spoke calmly, her face flecked with tiny shadows from an oil lamp that was not yet giving an even light.

Telephone, now electricity. Aoki stared at the daughter of the missing woman. Her face seemed one with the kimono, a fascinating effect. "I hadn't counted on weather like this."

She gave a delicate shrug. "The cold is coming up out of the ground."

Aoki wondered where her twin was, then wondered if Mori had reported to the proprietor that he'd asked for a woman—though unless she was already under the ryokan's roof, no woman would be coming to the Camellia Room tonight. He bowed and left the hall.

Half of Saito's face was lit by lamplight, the other half in shadow. He was quite still, looking like an art photograph. A faint smell of sake emanated from his kimono. He raised his head unhurriedly. "There you are. Piece by piece the technology goes down, and still the snow falls."

Aoki's eye was caught by movement, and he looked through the dining room door. A maid was setting the far corner table.

"Ah, yes," Saito said. "Despite events, they're going to dine again on regional delicacies, and doubtless they'll continue their conversation. A more urgent one." He rang the small bell; when a maid came, he ordered whiskey. "Will you?"

Aoki shook his head and seated himself. His stomach felt too nervous to drink whiskey. He studied the board and couldn't tell what new moves had been made, except that Black seemed to have massed at the top center.

Unobtrusively, the bodyguard entered the room and went to a chair in a far corner. Aoki glanced at him. It was cold over there, but that guy wouldn't feel anything.

Saito ignored the new arrival. "The Master was ill. They kept having recesses, and it seemed the match might be abandoned."

Aoki nodded. This man knew he was in the police, knew his personal history. Why hadn't he mentioned it?

"I find *this* fact interesting: The informant identified as X in the newspapers said both men had betrayed Madam Ito with other women. Do you remember that? X reported that Ito had shown his wife contempt in the carelessness of his complaisance, and that Yamazaki, after two years of enjoying her, was moving to cut the connection. Each, by his own route, was abandoning her."

Aoki did indeed remember.

"X described how in a garden teahouse Madam Ito wept while remonstrating with Yamazaki, how even as she wept she was charming, not once raising her voice." Saito paused, as if contemplating the image.

Aoki frowned. The scene was also in his head. He turned quickly. Ito and Yamazaki had appeared in the corridor door. Ito's face was taut; the soft flesh of it now appeared compacted into pronounced ridges and hollows like refrozen snow. With a tense flick of his head, the banker glanced at the two men at the Go board. In contrast, Yamazaki's easy arrogance seemed unaffected; his look deliberately traveled over the board. Aoki wondered if the man ever recalled the teahouse scene.

Across the room Shoba shot to his feet, bowing. Aoki licked his lip. His sixth sense, his street vibes, told him that something deep was in play, deep and complicated. He looked down at his hands, frowning. Here he was, talking about the old, unsolved case with this Go-player, as two of the main protagonists moved past like ghosts, while their future was being implacably carved out, or carved up, in faraway Tokyo.

A new question darted at him: Was Saito personally known to them? He'd observed a hint of wariness in their attitude to the Go-player, though most prominent men were suspicious of outsiders.

Aoki ate at the same table as before. The dark old timbers

strutted and braced high in the ceiling were different from the head-scraping rafters in the other parts of the ryokan. This room was a later addition. He leaned back and stared up into dense shadows. He was certain he could make out murky, painted faces, gazing back at him. The ryokan was getting into his mind, the cold was getting into his bones, but he had more appetite. When did Saito eat? Probably he dined early, in his room.

The two at the far table had settled into another banquet, and the maids brought dish after dish. The detective watched them drink a toast in sake. To whom, or what? *For me, it's all shadow play,* he thought.

In a swirl of kimono, Kazu Hatano came to them, bowing, inquiring with a cold smile about the meal in an impassive play of formalities. She bowed to Aoki. A maid went out to the anteroom carrying a bowl of sour plums. Aoki brooded over his own warm sake. He'd ordered a plebeian meal, tempura and yakitori, fare not on the menu. The maid had taken this order without query. Two or three nights a week he'd eaten at cheap restaurants, while his wife and father dined at home on Tokie's delicacies. Those days and hours, grief, guilt, a numbing sense of loss, were never far from the surface of his mind. Images of his wife kept emerging. In one, she stepped out from an alcove in this ryokan and watched him come and go. In another, her head was bent, her body erect, as she sat on a cushion making delicate yet sure brushstrokes on white paper, a breeze from the sea teasing at a wisp of hair.

Aoki's sake cup was frozen at his lips. That, and similar moments, he should've seized upon—prolonging and savoring them. Locked into his police life, he hadn't. He drained the cup at a gulp. The cold from the mountains was flowing into his soul, more and more freely. At least his mind was now occupied with new questions.

He got up and left the dining room. In the doorway he stopped and dabbed at his lips with a handkerchief. Blood. They were cracking in the astringent air. From the heart of the flickering firelight and darting shadows, Saito said, "On November 28 the match was drawing to a close. As is traditional, the players were 'sealed in cans,' shut off from the outside world, as *we* are. The aging Master was sealed into his own mind. It was his last match."

He'd spoken in a hard, judgmental voice. In the tricky light, Aoki couldn't make out the look on his face. The detective stopped near the board. When Saito looked up, his eyes shone like the black Go stones.

"My theory?" He'd reverted to Aoki's earlier question as if there'd been no time gap. "I see a woman with a brown paper bundle moving through the crowds of Tokyo Central station, going to a locker, setting a puzzle, giving those two trouble, symbolically abandoning a humiliating existence."

Aoki stared. "If you're right, where did she go?"

"Where do *you* think?" He spread his hands at their surroundings.

Aoki didn't respond, and the Go-player became reabsorbed in the battle. Aoki thought, *Can I penetrate to the heart of this case, get a breakthrough for Watanabe, for myself, unearth this woman, or find out what her fate was?* With her husband and her lover returning to the ryokan, her daughter here, and the old questions surrounding her disappearance blowing through the corridors like new breezes, maybe he had half a chance.

The woman was to come at ten, if she came. Aoki didn't care much one way or the other; his request had been impulsive. So far as sex was concerned, he supposed he might gradually find his way back to it.

In the Camellia Room the oil lamp cast feeble light; another chamber of shadows. He found the remaining half of the chocolate bar and bit into it. Dessert . . .

On his second trip to see Aoki in Kamakura, Superintendent Watanabe had turned into a proponent of mountain rest cures, but it had just been one of his smoke screens. Somehow his boss had learned of the Ito-Yamazaki junket, and he'd had to move fast. He must have asked himself why those men were going back to the missing woman's old home. Aoki frowned intensely. The cop who'd run the missing-woman case, who'd lost his promotion over it, had kept an iron in the fire, and Hideo Aoki was now the one holding it!

Aoki savored the chocolate. Yet was that really what it was about? No briefing? Not a word? It stank of double-dealing and trouble. *Forget the superintendent.* He dropped into a deeper meditation and in a moment believed that he was hearing the pulsating heart of the ryokan as it pumped blood through its aged arteries. In reality, the next thing he was conscious of was the sliding sound of stockinged feet moving over the corridor boards, and the door slid open.

Aoki gasped. A geisha in full regalia!

Kazu Hatano was kneeling in the doorway.

Aoki felt the hair on the back of his neck prickle. She bowed low, displaying the smooth sheen of her hair and its single gold ornament. Then, still on her knees, she moved into the room and bowed again, arms crossed, palms against her breasts. Her face was a powdered mask, aglow in the dusk.

"*Kazu Hatano!*" he breathed.

She was six feet from him, and a flowery fragrance enfolded him. "No, sir, I'm her sister." Her voice was a whisper. The kimono appeared to be of an azure color with deep red leaves dappling it. Aoki gazed at this woman sprung from the heart of old traditions, from the heart of autumn. The twin sister! He didn't know what to say.

But from now on words were redundant. A geisha of a certain type, she perfectly understood his mood and requirements, no conversation, no games, no food, no liquor. She turned the oil lamp down until the room was nearly dark. After a time she lay on him, his erection within her, her hair, cold and tensile, brushing his face. He was afloat in her perfume. Slowly she straightened up, arched her back, and began to move in a slight rocking motion within which her vaginal muscles gripped his penis in a delicate, yet ardent, separate movement. It seemed to Aoki that they were soaring above the ryokan and the snowy mountains, that stars were dropping past them on all sides, and then he was a falling star himself.

He awoke to the flickering sensation of her tongue and the pressure of her lips. In that warm, painted mouth his cock began to respond, and the moment of ejaculation brought a harsh gasp from deep in his throat. He slept again.

A draught of cold air striking his head woke him. The door had just slid shut, or was it part of the dream? She had gone, yet he could still feel her deft fingers tracing the long welt of scar tissue on his side, the legacy of a Tokyo gangster's knife.

He lay back amazed afresh at the geisha's identity, at her behind-the-scenes presence. Where in this rambling structure did the twin sister of Kazu Hatano reside?

Could the missing woman have been concealed here in the family's ancient home all this time? That must be Saito's conjecture! Seven years ago, surely the police would've had the same idea, and searched? Aoki hadn't been familiar with that part of the investigation.

Warm, heavy-limbed, half-dreaming, cocooned by the ryokan's creaking timbers and rustling fabrics, Inspector Aoki sent his mind drifting off along remote corridors, in pursuit of a rustling kimono.

Chapter Eleven

INSPECTOR AOKI HAD READ ABOUT such storms, and now he dreamed of them blowing down from Siberia, howling over the Japan Sea, drawing up moisture and dumping it as snow on the western "reverse" side of Japan. All life was flying to shelter, including Aoki. In midflight, up to his chest in snow, his eyes flicked open. He sat upright and was swept by dizziness. He put his head into his hands. Then he threw back the quilt and stood up, his right arm thrust out as though to ward off danger.

The kotatsu was cold ashes, smelling acrid and sour. He fumbled for matches and lit the wick of the oil lamp. Shivering, he put on the padded kimono and reached for the phone. Still dead. He checked his watch: 8:05 A.M.

On the futon, the cat stirred and stretched. Aoki gazed at it. "When did you arrive?" It rubbed against his leg, purring an answer, its eyes upturned to his face.

He turned and switched on the radio. Static crackled, then a voice surfaced.

Senior government officials are locked in discussions with directors of the Tokyo Citizens Bank. A team from the Bank of Japan is investigating the extent of the problems. Financial commentators report that the bank's fate is in the hands of the government. The bank's chairman and a senior Ministry of Finance official, last seen together, remain missing.

Not missing. Here! Just up to their necks in snow. Aoki switched off the radio and rubbed warmth into his hands. Today was the seventh anniversary. He wondered if it was significant only to him. For sure, Ito and Yamazaki would be rushing back to Tokyo the moment the road was open.

A woman's voice called him from outside the door, then it slid open: Mori, in her hands a small lacquer tray with his tea and a tube of ointment on it. She bowed. "For your lips, sir." She clucked her tongue and pointed at the floor, and Aoki saw that two dead mice were lined up there. "She's brought them to you, sir," the maid said.

A red woolen scarf wrapped around his neck, the ointment smeared on his lips, Aoki left his room. Last night flashed back, like the aftertaste of a delicious dessert, soon eaten and soon forgotten. Yet the appearance of Kazu Hatano's twin sister, in such a role, had amazed him.

Aoki walked the corridors. Saito's theory that the missing woman had deposited her bloody clothes in the station locker and fled to the family's ryokan might merely be the Go-player's fantasy, and how far could he be trusted, anyway? All his statements were sardonic, apparently infused with black humor. She'd been dead and gone these seven years, not hiding out. Her photo had been in every paper, on every TV screen. This Osaka guy could be just laying down a bullshit trail, following some personal, sardonic agenda.

Aoki shook his head. Now *he* was fantasizing! His own photo had appeared beside Tamaki's in the papers. Newspaperman Eichi Kimura's had also been bracketed with the Fatman on the front pages, but only once; then the party had killed the story. The journalist had come uninvited into his life, and he'd hardly known him, yet he'd died because of their wives' friendship.

Ascending the stairs to the hall, Aoki remembered the man Kimura had met the night before his murder. In a bar in Shinjuku, Madam Kimura had told the police, the mystery man had suggested to her husband that he back off writing about the Fatman. Big money was offered, and she said Kimura had turned it down. A mistake; he should've at least played along. According to his wife, he'd tried to question the man, whom he guessed was a government bureaucrat. Kimura hadn't described him further. By seven the next morning, her husband was dead.

Ito and Yamazaki—would they be able to claw back lost ground when they escaped from here, to surround and eliminate the forces against them, as that damned Saito was doing on the Go board? Maybe Saito *was* no more than an ardent observer of lurid crimes, who'd struck it lucky at this ryokan where he'd come to view autumn leaves and replay the classic Go match. Aoki shrugged and shook his head.

He was already at the Go board. This morning he wore a dark green kimono, which appeared almost black in the gloom. *Click-click-click*: stones in an unusual spurt. The big man leaned back from the table and motioned Aoki to take a seat. There was a glint in his eye. Instead of sitting, Aoki moved to stand near the fire.

"*So,* Madam Ito hurried back to the mountains and went into hiding within these walls. Have you thought any more about that?"

Aoki frowned. Again Saito had resumed a previous conversation as though there'd been no interval, one of his tricks. He said, "Where's the evidence for that?"

"The whole case was short on evidence." Saito placed his big hands on his lap. "Your personal case was almost as dramatic as Madam Ito's, wasn't it? Especially your wife. Please accept my condolences on that tragedy."

Yet again! The intimacy of these strangers' condolences was unreal to Aoki.

Saito shrugged, at the fate that life dealt out, and turned back to the Go board. Aoki, his face dour, went to breakfast.

At the moment Aoki returned from the dining room, Yamazaki entered the anteroom and paused to gaze at the board. The MOF official had on a padded gray kimono touched with red silk on the breast; his height, perfect grooming, and obvious composure under pressure gave him a power-edged elegance. An ivory-handled dagger, with a razor-sharp blade . . . Aoki grimaced. He *was* turning into a damned poet, sponsored by his family and the ryokan.

Yamazaki said, "The Master's play was affected by his bad health. The match was his swan song. After all, no one goes on forever." The nasal voice was as thick as syrup. Aoki's eyes narrowed. Yamazaki knew which match was being replayed. Saito smiled but said nothing. The MOF man gave an acerbic smile and went in to breakfast.

Saito asked, "Will we have our game of chess this evening?" Aoki bowed his agreement and went to the hall.

"This storm is really something," Kazu Hatano said, coming out of her office. "A different world from Tokyo, isn't it? It's a great inconvenience for our guests." *Yes, it most certainly is,* Aoki thought. Even at her most businesslike her voice intrigued him. She studied him, as though expecting a request, but he had no requests to make. Today she wore a dark blue kimono flecked with white, like falling snow against a night sky. Did she ever wear Western clothes? She lingered behind the counter. "Of course, now I must worry about fresh food."

Fresh food? What was she thinking about the seventh anniversary? It had to be in her mind. *Amazingly* like her sister, and where was the sister right now? Doubtless this woman knew of her visit to the Camellia Room; the charge would be on his bill. He glanced up. Under the snow's weight, the roof was emitting creaks as though a vise were being tightened on unseasoned wood.

From the bench, Shoba's eyes flicked at him, then away. The gray, snowy daylight hardly penetrated the small windows, yet the red birthmark on the bodyguard's head shone like a beacon in the gloom. "Beyond this place, the real world still exists," Aoki told himself as he headed back to his room. The twin sisters must have some idea of the circumstances of their mother's disappearance, might know it all. If alive, how would she look today? She'd be in her early fifties. At some point he was going to question Kazu Hatano about the case, but he needed an opening, and the circumstances and timing would have to be just right. Even then, it might be a useless attempt.

Ito waited on a landing, his expression stern and peering, his thick lips working over his teeth. He raised a small hand to stop the detective. His breath hissed. "Mr. Aoki, why are you here?"

An ambush. Aoki was startled at the impoliteness. The man's dark eyes were gleaming at him from their fleshy pouches. "I'm on vacation."

"Vacation?" The banker stared at the detective for a long moment, scrutinizing Aoki's face even more intensely. "Ah, yes." He nodded to himself and moved on up the stairs, stiff-backed with tension.

Aoki went to his room. Vacation! Even in his own ears it sounded false. The banker was wire-tight with nerves. *Join the club.*

The cat sat outside his door gazing up at the image of the camellia. She came to Aoki and brushed against his legs, and he stroked her. "You were doing some killing last night," he said, "before you bunked down with me."

Six months ago, a rainy night in Ginza. Aoki's classmate Shimamura was a thin fellow in a rumpled suit. At their junior high school he'd been a ball of energy, nicknamed "Mexican Jumping Beans." He worked at the Ministry of Finance. The MOF people were the cream—graduates of Tokyo University. Aoki was seeking a specialist's perspective as to how persons such as ex-governor Tamaki might interface with the yakuza—and the banking system. He couldn't mention Tamaki's name.

Shimamura's hair was plastered to his head; the poor brilliant guy couldn't manage to get himself an umbrella. Aoki signaled for a towel.

After they'd passed over schooldays and downed the first beer, his friend had been surprised at the subject Aoki raised. He sat back. "Straying into new territory, aren't you, Hideo?"

Aoki shrugged. "It's become a hot issue. My bosses have focused on the political middlemen in action between the banks and the yakuza, the guys who're the movers and shakers."

Shimamura frowned, as though at an unpleasant vista.

"What does the MOF think about it?" Aoki asked bluntly.

The bureaucrat gazed into his beer, then raised his eyes to Aoki's broad, tough face. "Hmmm...What I say is off the record." Aoki nodded. Shimamura put his beer glass aside. "It's not as simple as you've depicted it. *Sometimes* politicians are the go-betweens. Some of 'em have smoothed the introductions of the yakuza to the banks, but plenty of times, the yakuza deal direct."

He blinked a few times. "Listen, a banking catastrophe's been looming for over a decade. No one in government or big business wants the *degree* of the problem out in the open. No one knows what to do without causing a systemic collapse. They've been propping up weak banks, merging 'em with stronger ones, arranging phased write-downs of bad debts. None of this gets anywhere near the heart of the problem."

Shimamura kept his voice low. "There're still trillions in gray-area loans on the books. It wouldn't take *too* much to terminate our banking and financial world." His thin hands were locked together.

Salarymen were coming in, bar-girls were appearing at their sides, and the room was filling up with smoke and noise. Shimamura glanced around and leaned closer to Aoki. "Maybe up to half the bad debts still on the books involve the yakuza. Somebody's called our economic woes the 'yakuza recession.' Not exactly wrong. The borrowers either have strong links to the yakuza or are directly controlled by them. Most of these loans will *never* be recovered.

"How did this wonderful situation come about? In the 1980s big corporations were raising loans overseas, and some of our banks, to keep up their growth, started courting the gangsters, pushing loans down their throats. The yakuza saw it as a way to get into legitimate business. A lot of 'em invested in real estate at the crazy highs, and they've dropped an immense bundle. Now they're not paying back their new banker friends, and the banks are fighting to stay afloat." He sat back, picked up his glass, and drained it.

Aoki studied him. How did a forthright, abrasive guy like his friend, who wore awful suits, get into the MOF? In their student days, Shimamura often started fights he could never win. Frequently, Aoki had to step in to finish off what his friend had started and save him from being beaten up, collecting black eyes and split lips himself for his efforts.

Shimamura said, "The government's paralyzed. They've got to risk letting some of the worst cases crash, support the stronger cases. The ones that've been deepest in with the yakuza and the dirty politicians should be in the former category. *But they can't face up to doing it.*"

A girl approached, bringing more beer.

"The fellows of my generation are kicking the problem around among ourselves, but our bosses are sitting tight, gray suits, old gray minds—gray loans." He grinned painfully.

That was it. They drank more beer and revisited their youth, recalling old teachers and classmates. When they got up to leave, Shimamura turned suddenly to Aoki. "Bix Beiderbecke!"

" 'Krazy Kat!' "

They grinned at each other over the old jazz memories, over the old addiction, and parted with a warm handshake. It was 11:00 P.M. Walking away through streets ablaze with eye-aching neon, Aoki observed a flock of kimonoed women from the bars seeing their customers into black limousines, customers who weaved unsteady courses; doubtless some of them were bankers, some of them yakuza.

In the ryokan, reliving this, Aoki had been pacing the room. Now he stopped. Ito and Yamazaki would be returning to an inferno. Yet maybe they'd seen the Fatman coming. Maybe they'd come here to work on a counterattack, and the weather had stepped in to play a deadly, delaying hand. Nonetheless, they might have a plan.

Again he felt dizzy and sick to his stomach from the uncertainties. He'd been away from the job too long.

Maybe Madam Ito had taken her own life, and Ito or Yamazaki had sought to cover this up with the bloodied clothes to avoid the disgrace of the ménage-à-trois coming out—although it had come out anyway. Even that made more sense than Saito's theory that she was alive, but there was no conclusive evidence for either proposition. He wished again that he had that mountain of a dossier. He knew it would've been raked over and over. However, a vital piece of information might be buried there, waiting for the right brain to interpret it. *His* brain kept darting into alley after alley. Hyper-fucking-active! In this strange place, maybe *it* was being funneled toward the heart of the case.

Aoki's eye fell on the bonsai plants. One of them was missing, the sick one. It must've died. Shit!

Chapter Twelve

INSPECTOR AOKI AWOKE IN DARKNESS. He checked his watch with the flashlight: 5:15 P.M. The maid would not have wished to disturb him to light the lamp. He'd had no lunch; instead, he'd fallen into a deep and dreamless sleep. He pulled the quilt over his head. Presently he'd take a bath. Right now he felt drowsy, but his mind was again picking up the case.

Two maids at a Kyoto ryokan had told a reporter how Yamazaki had thrown Madam Ito to the floor in a violent outburst; how they'd heard her pleading as he'd perpetrated "terrible acts" on her; how the next day, she'd kept to her room, hiding her bruised face. Aoki doubted the story's veracity. In his opinion the MOF official would disdain such conduct, and it had come out that that paper was paying for information, much of which couldn't be verified.

It was weird, how these unchronological recollections were bombarding him—as if they'd been stored in the ryokan's guts, as much as in his mind, waiting for him and now were being pulled out by a mysterious hand, like rabbits from a hat. Crazy thinking. He sat up. He must stay pragmatic, yet flexible. Carefully, he extracted sleep from his eyes with his fingertips.

❖

He was no stranger to violence. He'd come to know himself, in that respect. He frequently dealt with scum who inflicted deadly harm on their victims and escaped justice. The frustration had occasionally boiled over in him. A few times he'd gone out of control. Once, a pimp-cum-pusher had been mocking and reticent about giving him an address. *Smack!* Aoki slapped him with bone-jarring force. The man, grinning, spat a mouthful of blood on Aoki's suit. The red haze smoldering in Aoki exploded. One-handed, he pinioned the guy against a wall by the throat, tore open the man's trousers and seized his testicles, and twisted with all his strength. Afterward, he'd taken a few deep breaths and rejoined his partner, and they'd gone to the address.

He stared at the Camellia Room. How long had the ryokan been in the Hatano family? He put on a yukata and went to the bath.

Aoki had washed and immersed himself when Yamazaki entered the bathhouse. The second time they'd shared the bath. Obviously Chairman Ito followed a different bathing routine. They floated in the steamy atmosphere. It was the stone bath, and the water temperature was higher than in the other. The detective noted that the MOF man's testicles were low-slung, potent-looking. Aoki shut his eyes. Today, he had balls on the brain.

"Abominable weather," Yamazaki said.

"But pleasant here," Aoki replied.

The tall man began to talk languidly about food, then about the specialties of Kamakura Inn. "You know about these places, do you, Inspector?" Aoki grunted noncommittally into the steam. "Ah. Well, each provincial daimyo had to leave his wife and children in Tokyo, virtually as hostages, and the daimyos themselves were required to live there every alternate year. As they moved to and from, each traveled with a retinue of a thousand or more servants—at great expense, to keep them short of funds." He chuckled. "The shoguns were very creative, very cautious in many ways. On his travels a daimyo stayed in *honjin*—the forerunners of ryokans like this one."

"This one isn't on a major road," Aoki ventured.

"This kind came later. Nonetheless, *honjin* were its prototype. One like this was for rich merchants who wanted to get away to enjoy the hot spring, the solitude, the change in the seasons. Our co-guest seems to fit that bill, doesn't he?"

Aoki had no comment. What he'd heard was some of the story he'd tried to remember from his father.

They luxuriated in the warmth. The crippled bank was away on another planet. Tokyo. Out of the steamy silence, the MOF man said, "I note your interest in Go." Aoki grunted, noncommittal again. "Our co-guest is possibly a high-grade player."

Aoki thought for a moment. "He says he plays as a spiritual discipline."

Yamazaki laughed, a gurgle of phlegm. "D'you believe that? In the old days, that might've been true for some. I think this fellow sees it as a test of strength—a sedentary martial art."

The detective nodded to himself.

When Aoki returned to his room, the kotatsu had been refueled and stoked up. He looked down at it, thinking. After his wife's funeral, he hadn't changed the routine that he'd adopted since his suspension. The surveillance on him had been reinstated. Moving from the coffee shop to the park and his observation of the neighborhood's juvenile and geriatric life to the bar must've become wearisome to his anonymous police watchers. However, Watanabe had been right to upgrade their vigilance, and the police shrink had been right to ring an alarm bell. After Tokie's death, hatred for the

Fatman had been implanted in his brain like a rock placed in a raked sand garden. Another crook who was escaping justice and retribution! Nonetheless, he was incapacitated, and powerless.

Watanabe. He stopped in the middle of dressing. Whatever it was the superintendent had in his sights, Hideo Aoki was expendable. With a jolt, Aoki knew that.

Before, he'd felt something coming. Leaving the room, he smelled a smell he couldn't identify, and there was a foul taste in his mouth. He grimaced, uneasy. He heard an echo of music, a calming melody. From a samisen! Tokie had played the instrument. Was she trying to talk to him in that way, too?

It seemed all his senses were hyper, including the sixth.

In the anteroom, Saito was surrounded by guttering candles; the room had become a grotto of slippery light and shadow, a feast of mysteriousness. The Go-player appeared as immersed in it as Aoki had been in the bath. Locked in battle, the stones glinted. "Ah, you reappear, bathed and fresh for the evening. For the anniversary night! And *they* are here!"

Aoki stared at Saito. So! He knew about it, but that figured.

"How does a *detective's* mind view it?"

Aoki gave a shrug. The bank's predicament was overshadowing everything. How could it be otherwise for these guys? *Financial* life and death.

Aoki went in to eat his dinner. He wore a clean padded kimono, which had been laid out in his room by invisible hands from the ryokan's underworld, maybe Mori's. He would be especially watchful tonight. The sensation he'd had in the corridor outside his room had shaken him up. He did feel alert, and fresher.

Ito and Yamazaki bowed to him as they went to their table. Ito looked grim but more in charge of himself, and Yamazaki had the same cool demeanor. Side by side the tall MOF official and the stubby bank chairman were an incongruous pair, yet their minds must be pretty well in tune. Yamazaki was just as exposed to the banking drama as Ito. An MOF official absent on a junket with a bank's delinquent chairman when it crashes! Any ordinary official would be sweating blood.

The unseen chef and kitchen staff had been hard at work. Aoki stared across the room. More out-of-sight inhabitants of the ryokan. The dishes came and went for the anniversary banquet. *It must be that.* Aoki drank three small flasks of sake, and the warm scented alcohol lulled his brain. In the far corner, they conversed as they ate and drank, the same guarded talk. They didn't look in his direction, but Ito, at least, had revealed that he was agitated about Aoki's presence, and Yamazaki had talked to him in the bath.

Aoki's fingers stroked his mole. He'd drunk more than he'd intended.

At nine, he went out to the anteroom to play chess with Saito. He was annoyed with himself for agreeing to it. How could he concentrate on chess? They played beside the Go board. Aoki received a rook's handicap and lost the first game in fifteen minutes; the next lasted only ten. They stared at the board, at the last massacre.

Saito jerked his head toward the dining room. "Why doesn't the food choke them, Mr. Aoki? Two of the chief players in our catastrophic financial system, as blameworthy as hell. In medieval days our country was covered by entangled forests. These days the myriad banking bad debts are those forests—*even more dangerous.*"

Aoki's head was a little fuzzy, but he caught the flicker of Saito's smile. The man *was* amused by it all, was mocking the players—the system. Did he really give a fuck about the critiques he was laying out, or was it all a game, like his Go?

Saito said, "In your own niche, you've looked up the system's backside, and it's shit on you."

Aoki took out a toothpick and went to work on his teeth. This guy was an outrageous mixture of rough edges and old Japanese culture. His father had had the last, but otherwise his character was as remote from this fellow's as Hokkaido was from Kyushu.

The Go-player sat motionless. "What do you think? Are all the facts being laid on the table? Are they emptying their minds of Madam Ito's case—bits and pieces the police never knew, the papers never dug up? But will it give them an answer?"

Aoki sucked at his teeth. "How can we know what they're talking about?" he said harshly. Abruptly, the man's unrelenting ego was angering him. "They'll be talking survival." His face felt flushed from the alcohol.

"That's for the daylight hours. Today they've exhausted themselves planning a counterattack for when they can get back. Each hour, Ito's been annoying Madam Hatano about the phone, but fate has cut it off, and fate is controlling its reconnection."

To hell with this, Aoki thought. He tossed the toothpick into an ashtray. "How could Madam Ito be concealed here for so long? Somebody would know, and talk."

Saito gave the room a sweeping look. "The public areas of the ryokan are like the tip of the iceberg. Beyond them lies a labyrinth, a headache for any searcher. The minds of the builders of these places were complicated! And old servants are loyal."

"They would've brought in dogs."

"Places like this have always known about dogs."

The cavorting shadows from the firelight seemed to breathe

danger to Aoki. He said, "How d'you know *so much* about this damned case?" It was the sake talking.

"I told you before, I'm a collector."

Aoki was squinting at the dark face. "Are you an economist?"

Saito laughed quietly. "Merely a businessman—"

A wailing sound had begun in the dining room. At first Aoki barely heard it, then: *"Oh-oh-oh-ah-eeee."* Higher and higher it went. The hair on the nape of Aoki's neck crackled. *An imitation of a woman coming to her orgasm!*

It was Yamazaki's voice!

The sound cut off. In the dining room Yamazaki was laughing now—unmistakably him.

Aoki was shocked. He looked at Saito. The man from Osaka's head was tilted to one side, his face like stone. Without a word Aoki got up and left the room. The sake had cleared from his head. In the corridor to the hall, he thought, *the anniversary night.* But what dominated his mind was that sound coming from deep in Yamazaki's throat in the thick voice.

His brow creased in concentration, he pulled up and stepped aside into an alcove. Neither man had cared for the woman; each had disdained and dishonored her. Perhaps each was here out of morbid curiosity or to probe for an advantage against the other. Perhaps, years ago, Yamazaki had mocked her with that cry. Aoki rubbed his cheekbone. He stepped out of the alcove and continued on to the hall.

A raucous belch came from behind him. He whirled around as Ito caught up to him. The bank chairman's face had changed: It was flame-red and contorted, as though flesh and bone were about to explode. He rushed past the stock-still Aoki, almost bumping him, as if the detective were invisible, and lurched into the hall. He

117

pulled up, rocked on his heels, and rapped hard on the counter. Shoba was on his feet, his face alert. Kazu Hatano came out of the office. Aoki drew in his breath. She was moving like a sleepwalker, and there was a look on her face far beyond the one he'd observed when she'd faced Ito before—ceramic-hard and nerveless. From the corridor, he watched, spellbound.

"When'll the road be clear?" the banker demanded in a slurred voice.

"I can't say."

"*The phone?*" He swayed against the counter.

"Is not yet in order."

"The *instant* you're reconnected . . ." His plump hands thudded again on the counter. He gave a peremptory bow, impatiently beckoned the bodyguard to follow, and weaved toward the staircase.

Aoki gazed after the pair. Had the cuckold stepped out of the shadows? Had that gross simulation unlocked some latent core of feeling for his missing wife? He turned to find the proprietor standing there like a ghost. She'd heard that terrible sound. The ritual dishonoring of her mother had gone through the rambling rooms and corridors like a breath of evil.

Aoki needed to speak to this woman who stood before him; instead, he stared at the shape of her head, her neck, the curve of her cheek, seeing her sister as she'd kneeled in the doorway of the Camellia Room. He blinked hard, sending the picture flying. Then he crossed to the counter and said quietly, "Could I speak with you?"

The slender woman's eyes moved slowly to his as if suddenly registering his presence. "Of course. Please come into the office."

Aoki followed her. A copper kettle purred on a brazier. Account ledgers were neatly stacked on a wooden chest. She offered him a seat beside an old-fashioned desk. A single sheet of paper lay on it, and Aoki glanced at it: a menu. He said, "I wish to introduce myself more formally. I'm a senior detective with the Tokyo Metropolitan Police, at present on leave."

She gave a brief nod. His occupation wasn't news, but from his first minute here he'd known that. He hesitated. Was it his curiosity or his ingrained police mentality that was making him take a step like this? Though fate might be the guiding hand at work, as Saito claimed.

"As a junior detective, I was on your mother's case." This time her eyes reacted. *Yeah,* Aoki thought, *when she heard that prolonged cry her blood must have run cold.* His had; even Saito had seemed momentarily paralyzed. Yet she'd emerged from her trancelike state and was watching him now, her eyes clear and acute.

Aoki paused. "I presume the police haven't interviewed you for quite a while. With the hindsight of seven years, have you had any fresh thoughts on what happened?"

A long moment. "No." Unemotionally spoken; she seemed to be staring at him out of her past, the unchallenged mistress of it.

"No theories at all?"

"None."

"Tonight's the seventh anniversary."

"You're well informed."

No inflection in her voice. Seven years ago, Superintendent Watanabe must have given her and her sister a hard time as he'd questioned them. Aoki glanced down at the menu—quite a banquet, seven courses, hungry guys. His eyes stopped at the last. *Vegetable dish: Chestnut dumplings with fern shoots and pickled plums.* He said, "The two gentlemen from Tokyo being here must've brought back unhappy memories."

119

"The subject's never far away."

He raised his eyebrows. "It surprises me you'd have them here."

He thought she wasn't going to answer; then, almost in a whisper, she said, "This ryokan has a 250-year tradition of hospitality. It's an obligation that stands above personal feelings." Her gaze was unwavering. "They were here once before, on the *first* anniversary."

Aoki absorbed this. The first year, then a gap of six. He frowned. All that Saito had said to him struck him as accurate, yet he had an even stronger impression now that the Go-player's agenda, for some reason, was to push him down the wrong path. He had similar thoughts about the owner of the mountain ryokan, but, staring at her pale face, into those steady eyes, he couldn't be sure of a thing.

In the Camellia Room, Aoki found jazz on the radio. He owned no books and not much other stuff, just a big collection of jazz records. It had been his interest since his teenage years, the only real one outside his work. Only half-humorously, Tokie had said once, "You could pack your life in two suitcases and disappear." But she was the one who'd disappeared. He turned down the radio's volume.

He'd seen photographs of the bloodstained clothing and the other items recovered from the Central station locker. He screwed up his brow. A light green silk kimono finely embroidered with gold thread, an obi with gold cranes in flight, a beautiful amber crescent hair ornament, and a purse containing the valuable diamond ring Ito had given her at their engagement. Everything she'd been wearing that evening when they had dinner, Ito had confirmed. Only an antique ruby ring, inherited from her mother, had been missing.

Aoki smoked a cigarette, puzzling over the locker and its contents. *Did* they stand for the abandonment of a wretched, dishonored life, and a payback? Or murder, or suicide? He yawned. He could still taste the sake on his palate, and his eyes were dead-heavy. It had stopped snowing late in the afternoon.

Aoki was weary, but he had an urge to leave the Camellia Room, to walk the corridors, the staircases, through the dark halls, as though a door might open and lead him into a secret chamber where the mysteries at the ryokan would be graphically displayed on whiteboards, a place like the incident rooms at headquarters.

He grimaced at this thinking and left his room. Coming down the staircase he crossed a lamp-lit corridor. A man came hurriedly out of it without warning and nearly collided with him, a man in a chef's white uniform. Aoki jumped back, as did the man, then face-to-face they regarded each other for a moment. With a half-bow, the white-coated man stepped around Aoki and hurried down the staircase.

Aoki stood transfixed, staring after him. All kinds of things were coming together in his head, but the key one was the front page of a Tokyo daily at the time of Madam Ito's disappearance, showing separate photographs of the faces of four persons: Madam Ito in all her mature beauty; her husband, Ito; her lover, Yamazaki; and underneath that trio the identity-card-type shot of a man with a white scar over his left eye, her ex-husband, Hatano. The face of the man Aoki had just been staring at.

Aoki turned and went straight back to his room.

Inspector Aoki awoke at 3:10 A.M. instantly clearheaded. He wondered what had wakened him, and listened; just the faintest stirring of coals in the kotatsu. The memory of the incident late last night jumped into his mind. What in the hell was Hatano doing back at the ryokan? The ex-husband had been thrown out by Madam Ito, who'd then divorced him, long before she'd met Ito. Watanabe had tracked the chef down in Osaka and tried to pin his ex-wife's disappearance on him. It hadn't worked, and presumably he'd dropped from sight. Now he was here! The interesting questions were: Did Watanabe know he was here? Did Ito and Yamazaki? For sure, Kazu Hatano knew. For an hour, before he'd slept, Aoki had turned this over and over in his mind, wondering if there had been something to Watanabe's last line of inquiry: that Hatano and his daughters had conspired to take Madam Ito out of circulation.

Aoki threw back the quilt, put on his padded kimono and slippers, slid back the door, and played his flashlight beam into the corridor. Stepping out, he paused and listened again. The frigid air stung his cheeks, sharp as razor nicks.

The cat's eyes flashed. He started. It was sitting there, watching him. It came forward, rubbed its body against his legs, and meowed softly, a lonesome sound. Briefly, he stroked its back.

He set off, walking quietly through the ryokan to the anteroom. He seemed to be on a mission of an indeterminate nature, but he was wide awake.

In the anteroom nothing had changed, except that the last log had burned to ashes. He looked toward the windows and did see change. Huge icicles resembling daggers hung from the eaves. Daggers that could pierce your heart. Astonished, he stared at them, then swept his eyes over the snow-lit room. On the Go board, the stones were frozen in their own unique killing formations, just as Saito had left them.

He retraced his steps to the hall, descended the stairs, and took a corridor. Another exploratory move on this unclear mission. Ahead, a door was partially open, the ghost-flower painted on it glimmering in the beam of his flashlight. Within, there was an incandescent glow like one from a bedside lamp. Aoki paused, then slid open the door fully and peered down the flashlight beam.

His breath came out in a long hiss. The light had jumped with his reflexes but now held steady on the naked figure. Between the slender legs last seen afloat in the stone bath, the white bedding on the floor was drenched with blood. Mouth open, Aoki stared at the carnage. Probably the stab through the heart had been first, then the work down below; maybe a couple of swift slashes, then a more deliberate one—a big cut across the abdomen. Aoki smelled strong odors. He moved the flashlight, checking the room, and found the alcove and what was missing.

The long penis and the pendulous testicles, raw and bloody as butcher's meat, were displayed in a lacquer box beneath the hanging scroll, artistically arranged—as much as the objects would allow. The gaping wound on the abdomen looked surgical, and instantly Aoki knew an organ had been removed; he'd seen enough autopsies. He stared at the butchery as though mentally photographing it. He'd witnessed much more chaotic rearrangements of human bodies; this seemed highly organized in comparison.

Yamazaki's eyes were open. The bleeding had ceased. It was useless to check for life; the MOF official's arrogant spirit, his leasehold of power, had been terminated, his elegance despoiled. It was going to create a sensation. With this ending, Yamazaki would be less of a forgotten man than if his career had merely finished in humilating ignominy.

This was Yamazaki's room, but it was the one Ito had stepped out of to peer after him. Aoki could feel a fluttering pulse beneath his left eye. He fumbled for his cigarettes and lit one quickly, tucking the flashlight under his arm. He wasn't as inured to scenes of sudden death as he'd thought.

The bitter chill in the air had invaded his heart. The severed genitalia were on display, but what of the other organ that appeared to have been taken? He exhaled smoke and moved the beam of light over more of the room. Big drops of blood had stained the tatami, but most of it was on the bed. Aoki stepped back. His dinner was churning in his stomach.

Chapter Thirteen

ENTRANCE FORBIDDEN. POLICE. AOKI SEALED the Azalea Room and placed the notice, written on a piece of cardboard torn from the bonsai carton, outside the door. Suspended from duty, he had no authority to do this—in a strict sense, no authority to do anything—but it was the automatic action of an experienced CIB detective.

The ryokan remained mute and freezing and steeped in predawn darkness. He looked along the corridor. What hole had the perpetrator crept away to?

Grim-faced, Aoki returned to his room and lifted the phone. Dead. The place should begin to come to life about six. He had no idea where the proprietor's quarters were, nor Ito's room, and he wouldn't blunder around in the dark, maybe disturbing evidence.

He lit a cigarette, noticing that his hands were shaking. Tension had locked his chest muscles rigid. Flexing his shoulders several times, he tried to relax, but Yamazaki's slaughtered corpse was a vivid picture in his head. His street smarts had warned that something bad was coming. Whatever Watanabe's reason was for sending him here, it had transported him back to the Madam Ito case, and now it had spiraled downward into murder. His boss couldn't have foreseen this. Whatever his agenda was, had this brutal murder advanced or derailed it?—Staring at his disarranged bed, he shook his head. Maybe it'd been the murderer slipping along the corridor that woke him up. Or the cat.

He switched on the radio and found NHK. Nearly 5:00 A.M. Impatiently he waited for music to finish, then heard the world headlines. The latest on the bank soon came:

> *The Tokyo Metropolitan Police disclosed that a man answering the description of Hiroshi Ito, chairman of the Tokyo Citizens Bank, was seen at Tokyo Central station boarding the 7:45 A.M. bullet train for Akita on Sunday. He was accompanied by a man who police say may have been Haruki Yamazaki, an official of the Ministry of Finance. The MOF advises that Mr. Yamazaki is temporarily away from his office. At the bank's annual general meeting last year, allegations about a connection to the yakuza were leveled at Mr. Ito. These were denied. Mr. Yamazaki, in a statement issued by the MOF, confirmed that the allegations were groundless. Fresh police inquiries indicate the men may have traveled to a mountain inn in Hokkaido. Since Tuesday the region has been blanketed by heavy snow, and the inn is presently cut off from all communication.*

Aoki grimaced. Yamazaki was cut off, for sure, but at last the cops had gotten a fix on where the two were.

At 6:00 A.M. he went upstairs. The brazier was out in the hall, though the oil lamp there was still alight. He turned it up. No one was stirring yet. Where was Kazu Hatano in the labyrinthine building, and Ito—and the murderer? Where was the ex-husband, Hatano? The brief and startling late-night encounter with him was stark in Aoki's mind. He paced the hall, rubbing his hands and swinging his arms. Kazu Hatano had had a shock last night, and this wasn't going to improve matters.

At 6:30 A.M., in a swishing of kimono and a sliding of slippers on boards, Kazu Hatano emerged from a corridor and stopped dead. Her hand raced to her throat, as though she were seeing an apparition. Aoki stepped forward. "Mr. Yamazaki is dead. In his room. I regret to tell you, murdered."

A soft gasp. She was gazing at him, very disturbed but not deeply shocked. Aoki could read nothing more than that. She turned, entered her office, and checked the phone, then shook her head at him. From the door, he said, "The room must not be entered by anyone. Please instruct your staff. How do I get to Mr. Ito's room?"

"The Lily Room. I'll show you." Her voice was barely above a whisper.

Aoki found the banker, fully dressed, hands joined behind his back, gazing at the frosted windowpanes. The fusuma door was open, and Aoki observed the small man for a moment. The room stank of rancid pickles. Aoki cleared his throat. Ito's face swiveled around on his plump neck.

"Sir, I'm sorry to tell you, Mr. Yamazaki is dead. Murdered."

A sharp hiss came from the banker. His heavy-lidded eyes popped wide open; then the lids dropped again, like shutters.

Aoki was startled. "I must ask you some questions—"

The banker was staring glassily at him. Aoki moved forward and peered into his face. Amazing! In the space of a microsecond, the moon-faced man had shut down. He seemed totally out on his feet. Aoki withdrew from the room to find a maid to bring tea for the shocked man.

At breakfast, the malignant atmosphere of disaster hung over the snow-besieged inn. Mori hadn't turned up with Aoki's tea, and the dining-room maid had the fumbles, clattering dishes on the lacquered table. When the detective came out to the anteroom, Saito was standing beside the Go board, peering out the window as if to a point beyond the range of his eyesight. He swung his eyes to Aoki. This morning Aoki was a student of eyes; the big man's were dark and contemplative.

"So! Something *has* happened."

Aoki nodded curtly. "Who told you?"

"My room maid."

Aoki scrutinized the Go-player's face. "Did you hear anything last night?"

Saito smiled sardonically. "The nightlong roar from these frozen mountains, the timbers creaking in this old place, nothing else. Will you investigate, *Inspector* Aoki? *Can* you investigate, or will you leave it to the prefecture police?"

Aoki didn't respond. The new fire crackled in the room.

Saito shrugged. "And Mr. Ito?"

"In his room."

"Doubtless considering his own situation." That word "situation" was meaningful in Aoki's ears. "Emasculation?" Saito pondered aloud.

Aoki gaped. "*Who told you that?*"

"My room maid. The people here already have all the details."

The detective rubbed his jaw. What in the hell? He turned toward the windows. His mind had gone off on a tangent—back to other murders, seemingly of this type. *Crimes of passion:* male and female perpetrators. *Crimes of revenge:* ditto. He'd found a severed penis in an alley where a vengeful wife had thrown it, held it in his handkerchief as they'd raced to the hospital with the amputee-victim. Speeding through the dark city, to the accompaniment of a siren, another man's cock in your hand . . .

Saito broke into his thoughts. "On December 1, the Master played chess and billiards. The night before, he'd played mah-jongg till midnight. Was he escaping from a match that he was losing?" Saito's voice was pragmatic, his eyes fixed on the board.

Aoki blinked in amazement. Was this guy for real? For himself, the match had been relegated to the 1930s—where it belonged—but in Saito's mind, clearly, it had parity with the vicious drama played out last night.

Aoki shook his head, gave a perfunctory bow, and left the anteroom. *Investigate?* That was the mode he'd fallen into. Suspension or not, it was what he was trained to do. Grimly, he thought, *What I am going to do.* Well, he'd quarantined the room, though ineffectually. He felt certain that no human being could've left the ryokan. However, the snow would begin to thaw soon, and their isolation couldn't last much longer. The local CIB would want the crime scene left undisturbed, and he couldn't afford to make more mistakes, so he'd have to tread carefully. He traced his tongue over his split lips.

For the second time, he entered Kazu Hatano's office. She rose and moved to the center of the room, one slender hand resting on the desk. Aoki's eyes settled on that delicate white wrist below her kimono sleeve—delicate, but strong, too. She would do some of the

physical work of running the ryokan. He said decisively, "I'm starting an investigation. When the local police can get through, they'll
take it over." He paused. She was without makeup, a different and
far more beautiful woman. "Please give me a complete list of everyone in the ryokan, their occupations, how long they've been here,
and the rooms where they slept last night."

Aoki dropped his gaze to the dark, polished wood of the old
desk. There'd been no knife in the Azalea Room and no apparent
blood spots in the corridor, and he'd examined the environs closely.
A few minutes ago, from the hall, he'd looked out to the vestibule
and seen the snow shutters locked in place. He'd found out yesterday that the other entrances were snowed in even deeper than the
front door.

He looked up sharply. "Do you have any information that might
assist me?"

She shook her head. "No."

Hmmm, an automatic response. His fingers stroked his right
cheekbone. The faces of Ito and his bodyguard came to him. What
had that blazing row—from Ito's side, anyway—been about in Yamazaki's room, the Azalea Room?

Chairman Ito's reaction when he'd heard the news had verged
on the surreal. The man was an experienced operator in the brutal
business world; he must've cut more tension-charged deals, more financial throats, than Aoki had had plates of yakitori. His being
thrown into an immobilizing trance was a reaction about as believ-
able as Superintendent Watanabe's sudden concern for Aoki's
health.

Burning with annoyance, Aoki stood immobile and silent. He
was conscious of Kazu Hatano watching him, but the thoughts
were ricocheting around in his brain. Starkest was Yamazaki's sick

simulation of a woman reaching her climax; almost as vivid, the bank chairman's face as he'd stormed into the hall.

And this woman's!

And her father's, as he'd hurried through the ryokan.

Devoid of electric light, cut off from the outside, the atmosphere in the ryokan on the seventh anniversary had been deeply bizarre, with all the major players in the missing woman's life present. Aoki had screwed his eyes almost shut, concentrating. He jerked his head up. "Someone other than myself and the perpetrator has seen the corpse. Details of its condition are known. What do you know about that?"

She flicked him a surprised glance and shook her head. Aoki studied her. Then he bowed, turned, and went to see Ito again.

Tea had been served to the bank chairman, and he was on his feet, cup in hand, eyes now alert, but otherwise unreadable. He gestured to the detective to enter. Aoki frowned. The banker had snapped out of that stupor fast.

"A shocking affair," Ito murmured hoarsely. "A great tragedy. *Who?*" He put down the cup and examined his small hands. Aoki stared at the downturned face; it resembled a piece of discolored marble. What he had here was the chairman of a bank that had imploded and pancaked down on itself like a skyscraper being demolished, the cuckolded yet reportedly complaisant husband of a woman who'd been missing for seven years, the holiday companion of the man who cuckolded him—the man who was now a stiffened corpse in a room of this snow-entombed ryokan—and in the background, like a shadow, the woman's ex-husband. That was all, or all that he could see at present!

The heavy-lidded eyes met the detective's. "Well? We're totally locked in. No one can get in or get out. So?"

Aoki weighed the inference. "Yes, the murderer's still under this roof. Unless there's a factor I can't see."

Ito gave him a hard, puzzled look. Abruptly, he put his hands into the kotatsu. "Stabbed through the heart, his genitals cut off and placed in the alcove."

"*How do you know that?*"

Ito quickly withdrew his hands. They'd turned red, looked almost bloody, and were shaking slightly. "I went to the room after you were here."

Aoki's face muscles tightened. "You should *not* have done that. The room's a sealed crime scene." He shook his head in disgust. "Who did you tell those details to?"

"No one." Ito shrugged his soft, padded shoulders. "Insane!" he muttered. He was having difficulty breathing.

Aoki controlled his anger and gazed into the alcove. Ito was showing definite signs of pressure. Maybe he'd misread the man; perhaps his reaction when he first heard the news had been genuine. For sure, the fellow was sending out mixed signals, and the position was awkward. He should have a colleague with him before asking questions that might have incriminating answers. It was irregular, but everything about his situation was. Aoki stared down at the glowing coals, gathering energy.

He turned on the banker. "*Who's* the murderer? *Why* was he murdered?"

Ito's face froze. The round head shot back on the thick neck. He sneered, "*How do I know that?* How in *hell* do I know *any* of that?" He flung out his hands.

Aoki stepped back and said forcefully, "Did Mr. Yamazaki fear himself in danger? Did he speak of such?"

"No," the banker snarled. Sharply, his hands dropped to his sides.

"Or show it?"

Ito gulped in air. "Yamazaki feared nothing. He could accept danger or reversal of fortune with equanimity." He stopped. "*If* he apprehended danger, he didn't tell me."

A rare type, if it were true, but it might be. Aoki recalled the man's arrogant progress through the corridors, his condescension in the bath. *This* man, though, despite his anger and contempt, was badly shaken. He'd got that now and wondered how the fellow had stomached viewing the corpse. *If* he was an innocent party. *If* he'd actually gone there as he claimed—and what about his bodyguard?

His face severe, Aoki said, "Last night after you retired, did you leave your room again?"

"No!"

Aoki raised his eyebrows.

"Do you think I'm lying?" A menacing undertone, but Aoki'd heard an infinity of them.

"What happened to your man after you left the hall?"

"He went to bed."

"Why did you beckon him to follow you?"

"To give him instructions for today."

"Yes?"

"I was hopeful the road might be cleared."

"Where is he now?"

Ito blinked angrily. "Probably having breakfast in the kitchen."

Aoki retasted his own breakfast. He was dying for a cigarette; his fingers tingled for one. What had Ito been shouting about last night in the Azalea Room, and what had been said in those conversations over the banquets? Had they been an overture to the murder, or the murder a result of that talk fest—or was it totally different territory? A new caution held him back from asking these questions. Delicate territory, *not* to be contaminated by a wrong move.

Aoki paused. Instinctively, he had a strong feeling that this man knew why Yamazaki had been murdered. His reticence, his whole demeanor, had the stench of concealment and insincerity. Lies had come out of the fellow's mouth, Aoki was sure. For one, Yamazaki was the kind of man who'd know who his enemies were, where threats lay.

Aoki bowed to the banker. "I will speak to you again later."

Shoba was outside Ito's door, motionless and solid against the corridor wall. Aoki pulled up and swept his eyes over the bodyguard, examining the gray suit: creased but unmarked. "I'm a detective in the TMP. I've got some questions to ask you." The man bowed his conical head, and the red birthmark blazed in the dusk. The muscles of his arms and torso rippled beneath the gray serge. This close, he appeared almost as wide as he was tall. Aoki spat out, "Concerning the murder of Mr. Yamazaki."

The small eyes examined Aoki. "Your badge, sir?" The voice was thick and labored but deferential.

Aoki nodded slowly. His badge and gun were locked in Watanabe's desk in Toyko.

The man looked almost apologetic, but Aoki knew that these were the mini sumo's little tricks.

The door to Ito's room slid open, and the banker stood there. He'd overheard. "Answer his questions," he snapped.

Shoba had nothing to tell—the way he told it. He'd followed his boss to his room, received his instructions, then gone to his own room on a lower level. He'd heard nothing and seen no one until he'd gone to the kitchen for his breakfast at 7:00 A.M. and been told the news.

When the short, strangulated report finished, Ito grunted and went back into the room. The door with its pale painting of a lily slid shut behind him. Aoki stared at Shoba. At some point, the minder's voice box had received forceful attention, but that didn't make him a liar, or a killer—though he had apparent credentials for both roles. Aoki sighed inwardly and turned away.

He headed back to the main hall. Motive? A crime of revenge and retribution—after the amazing scene played out at the end of the banquet? The obscene simulation by Yamazaki, the sinuous cries, sounded afresh in Aoki's mind. It was the deduction crying out to be made, yet maybe the emasculation was merely dressing on the salad, a premeditated or spontaneous act to muddy the waters. And that other big incision—what in fuck's name was that about? According to Superintendent Watanabe's old investigation, ex-husband Hatano slotted into the picture, with jealousy and retribution figuring. But that had been against his ex-wife . . .

It wasn't unpleasant to see a man like Ito sweat. Bitterly, Aoki thought how ex-governor Tamaki had gone smiling into his future, one as golden as his past, unaffected by *any* retribution, leaving Hideo Aoki with a suicided wife, a heart-failed father, and a ruined career. Even in the face of this horrific crime, hatred turned over in Aoki's stomach.

He paused on a landing of the wooden staircase to get a cigarette going, drawing the smoke and aroma into his lungs. The perpetrator was still in the ryokan. Aoki had a sudden compulsion to run through the place tearing open the door to every room, every cupboard . . . Not that simple.

However, he did begin to roam farther afield, exploring areas he hadn't entered before. He descended several short stairways to lower levels, progressed along corridors, went through small empty rooms that seemed to him like forest clearings, passed doors whose paper paneling was browned with age. A rambling structure, obviously added on to over the centuries; a labyrinth. He wished he'd studied the layout from the overlooking road when he arrived. He was staying on the move, trying to keep warm.

At the end of a long corridor hung with ancient scrolls, he found a small courtyard submerged by snow as high as the lintels of the two windows that looked upon it. His wife said, *Some corridors lead to places of silence that bring true rest and induce insight.* Then: *We are very close to you.*

Very close indeed, his father added.

Their voices were inside his head, but absolutely clear. "Am I losing my way even more, or starting to find it?" he asked. But they'd gone, or had no comment. He'd been asking about the poetic impressions and images that were emerging in his mind, as if a door had sprung open between a pragmatic cop's world and the cultured world of old Japan. A floating world. *Their* world. "Find out for yourself," he told himself.

To his left, abutting the courtyard, was a gallery about thirty feet long, its flooring formed by wider planks. At its end was a door. Aoki stepped into the gallery. The floor leaped into life—into an urgent birdlike twittering. He froze. The twittering ceased. Aoki knew what it was. He was amazed. *A nightingale floor!* His father had introduced him as a young boy to the famous one at the castle in Kyoto—an ingenious floor, clamped and nailed into place; walking on it caused friction between the nails and their clamps, emitting the giveaway sounds. There was no way to move silently on it

and it had been the shoguns' warning against spies and assassins—
another bit of their paranoia.

"A nightingale floor," he breathed.

You remember that, do you? his father said. They were still here!

This special floor could be protection for a hidden space. He
went on, the agitated sound scraping his nerves. The door at the
end was unlocked. He opened it and looked into two more corridors, one going ahead, one to his right. He closed the door and retraced his steps. Brooding on this discovery, he lit another cigarette.

At 2:00 P.M. Aoki entered the service area. He did this by sliding
open a door Kazu Hatano indicated and stepping into a dim corridor lit by a few oil lamps. She followed him and then took the lead.
They walked for a minute and came upon the kitchen, a room with
smoke-blackened rafters from which hung burnished pots and
pans and bunches of dried mountain herbs. Along one wall a massive woodstove with banked-down fires glowed. A stone-flagged
floor was spread with old tatami mats, insulation against the chill
spearing up from it.

Fifteen people waited in the room: four men, eleven women, absolutely silent. They must've been listening for the approaching
steps. "Is everyone here?" Aoki asked Kazu Hatano. Already his
eyes had found the face with the white scar over the eyebrow.

"Yes." She stared straight ahead. Obviously, that wasn't true.
Where, for instance, was her geisha sister? Aoki tightened his lips.
The staff watched him. His glance fell on Mori, and she looked
down. The light gleamed on steel: His eyes shot to a side table
where a dozen kitchen knives were ranked, shining, deadly.

All this at the service of Ito and Yamazaki's banquets, his own simple meals, and Saito's sour plums! Faces tense, they were waiting for him to speak. He might've been studying the cast of a Kabuki play before they got into makeup and costume. He cleared his throat. "I'm a police officer. You know what happened last night. I, or other police, will require to speak to each one of you. No one is to leave the ryokan, even if it should become possible."

He'd made his voice hard and official. Again his eyes came to rest on Hatano's face: fifties, dressed as a chef, probably the head guy. A lean fellow, with an intense, tough look about him. Aoki modified the observation: more a brooding anger. It was a singular face that matched neither the artistry of the delicacies borne to the corner table on the last two nights nor the worried curiosity of the others in the room.

Aoki's glance moved on. He was putting them on notice that he was here, in charge, and that more was to follow. In his hand he held a list, in Kazu Hatano's neat characters, of their names and where they'd slept last night. His eyes paused at one name, then continued down the list. What he needed now was a plan of the place. He looked up.

"The murderer's in the ryokan. Where else can he—or she—be?" He gave them a hard look. "Anyone who has any information, no matter if it seems unimportant, must come forward *now*." He slapped the palm of his hand against his thigh; like a muscle jumping in a face, they gave a collective start. "Don't wait for the interview if you heard or saw or even felt something. I want to know about it. It'll go hard with anyone who holds back. You can ask for me at the office." He spun on his heel and strode out, with Kazu Hatano hurrying behind. Nervous tension seemed to flow after them.

Aoki went straight back to the murder scene, thinking about the

questions he wanted to ask the proprietor, but Kazu Hatano realized where he was going and didn't follow, turning instead for the
office. He paused at the door to the Azalea Room; his improvised
sign remained in place. He stood listening. Deep silence. He slid
the door open. The room was faintly illuminated by a fragment of
dull afternoon light from the window. He took the flashlight out of
his pocket. The corpse was exactly as before; the severed parts in
the alcove continued to make their grotesque, mysterious statement. The air was limpid, the odor unpleasant, and the cold seemed
excluded from this room; his illusion.

Aoki noticed the scroll in the alcove, played the light on it, and
read:

If you meet a Buddha, kill him.
If you meet a patriarch of the law, kill him.

He studied the characters again. It was difficult for him to render
them into modern Japanese. The brutal message stood in stark
contrast to the ryokan's floating world. *Maybe.* For sure, the poem
fitted this horrendous event, as much as the nightingale floor fitted
that remote gallery. He brought out a pen and, holding the light under his arm, copied the characters onto a scrap of paper taken from
his wallet.

He stepped out of the room and closed the door. There was a
prickling on his back, a tightening in his genitals. A vision of the
professional knife work was engraved on his brain.

Kazu Hatano was extremely tense, yet strength emanated from her
as she gazed at Aoki: a police type, who'd stepped out from behind

the guest. How had he come to be here? Aoki read that. He'd had enough dealings with businesswomen in Ginza bars to know, despite appearances, how tough they could be. He folded his arms and leaned against the doorjamb. "And the guests. Three of us remain. No one else out of sight, is there?"

"Of course not." The freckles under her eyes were very clear. Aoki nodded. A sneeze overcame him, and he dug for a handkerchief. He'd been holding the scrap of paper in his hand. The poem seemed Zen-like to him. He gazed at it afresh; he wished to ask her about it, but it could wait.

"Where is your sister?"

He saw she'd been waiting for this.

"She has disappeared."

Aoki regarded her. Her dark eyes held his. The silence endured, deliberate, on his part. "Do you mean she's left the ryokan?"

"That isn't possible."

"What are you saying, then?" With an effort, he held his voice down.

"There are hidden places."

"Unknown to you?" he said, incredulous, but Saito's words about this came back to him.

She nodded abruptly. "There're chambers and spaces that were designed for hiding in times of trouble. Not all of them are known."

Beyond the walls he heard the faint whining of the wind. "Why didn't you tell me this before?"

"We haven't completed our search."

"When was she last seen?"

"Last night at about eight-thirty by one of the maids."

Aoki screwed up his brow. "Why would she disappear?" Her face was blank; her gaze had lifted and seemed to be passing him, communing with someone elsewhere. Her only answer was a slight movement of her hands. Aoki's fingers rubbed his cheekbone. He said tersely, "A man's been murdered, an honored guest who might've called on the services of a geisha. No doubt the room maid will know about that. Please ask her to come here."

She hesitated. Her breasts beneath the kimono rose and fell noticeably. "*That* has nothing to do with my sister," she said, her voice firm and low. Giving him a look, she went out.

"Maybe, maybe, Kazu Hatano," he said to himself, and turned to inspect the room with more attention, especially the desk, with its many closed compartments. He gazed at these as if to X-ray them, then paced the room, his slippers whispering on the springy tatami.

She knew *something* about her mother's disappearance, perhaps something about Yamazaki's murder—and how in hell couldn't she know where her sister was? The tiny fractures in her demeanor were telling him that she was being selective with the truth. He turned and gazed at the desk again. She must have been like this with Watanabe, which would have strengthened the superintendent's suspicions. Her mother had been a famous beauty when Ito'd found her. *If* those bloodstained clothes stood for the facts, she'd finished up a bloodied corpse, but "if" was the operative word. The Go-playing Saito had gotten into his mind about that.

The Kabuki-like scene in the kitchen flashed back. Last year his father had taken Tokie to Kyoto to see the Kabuki plays. In his father's opinion, Kyoto had the best atmosphere for them. Tokie wore her finest kimono to compete with the famed finery of the local ladies. Aoki stayed home, immersed in the case of a proprietor of a dry-cleaning firm who had stabbed a moneylender to death and clammed up. His own bit of Kabuki. He nodded to himself. As for the ex-husband, her father? The investigation was beginning to pulse stronger in Aoki. He'd get that fellow alone . . .

At a slight sound, his head whipped around to the door. Paler than before, Kazu Hatano stood there holding a wide-eyed Mori by the hand.

Chapter Fourteen

SHAKING WITH NERVES, MORI LOOKED at her employer for reassurance, but, except for holding her servant's hand, Kazu Hatano was unresponsive, apparently lost in thought. Aoki glanced at her, then gave the middle-aged room maid a friendly nod. "Mori-san, last night, did Mr. Yamazaki ask you to arrange for the company of the geisha?"

"Yes, sir." Her voice was barely audible.

Aoki breathed in, nodded again. "Did she go to his room?"

"I don't know, sir."

"You arranged the appointment?"

"Yes, sir, for nine o'clock." Her breathing was coming in shallow puffs. She darted another frightened look at her mistress.

Aoki sighed to himself, but he was patient with her. Little by little he heard that she'd gone off duty at eight thirty, and what she'd done then. She repeated that she hadn't seen the geisha go to the room. Aoki stared at her for a long moment, then gave her permission to leave. With a hurried bow, she fled the office.

◈

He turned to Kazu Hatano. "You can see why it's vital to talk to your sister."

With a start, Kazu Hatano emerged from her thoughts. "We will continue our search." She looked away quickly, but Aoki caught the gleam of tears.

The inspector went out to the hall, trying to interpret that. Lies were as prevalent here as the icy drafts penetrating the ill-fitting window frames. Granted, the place was a labyrinth, yet it was unbelievable it would take so long to uncover the sister. *If she was alive.* That pulled him up. He should look over the sister's room.

The terrified Mori had brought back to him an image of Ito's trembling hands—and his anger and sarcasm. Had the media stories regarding the banker's complacency over his wife's affair with Yamazaki been another fiction? Yamazaki's murder had the seals of both jealousy and revenge. Last night, the banker had been enraged on two occasions; this morning, his agitation could equally well have indicated a murderer fearful of discovery or a person appalled by the death of a close associate. Yet maybe the killing was for an entirely different reason. For sure, the banker knew more than he'd said. Aoki ran his tongue over his sore lips. Whatever the answer, the cruel cry that had sinuously traveled the corridors might've been the trigger for the murder.

Had he and Yamazaki known that their meals were being prepared by Hatano, their predecessor in Madam Ito's bed? Aoki rubbed his jaw. How much of this, of the past and the present, was in the reticent Kazu Hatano's beautiful head?

Minutes later Aoki slid back the door of his room. The charcoal glowed bloodred in the kotatsu. He lit a cigarette and glanced at his watch: The second hand swept past 6:00 P.M. He switched on the radio and was back in the company of NHK. The transmission was much worse than before.

. . . Tokyo Citizens Bank continues to send shock waves . . . new speculation . . . allegations . . . yakuza connections . . . informed sources advise Bank of Japan . . . turned up substantial loans to front corporations controlled by gangsters . . . bank recently withdrew from a commitment . . . property developments in Yokohama . . . Yakuza client facing crippling losses . . . police search . . . Ito and Yamazaki still hampered by weather conditions . . .

Aoki switched it off and gazed into space. He'd heard enough. Someone inside the Citizens Bank was leaking. The Bank of Japan played close to the vest; there was no way it would've released information about an investigation so soon. He stubbed out the cigarette.

The yakuza. That was something to think about; they didn't tolerate anyone crossing them. Retribution could be brutal, but since the onset of the storm, it had been impossible to get anyone into the ryokan, and it was highly unlikely they'd have a sleeper at this remote place. Besides, Ito, who must've made the decision to cancel the loan on the Yokohama project, was still alive. Yet the killing had the pro stamp, though what hit man would play around with sexual organs like that? As for the surgical cut across the gut—

He stared around the Camellia Room. He felt caged in the snow-besieged ryokan, suffocated by the multiple speculations insinuating his every brain cell.

Saito appeared to be extracting maximum stimulation from the situation. Aoki had checked with Kazu Hatano; Saito had given an

Osaka address, all right. When Aoki could, he'd look into it. His fingers touched the scrap of paper within the kimono.

Inspector Aoki cleared his throat. She looked up quickly from a ledger. Here he was again! Was that what the look meant? The black hair, smooth as water coming over a weir, had that bluish shine and the same gold ornament. The scrap of paper was in his hand. "Excuse me, I have a question about the scroll in Mr. Yamazaki's room—" He stopped. Her face had shot up in response to his "excuse me," and for an instant he'd seen a simpler, worried woman. He came forward and handed her his note. "Please tell me about this."

He watched her eyes widen in surprise as she read, then let the hand holding the note fall to the desk. "It's an old Zen motto. The scroll doesn't belong to the ryokan."

"You mean it's replaced another?"

"Yes. It's been brought from outside." Her face had become even paler. "It is not something we would have here."

Aoki nodded. Nor would any inn proprietor. Two exhortations to murder; not a restful sentiment for guests. If the killer had done it, was the motive the same as for the severed genitalia left on display beneath it?

Maybe Yamazaki had brought it in himself. The fellow's personality, apparently, had been weird enough to play private jokes like that. He cursed under his breath.

He'd seen no signs of searching going on, though if they were doing any at all, it would be in parts beyond the guest areas. He gave a slight bow and left. None of the staff had turned up at the office asking for him.

He paused outside the office, a deep frown on his brow. Too much was going on in his head. He was missing the usual discussion and interaction with a colleague—just like he was missing his badge and gun. Bleakly, he considered what to do next. He reached into a pocket for the lip salve. As he applied it, as if sent to him as a respite, the fine blue veins on the back of Kazu Hatano's hands came into his mind's eye.

Aoki descended the stairs at the southwest corner. Something was impelling him to undertake these explorations. Perhaps he was half-expecting to ferret out the missing sister, but he met no one and heard no human sounds, only the creaking of timbers and the fainter whining of the wind. He could hear his own breathing. It was the same scenario: dusky, wood-paneled corridors with many doors; small, empty rooms; ceilings almost scraping his head. His slippers moved softly over dully glimmering floors polished for centuries by a legion of departed maids. An empty, but clean, labyrinth. How did they keep up all the floor polishing? Was it ever filled with guests, even in spring? It was so dim in places that occasionally he flicked on his flashlight. At last he turned a corner into a day-lit gallery and realized that he was on the other side of the snow-drowned courtyard, opposite the cunningly built nightingale floor.

Aoki stopped dead. A voice was chanting, hands clapping, and he smelled the cloying odor of incense. A Shinto ritual. Abruptly its sounds ceased, replaced by footsteps. Ito came out of the gallery and walked quickly past, his eyes fixedly ahead. The detective might not have existed. Akoi watched him go. Ito saying prayers!

The inspector turned and entered the gallery. The shrine was built into an alcove, filling the space from floor to ceiling, gilded and ornate, red and gold—a family altar.

A shrine to appease a restless spirit, Tokie said.

I'm afraid so, his father commented.

Aoki stared at it as the voices faded in his head. Had Ito been praying for his wife, for Yamazaki—or for rescue from the Fatman's clutches?

"So he's gone. The Don Juan of the Tokyo finance world has stepped through the curtain—minus his sexual equipment."

Saito spoke in a pragmatic voice. They were in the anteroom. Aoki looked at him, hard. He'd located this man's room on a lower level than Ito's, about two minutes' walk from the Azalea Room in the northeast part of the ryokan: the Chrysanthemum Room. "Do you recall the information submitted to the police by Madam Ito's friend, identified as Person Y—the Kobe incident?"

As Saito looked at him for confirmation, Aoki remembered. Yamazaki and Madam Ito had visited Kobe, staying at a hotel in the hills. While she was out, he arranged for another female friend, from his rich gallery, to come to their room. He "arranged" to be in this woman's arms, in her body, precisely at the time Madam Ito returned. She rushed from the room and cut her wrists in the hotel ladies' room with a nail file. She'd spent several days in a Kobe hospital. The hospital stay had been substantiated; the story about the other woman hadn't been.

"A *torture* point," Saito said. "She'd never loved either of her husbands, so the papers said, but Mr. Yamazaki was a different matter. She was intelligent and must have known what kind of man he was. Nonetheless, concerning him, she had no power over herself."

How had Ito reacted to the attempted suicide? At the time, they'd kept it out of the news. Aoki recalled that a paper had written a sly comment on the MOF man's morals: "Each night, Mr. Yamazaki lies down on a new tatami mat."

Aoki studied this student, or addict, of sensational crimes. What a recall for detail he had.

"I continue to hear interesting things on my radio." Saito's big hands rested loosely on his knees. Aoki waited, his own hands behind his back. "They're saying now a trillion has blown clean out of the bank's books like chaff. Of course, it was gone long ago, but they've kept the lid on that. The amazing thing is the government might let it go down." He gave a harsh chuckle.

Aoki pulled out his pack of cigarettes, wondering if Saito had heard the report at six about the bank's yakuza links.

"And isn't it even more amazing that as the bank crashes, the chairman's trapped at a mountain ryokan, incommunicado, and the supervising MOF official lies murdered in the same ryokan?" He looked up at the detective.

Aoki was unresponsive, thinking. Ito and Yamazaki had made reservations at the ryokan for three nights only, so their absence from Toyko was enforced by the weather. An act of God, as they said in the West. Even so, with the bank in the shithouse, how could they have afforded to be absent for even one hour?

Saito said, "Citizens caught up in the bank's demise are legion. Ito's the figurehead upon which waves of hatred will be advancing, and Yamazaki, complicit in the disaster, shares the blame. They were locked together in a deadly embrace."

Aoki stirred from his thoughts. Deadly embrace? A new thought came: The two might never have intended to return from this rendezvous, might've made a pact. For sure, they'd been locked together, but Ito was still here, and Yamazaki's exit hadn't been suicide.

Fiercely, he frowned at the fire. More likely, they'd been working out a plan to save the bank. Key in the fast-moving Fatman in his banking committee role, the snowstorm, and a hand with a razor-sharp blade—and that'd hit the scrap heap.

Saito shrugged. "And perhaps, after all, nothing has been dis-covered or decided about Madam Ito."

Aoki was only half-listening. The Fatman and his yakuza friends wouldn't want the bank to go down. Until recently it must've been a goose laying golden eggs. He said tersely, "Yamazaki's murder has put her case into the background."

This man's story that the pair had been engaged in a retrospec-tive on the missing wife and mistress could be total bullshit. Yet Yamazaki's horrible simulated wailing was back in his head.

Aoki turned and moved closer to the fire. Whatever had been discussed between the two men each night now resided solely in the mind of Ito.

Saito picked up a black stone from the bowl. "According to my maid, the twin sister has disappeared." He placed the stone with precision. "Disappearances seem to run in the family."

Aoki moved his eyes away from the dark, craggy face, the thick, glossy hair. News ran through this place like an electric current. What about the electricity, the phone? He gave an impatient nod and left the anteroom.

Massaging the cold from his fingers, he couldn't decide whether to speak to Ito again, whether to risk trampling the ground for the local CIB, who must surely be here tomorrow—

He was staring down a corridor as if at a suddenly revealed vista: the chef, Hatano, hurrying through a remote corridor of the ryokan last night. The fellow Superintendent Watanabe had fingered for Madam Ito's disappearance, the fellow who'd been mad with jealousy when she'd married Ito—according to Watanabe. In sending that awful sound through the ryokan last night, had Yamazaki stepped into *that* deadly quicksand, and was Ito the next in line?

Aoki began to pace up and down, hardly aware he was doing it. *If* that was the way it was playing, it tossed out Saito's sardonic take, that Ito was the one who'd exacted revenge on his wife's seducer—as well as his own emerging thoughts about the yakuza. Watanabe couldn't have predicted any of this.

He pulled up and stared into the darkness at the end of the corridor. His boss's agenda in sending him here continued to float like smoke in his head, but what if Watanabe had known that Madam Ito's ex-husband was here, that the three men closest to her disappearance had suddenly assembled at the ryokan? Had the superintendent, in his convoluted way, thrown his best investigator into the situation, like bread on the waters, hoping for a breakthrough?

Chapter Fifteen

"*WATANABE-WATANABE-WATANABE,*" AOKI MUTTERED in the Camellia Room. He smacked his right fist into his left hand. He backed off, took in air in a deep breath. Figuring out his boss's reason for sending him to the ryokan *was* like trying to grab hold of smoke, but all his experience, his sixth sense, told him that it was at the heart of what was being enacted here. Maybe what he'd just thought about his boss's agenda was right on. Yet they'd tracked him out to the Fatman's Hakone house that night, and the police shrink, obviously, had reported his paranoia about the ex-governor's escape from justice, and his part in Tokie's death, and the journalist Kimura's death; and his grief and guilt about Tokie. The surveillance they'd put on him showed their concern about how dangerous he might be, but did he need to go down deeper yet to uncover Watananbe's agenda?

Aoki pulled a cigarette from the pack, lit up, and exhaled spasmodically. He could hear the stream flowing again; the ice was melting. He gazed into the alcove. The ryokan must've borne witness to a host of tragic events, and the MOF man's murder was merely another in the stream of time. Like clockwork, this new way of thinking was rolling out of his brain, almost as a respite from the other grinding thoughts. Carefully, he brushed his lips with his fingertips. Kazu Hatano's face had flashed fear and worry—and the hint of a straightforward woman. Her missing sister must be the *foremost* worry. Unless . . . He stubbed out the cigarette and left his room.

At 3:20 P.M. he stepped through the door into the ryokan's subterranean area. A minute later he stood in the kitchen's doorway. His eyes swept the large space. The Kabuki cast had vanished. Only two persons present, each frozen, staring at him. The woman kitchen-hand dropped her eyes first. "Carry on with your work," Aoki said. The chef was filleting a large fish. He made a short, smacking sound with his lips, then lowered his eyes to the task. Hard, wary eyes, and his face had flooded with color. *Zip-zippp*—a slight but sinister sound. Aoki watched the razor-sharp knife slice a fillet from the backbone. The man's hairless, wiry forearm flashed over the rich flesh. He was concentrating on his knife work; his face had become closed. *Adept.* Two dark shadowy spots stood out on his forehead. *Fast.* His latex-gloved hands flipped two fillets onto a stainless-steel tray; he flicked a trace of blood off the metal with a cloth, then washed and dried the gleaming blade.

Child's play for a man like this to excise Yamazaki's genitalia; to display them in the black lacquered box. The thought chilled Aoki. Though thrusting a knife into *living* human flesh mightn't be so easy.

No stoves were lit yet, and the room was like a meat locker. The chef crossed his arms and regarded Aoki. His black eyes didn't deviate from the detective's face.

"Why did you come back here?" Aoki said.

The chef looked at the woman and pointed to the door. She

stopped beating eggs and went out. When it came, his voice was rough and intense. "That's my business."

Aoki nodded slowly. "I know who you are. I suggest you answer the question."

The man's face had turned dark. His tongue licked over his lips. "How long ago, Mr. Hatano?"

He lifted his eyes and stared beyond Aoki. "Two years."

Aoki had expected a longer period. "Before that?"

"I had a restaurant in Osaka."

For a long moment Aoki considered this, continuing to gaze at the man's face. What had brought him to the mountains—a business failure, filial duty? His daughters? Aoki knew there'd be a story behind that, but this man wasn't going to say anything more, and he was in no position to force him to. "Where were you going last night?"

"To my room." Hatano's gaze dropped to the spotless bench. The two shadows on his forehead were dark as bruises. His mouth was small and tight-lipped: a fish's asshole of a mouth. Aoki nodded, turned, and left, the sound of the knife slicing the raw fish still in his head.

In the corridor, he stopped. *Three* Hatanos at the inn, but one missing. The chef's take on his missing daughter wouldn't differ from Kazu Hatano's. Family business.

Aoki turned his head sharply. A snatch of jazz: Bix Beiderbecke, playing "Tiger Blues." He remembered his classmate Shimamura, the innumerable concerts they'd attended together in their youth. Lost days. There was no jazz here; it was the ryokan playing its tricks, or his damned nerves.

He went on along the corridor and stepped back into the public domain. At the foot of a stairway he paused, pulled out a chocolate bar, and bit off a piece, chewed, and meditated. Yamazaki, in a speech to the Bankers' Association, had attacked the yakuza as "a cancer in corporate life." Big surprise, though perhaps he'd been laying down smoke over his own complicated official activities. If the yakuza *had* placed an assassin in the ryokan, it could only be with the aid of someone here. He was back to that.

Aoki swallowed the delicious chocolate. The time factor was too short. Revenge and retribution at the hands of the cuckolded Ito stayed on the screen as a motive. Ditto with Hatano. As for Kazu Hatano, loathing for Ito exuded from her every atom; he hadn't observed her face-to-face with Yamazaki.

Reluctantly he put it all aside and went to the office.

In the hall, Shoba sat on the bench he'd made his own. He stood up, folded into a bow, his eyes on the detective's feet. Aoki grunted. Yeah, those hard fists could pound you to a pulp, but how was his knife work?

"Everything's up for grabs," Aoki told himself.

Kazu Hatano must've been working hard to restore the place to equilibrium and settle the staff down, not an easy task with a murdered corpse in situ, not to mention the disruptions from the snowstorm. She looked up from her desk, and a black ringlet of hair escaped and curved down beside her pale cheek. Aoki wished he could enter through those eyes into her thoughts. The mother had been a famous mountain beauty, and the daughter had a comparable allure, though her looks weren't exactly of the classic type. She rose, her eyes questioning.

With a shock, Aoki realized that this woman was stirring something in him, that each time he was seeing her in a different light. The slender hand brushed back the ringlet and withdrew down her cheek and under her chin to spread against her throat, revealing her shapely forearm in the kimono sleeve.

Aoki's heart was pounding. The simple gesture had aroused his passion. It *was* as simple as that. He swallowed. "The phone?"

"It's still out of order. My housemen are going to start digging out the front door today. The snowplow will already be at work down the mountain. I do hope so."

"Your sister?" Heat was moving across his face.

Her eyes dropped. "She can't be found."

Aoki swallowed hard. "I find that incredible."

The shapely shoulders moved in the slightest of shrugs. "It's the fact."

He coughed. The damned tobacco—no, this damned emotion. "Do you have any new thoughts on Mr. Yamazaki's murder?"

She hesitated, then gave him a direct look. "It's connected to the present, not the past."

Aoki blinked. "Please be more specific."

She shook her head.

Specific! His eyes flicked away. Information was locked inside her head about her mother's disappearance, and about Ito and Ya-mazaki being here, that was for sure—information he needed. "Why did your father come back to the ryokan?"

Her eyes widened. This had surprised her. "You would have to ask him."

He could only gaze at her as he absorbed her reticence. One, maybe two nights to get through, then all of this would be opened up like a can of sardines by the CIB. He hoped fervently it wouldn't prove personally disastrous for her.

At five, with a sense of relief that the day was ending, Aoki went to the bath. Shoba was waiting in the corridor, and Aoki ignored the man's bow. The bathhouse was steaming—tonight the stone bath. Ito's rotund white body was adrift in the water, and his eyes flicked open at the newcomer. Aoki soaped and rinsed and lowered himself in. Immersed, he gazed across at the bank chairman and remembered Yamazaki's long pale legs, visualized the savage yet clinical cutting that'd been done between them.

After a few minutes, Ito climbed out and sat on a stool, his stomach subsiding in gross rolls of fat. "Buddha" was right on, Aoki thought. Ladling cold water over his head and body, drying himself, the banker appeared deep in thought. A few times his eyes darted at the Tokyo police officer.

Was the banker in danger? The question hovered beyond Aoki's closed eyes as information and priorities shuffled continuously in his brain. After his enforced absence from the force, the disgrace that had been unjustly laid on him, it seemed the impetus to throw himself into this case was building in him like a fever.

Saito's slicked-back hair gleamed in the lamplight like old lacquer. He was sipping green tea and, without looking up from his seated position, bowed slightly to the detective. He wore a black kimono devoid of decoration. Aoki realized that these meetings by the Go board were forming a thread of familiarity between them. "The type that adversaries have," he told himself. He moved nearer the fire and warmed his hands. When would Saito get around to his own case, in depth? When he was ready. The man liked to throw in observations from the margin, stir things up, yet maybe he *had* come to view the fall leaves, to replay this historic match in seclusion. Maybe he was nothing more than what he said he was, just an eccentric.

Still concentrating on the formations before him, Saito said, "Are you bitter?"

Aoki exhaled his breath softly.

"Is my question impertinent?"

"No." *Retired* was the entry against the man from Osaka's name in the register. Did retired businessmen become hobbyists on the nation's crime spectaculars, Go-players, and commentators on the financial world? Was *that* it?

Aoki touched his mole. Lateral thinking, or was it surreal? In these frozen mountains his ideas, his theories, were changing direction like wind shifts. He cleared his throat. "I wouldn't say bitter. Hatred for the system."

Saito's eyes swept the board. "Ah, the system. Weren't you a little naive? I mean, a TMP investigator of your experience taking on ex-governor, ex-minister Tamaki, the ruling party, and ultimately your own superiors in the police? From a base of no power whatsoever!" His eyes had become slits. "It's the move a samurai with no wish to live longer might have made in *his* world."

Aoki reddened. What choice had he had? He'd been under orders, and then Tokie had played her hand, and down he'd spiraled. His own case was beginning to feel like one he'd studied at the academy, not his life. He had several questions in his mind to put to Saito, but they should wait till the prefecture cops arrived. The same with Ito—and with Hatano.

"No comment?" Saito threw him a calculating glance.

Samurai! He'd just been doing the job he'd been assigned to. This man had misread the situation—just as Tokie had apparently seen him as engaged in a noble cause against corruption in high places. Sure, he'd wanted to see justice done, to do a pro job, but it'd been his personal angst, after putting in a horrendous amount of work and driving himself and his team into the ground, that had hit him like a pile driver.

Click-click. Saito's hand was in the bowl of black stones. "Your superiors went down like rice stalks before the wind. It was unfortunate your wife took it to the journalist. No—tragic. Hatred of the system? Ito and Yamazaki are icons of it, of the same tarnished caliber as Tamaki. 'The gray men who destroyed your life.' I quote the *Tokyo Shimbun*." Aoki grimaced; quite a bit of such stuff had been printed. Saito smiled cryptically. "Not bitter?" His voice resonated disbelief.

Aoki was becoming angrier. Damn his teasing questions. Was this Osaka fellow saying his mind might be off the rails, that he might be targeting this class of guy? That was crazy, because it was only about Tamaki. If he could ever drag the ex-governor under the spotlight of justice, he'd do it; if not, there was another option, and that was where the Go-player's thinking had gone. Even ahead of his own!

Aoki held up his hands and studied them in the firelight. They were bloodred. He realized that, in his subconscious, he had made an appointment with Tamaki of that kind—if he could find no way to bring the Fatman before the law. He gazed at the Go board. The Go-player had cut very close to the bone.

Saito looked up. "The wonder of our country is that the old ways survive. From the furthest mountain village to the quiet suburban garden, the old Japan remains, despite the chaos of the markets. It goes on singing its song like the evening wind in pine trees, even in the records of the Go association! Change, with all its clatter and racket, might seem the main game, but in the end it's an echo of history."

Aoki stared at the big, hunched, black-kimonoed figure. In a burst of energy, the fire crackled and sparks flew.

Saito said, "The match finished on December 4. The last session was intense, close combat. All their combined art was in the moves. Each reached for stones with great rapidity. 'The sky clouded over from shortly after noon, and crows cawed incessantly'—Kawabata's words about this phase."

Aoki frowned. The cawing of crows was a death knell. His father had said that once.

"The last play was Black 237. At forty-two minutes past two it was over, and the Master had lost."

Saito smiled up from the board as though the old dead master had just died again, under his hands.

Ito entered the room and went in to dinner. Aoki followed. The bank chairman sat at the table he'd shared with Yamazaki, having a solitary banquet, a farewell to the ryokan and this bizarre and tragic interlude, Aoki thought. And to fame, reputation, and fortune. Tomorrow, or the next day, the road would be open, and the outside world would pour down on them like an avalanche.

Inspector Aoki walked through the semidarkness checking out the status of things. He stood in the shadows near the mouth of the corridor that led to Ito's room. Ito had retired, and the squat and muscular Shoba was seated on a chair outside the door, settled for the night. Aoki retraced his steps. Ito was taking precautions. Was that a mark of his innocence?

He lingered on the small landing on Ito's floor. Mounted on the wall near his head was a sword, a samurai weapon. Even in the dusk the elaborate enamel-and-gilt scabbard glowed. He gazed at it.

The Go-player has the killer instinct. You used that phrase, Hideo, one of the few times you talked to me about your work. That is a murderous match he is playing—one of the turning points in the history of Go, when a way of art, of symmetry, surprise, and nobility, was smashed like a beautiful ceramic bowl.

His father!

It became merely a test of strength, a testimony to victory and defeat.

In the freezing, empty stairwell, Aoki said, "But this man just replays a match that originated with others."

Replays this match year after year. There are a myriad classic matches to choose from. The voice sounded weary.

"So—what are you saying?" Aoki said urgently. "That he's a killer in real life?"

But the old man was saying nothing more.

What had been smoldering in his subconcious burst into flame in Aoki's mind like the anteroom fire, knocking his father's voice clear out of his head. There was no missing sister—not here at Kamakura Inn. Another lie! Kazu Hatano had been the geisha who'd come to his room!

Chapter Sixteen

KAZU HATANO THE GEISHA! IN the dark of the Camellia Room, with the somehow softer voice telling him that she was the sister, in the height of passion, could he've been fooled? Aoki had returned to the corridor outside his room, a cigarette dangling from his lip.

Easily. In the semidarkness and slipperiness of this world, it was hard to take a firm grip on anything, yet a doubt about it nagged at him. Impulsively, he turned to go back to the office.

Ten minutes later he was shown into a small bedroom on a lower level. The sister's room. The maid whom Kazu Hatano had instructed to bring him here lit the oil lamp and went out to the corridor to wait. He glanced around. The only personal item in the room was a framed photograph on a table. He gazed at it. The twin sisters. For sure, they looked identical; who was who, he couldn't tell. He grunted and opened the wardrobe. It held female clothing, including several elaborate kimonos. He moved the hangers and sighed. Here it was, the azure kimono dappled with the deep red leaves. He'd begun to think that he might have dreamed that night. But who had been wearing it?

Dinner was well over, and presumably Chef Hatano would've

finished for the night. Aoki had consulted the floor plan Kazu Hatano had given him and knew where the father's room was. He'd decided to step over the line of his suspension and go for the guy. The bastard had clammed up earlier. "Let's see what we can do about that," Aoki muttered as he descended the stairs.

Minutes later, a door slid open and the wiry man's eyes flicked over the detective. Aoki thought tensely, *With the speed of his filleting knife.* A modest room, from what he could see past the blocking figure. He said, "I want to ask you some more questions."

Hatano said nothing. His face was shadowed, yet the two dark patches on his forehead stood out. Aoki coughed, clearing away the last cigarette. "Okay, what *did* bring you here two years ago?" Forcefully he said, "And I want to know what happened in Osaka, or here, for you to make the move."

Aoki scrutinized the face before him. Every gram of this man exuded anger and menace. Did he have a tongue? The detective snarled, "I haven't got all night; I've got *murder* on my plate—not fancy-cut sashimi."

The chef came to life, exhaling a violent hiss through his teeth. "*Murder.* So what! There're other things as deadly."

Aoki blinked at the force of the man's breath. He'd hit a nerve. "So?"

"*Sssss*—I owned a restaurant. My food was the best in Osaka, but you'd need a *palate* to know that. Yet I went bankrupt. So what? It happens, but it *always* happens if the loan sharks've got you by the balls." He thrust his torso forward. "You cops should look into *them.* Banks don't want to know the small businessman, so desperate fools take a month's loan to get over a cash-flow glitch at forty-nine fucking percent a month! Fifteen times the legal limit! The glitch is longer, you're trapped in a fucking repayment-borrowing cycle, business and house go down the tube, and maybe your fucking sanity." He spat out, "These sharks are business-*killers,* life-destroyers!"

The savage bitterness came directly into Aoki's face. Of course, he knew about the small-business warfare in the nation. It bred crime. But it didn't shift murder from dead center in his mind. What Hatano said sounded like the truth, but the whole truth? This chef seemed like a candidate for deeper and dirtier problems, including his ex-wife's disappearance and maybe Yamazaki's brutal demise.

Aoki rocked slightly on his heels. Their faces were eighteen inches apart. He was at home dealing with this kind of shit, unlike the Itos of the world. "So you dragged your ass back here."

Hatano's eyes burned in the gloom. "Bankrupted, personally fucked, where else d'you go but back to your family?" He had locked his right fist in his left hand. He sneered, "There's a lot of people I could take a knife to, but they're in Osaka."

The snarled phrases seemed to be curving through the air at Aoki like knives. He'd picked up the slur about his plebeian food choices. He frowned. He'd thought of something. "What was the name of this amazing restaurant?"

"Osaka One." Hatano almost choked on the words, as if reluctant to speak of the dead.

Aoki gave a brusque nod. "So you're an expert on *that* kind of mayhem, but what's your take on this murder? Right in the bosom of your family, a family with a lot of interesting history."

Hatano's small mouth had snapped shut.

"What's your take on your long-missing wife, your missing daughter?"

But the chef had clammed up again. A rush of blood to the head had brought the Osaka debacle spilling out, but family matters were something else. Now his eyes said, *Fuck off.* Aoki grunted, turned his back on Kazu Hatano's father, and headed uphill through corridors, stairways, and semidarkness. It was 8:25 P.M.

Her office was quiet with the stirring of the charcoal fire when Aoki knocked and entered. His heart was going faster. She was there, seated at the desk; seemed always there. Presumably she slept, ate, washed and groomed herself, had conversations, but in any of those manifestations she was a mystery to Aoki.

He decided, *Quiet with her thoughts*—and what thoughts! She wore the dark blue kimono. Was it she or her sister who'd worn the azure one with the deep red leaves—in the Camellia Room?

Face-to-face again! The thrill that had surged through his system at 3:45 P.M.—he knew the time precisely—hadn't subsided, but now it was mixed up with everything else in his mind. Had he had this woman in the most intimate way, or had he not? It was amazing to him that he didn't know. He cleared his throat. "Your sister?"

"We've concluded our search. She hasn't been found."

"And the maid was the last to see her—at eight thirty last night?"

"Yes."

Unconsciously, he was shaking his head. "No doubt the local police'll bring in sniffer dogs."

She watched him impassively, so calm in the face of yet another family disappearance—such an incriminating disappearance—and of his discovery that her father was here. That flash of the inner woman last night, the decent and troubled persona, seemed a total illusion. Now she was impenetrable.

She studied the desktop, then looked up. "Governor Tamaki

was here in the spring with a party from Tokyo." Aoki blinked hard. Tamaki here! "The Fatman's Club came for three days. Only one fat man, really."

Aoki stared at her, rubbing fingers along his cheekbone. He knew of the club from the investigation, a gang of the Fatman's classmates and sycophants, a kind of dining club and secret society. *So they'd been here.* His voice tight with curiosity and excitement, he said, "Were Ito and Yamazaki in the party?"

"No." She showed her surprise. "Those two would have their own secret clubs, and they'd relate to the defilement of women." She spoke with deep contempt. "I believe it was an inner circle of the club, all his old classmates."

A muscle in Aoki's cheek jumped. *Classmates.* The bond of a life-time. "Did you know or recognize anyone, apart from the governor?"

She hesitated. "No."

"What did they do here?"

"Drank and ate and talked. Once they went for a walk to look at the new leaves."

Aoki nodded. It was hard to imagine Tamaki coming to such a remote place. He remembered the Fatman had once described him-self in a magazine interview as "an urban animal."

"Strange men," she said. "They'd drink their sake straight down and then tap the cup twice on the table. They broke some. And they all wore a gold badge."

"What kind of badge?"

"A small one—the silhouette of a fat man. It was meant to be Governor Tamaki, I think. Not a flattering likeness. The belly was huge."

Aoki gazed at her, amazed that she'd volunteered this

information—and at the flow of words. Then he realized she'd created a diversion—away from the sister and her father.

The badge had stirred something in him that had the illusive flavor of both premonition and memory. He creased his brow, but nothing came. He moved his head from side to side, loosening muscles.

She gave him a measuring look. A brass kettle was singing softly on a brazier. "Could I offer you tea?"

Surprised, he nodded assent. She produced two old, unmatched bowls. The whisk she used in them made only a whisper, and in the bowls the tea became green froth. Tokie and his father had frequently engaged in this ritual. "A serene moment," his father had said, staring into Aoki's eyes. Usually, he'd gone to the kitchen and opened a beer—another facet of their lives he hadn't chosen to enter.

This tea warmed his insides. The bowl he held, hot in his hands, had an inner glow in the dusky room, and the firelight gleamed on its glazed surface. He found himself sinking into a quieter space; all his senses seemed more intense in these mountains. He shook himself out of this. He hadn't mentioned her father again.

Out of the quietude of the ceremony, she said, "In the northeast, a devil's gate has opened, and evil is flowing in." Aoki's face was blank. Was this some kind of mountain superstition? She was deadly serious. "In the old days, they'd cut off the northeast corners of buildings like this to counter such an entry. I regret my ancestors neglected to do it."

She looked beyond Aoki to the fire. Her voice had sounded depressed. Being in mountains when you were a stranger to them was a tricky business, but he couldn't pay attention to this. He'd been admiring the precise movement of her lips: sculpting words with a new vivacity. This woman was strung tight with sensitivity; she could well know of his newly aroused feelings for her.

He thought of something. "What's the ryokan's connection with Kamakura?"

"One of my ancestors was a cultured man. He admired the shogunate of Yoritomo, at Kamakura."

Aoki absorbed this. Finishing the tea, he stood up, gave thanks, bowed, and left the office. In the hall, he consulted his watch. It was getting late. What was Saito up to?

The Go board was now a tract of black stones. Aoki blinked at it. Winner take all. Throughout the re-created match, Saito had been sitting in the challenger's place—the executioner's, for in this 1938 match, the Master of Go *had* been "executed." No candles tonight; a single oil lamp glowed on a table, backed up by the light from the log fire. His father was right about Saito's killer instinct, and Aoki wondered if the old man was back in the shadows, watching them.

Saito, an apparently untouched whiskey before him, motioned Aoki to sit. "A drink?" Aoki chose warm sake; it would build on the toehold of warmth the tea had taken in him. The bell tinkled. The sake was brought while they remained silent. Decisively, Aoki thought, *I'll search his room after this, if I can do it.*

Aoki drank the first cup of the scented liquor straight off, and some little devil made him tap the bowl twice on the table. At the sharp double sound against the wood, Saito's eyes lifted to the detective's. He said, "Despite what the papers reported, Ito wasn't complaisant about Yamazaki's seduction of his wife. He saw himself as forced to accept it—needed Yamazaki to shield him and his bank from the storm hovering on its horizon, which Yamazaki was able to deliver." He shrugged. "When the banking committee and the Bank of Japan moved on the bank, that shield was destroyed."

Saito sipped at his glass, then also tapped it twice on the table, and his thick lips twisted in a smile. More of his mockery. Aoki watched, expressionless. Where was this black-humored mystery man heading now?

"Being a cuckold doesn't sit well with any man's ego. Especially a highflier like him. What were his thoughts when all of that came out? When the whole nation knew? And then last night's obscenity." He grimaced. "The police will be here shortly. Then, I think, Mr. Ito is going to be *grilled*. That ample pink flesh will become an even pinker hue." He laughed, a rough sound.

The only laughter Aoki had heard here was the Go-player's. No. He'd heard Yamazaki's at the end of the MOF man's imitation of Madam Ito in the height of passion. He frowned at his sake cup. Saito was still pointing the finger at Ito. Concerning Ito and Yamazaki, did this man have a game in play parallel to the one on the board—just as dark and intense? Yeah, "killer instinct"—from his father or his own subconscious; a suspicious character, anyway. Ito wasn't going to be the only one for grilling when the CIB arrived.

Aoki placed his hands on his knees and stared at the Go-player. "The Fatman's Club. Six months ago, Governor Tamaki and his cronies were here. Did you know that, Saito-san? This obscure ryokan seems to have a lot of connections to people and matters that've been in the public eye."

Saito had dropped his eyes to the defunct match. Osaka? Retired? What was the truth? Aoki was squinting to better pick up his reaction, but the other sat still and silent as a Zen monk at midnight meditation.

Aoki put down the cup. From the windows, the snow light flowed into the room, putting a nimbus around Saito's head. He used the man's name for the second time. "Saito-san, you're from Osaka. D'you know the Osaka One restaurant?"

He wondered if Saito had heard.

Then the voice came. "No."

Aoki drained the last of the sake and stood up. "Good night." He bowed and left the room. Saito had hardly touched his whiskey. He hoped he'd have time to search the room.

Out of the whirlpool in his head, as he passed through the hall, Aoki thought, *If the murderer put the scroll with its brutal Zen motto in the Azalea Room, Yamazaki's killing was premeditated, not due to any hot rush of passion.* It was a message from a tortuous and educated mind, a mind like the Go-player's.

Everything was still up for grabs—except suddenly he felt that Chairman Ito had stepped into the clear concerning Yamazaki's murder.

Chapter Seventeen

AT ANY MOMENT SAITO MIGHT down his whiskey and decide to retire. Aoki descended the staircase and traversed a corridor. Here: *the northeast corner, the devil's gate!* His lips tightened. He couldn't believe that stuff. Softly his slippers brushed over the boards; ahead, a glowing pale blob—a painted chrysanthemum. He paused beside it, listening.

Had Kazu Hatano told him about the Fatman's Club to send him in yet *another* direction? Though maybe she felt pity for the grief he'd had from the Fatman's hands.

He slid the door open. The oil lamp had gone out, the room maid's failure. His flashlight stabbed into a space as organized as Saito's stones on the board. Except for a suitcase on a stand, there was nothing to show that a guest was in residence. He opened the wardrobe door. The blue suit and a dark overcoat, hung side by side. A wide-brimmed black hat and a radio packed in its carrying case were on the shelf. The suitcase was unlocked, and he lifted the lid. Clothes, immaculately folded. Ready for departure?

Aoki, taking shallow breaths, listened again. Then his fingers probed down the sides of the layered garments and touched something different. Carefully, he extracted a folder. He flipped it open and held the light on the contents. He was looking at Madam Ito's face on a front page—at clippings on the missing-woman case! Then clippings on Kimura's story, Tokie's suicide, the follow-up stories after Kimura's murder!

Aoki felt as if he'd taken a stunning punch on the forehead. Here was the source of Saito's amazing knowledge! The guy *must* have known Ito and Yamazaki were coming here! And Saito had known in advance that Inspector Hideo Aoki was, too—undeniably! He'd only known himself on the morning of his departure.

A new chill invaded Aoki's heart. Superintendent Watanabe's face, curly hair, and yellow tie and gloves were glowing hazily in his mind's eye like a warning beacon in thick fog.

A faint sound in the corridor. Aoki twisted his neck toward the door, straining to hear, heard only the timbers of the ryokan excreting their usual creaks. His facial muscles felt tight against his bones. He replaced the folder, then checked between the layers of clothing. No weapon, no identification papers, no cardboard tube to carry a scroll in. He lowered the suitcase lid and clipped it shut. He must get out.

He swept the flashlight into the alcove and over a scroll. With the same difficulty he'd had with the one in Yamazaki's room, he read the old Japanese:

> *Frost! You may fall!*
> *After chrysanthemums there are*
> *no flowers at all!*
> —OEMARU

It seemed right for the season, to belong in the room. *He must go.*

He stepped out into the corridor and closed the door, tension coiling and uncoiling in his stomach. Should he grab Saito and put him under restraint? Mightn't be so easy. Anyway, did the possession of all that information from the past make him Yamazaki's murderer?

Aoki moved, quiet and fast, back to the stairs. There were too many things in play: Ito's nervy reticence, his bodyguard in situ outside his room—maybe there was a stew of passion, jealousy, and revenge in the banker's gut, as Saito was contending, but the Go-player's real role? Aoki needed a lot more resources than he had available to probe that fellow's depths.

The sly *zipp-zipp* of the chef's knife work came back—and the missing sister, if she was here at all. Had Kazu Hatano kept the assignation with Yamazaki? Shit! Aoki brushed fingers over his cracked lips.

The staircase was lit by an oil lamp, a dirty amber glow. His hand was on the bannister when footsteps sounded in the darkness above. Descending! Aoki turned and, passing the corridor to Saito's room, slipped back into another. He pressed his shoulders into a doorway. Turning his head to the side, he had a good view of the half-lit stairs.

A man came slowly down the staircase into the meager light. He stopped—a tall figure, head in an attitude of listening. Saito! He gazed into Aoki's corridor, then turned and entered his own.

On the wooden staircase, more footsteps! Aoki blinked several times, remoistening his eyes. A man in a padded kimono descended, carrying a tray, and the light gleamed on a silver plate cover. Chef Hatano! Aoki couldn't make out his face, but he recognized the figure, its malevolent intensity. The chef also took the corridor to the Chrysanthemum Room.

For a moment Aoki gazed at the empty hall, then retraced his steps and ascended the staircase. What in hell was that about? Room service—a late-night snack? Saito probably was taking his meals in his room, but at this hour? Why had it been brought by the chef? That guy wouldn't take kindly to a room maid's duties, and earlier Aoki'd had the impression that he'd retired for the night.

It was 10:55 P.M. and Aoki stood by the brazier in the front hall. Someone had put more charcoal in before going to bed, and he warmed his hands. Then he gingerly inserted a cigarette between his lips and lit up. The office was dark, the door closed.

"Wake up, Hideo!"

He started and looked up quickly as if to see the old man's face in the shadows. The voice had sounded tired and peeved. But a question lay in the air between them: How had Saito known that this suspended inspector of the TMP was coming to the ryokan?

Aoki dragged the fragrant smoke into his lungs. Like a jolt of electricity from bad wiring, the connection to the gold Fatman badge leaped out of his subsconscious.

One night, in the Ginza, a door had opened across the narrow street from where he'd paused in a doorway to light a cigarette. He'd been about to flick the lighter when a figure emerged just as an electric light snapped on in a room above, illuminating the face.

"Watanabe-san," Aoki called out, then regretted it. Maybe the boss had a girlfriend and was keeping it quiet. The superintendent's head swiveled in the direction of the voice, and Aoki stepped out into the street.

"Ah, Aoki-san, working late?" Watanabe was squinting at him.

"Off duty, on my way home." Aoki smelled alcohol on his boss's breath.

"Ah! Good night, then." Watanabe had hurried off. It had been a week prior to the morning Aoki had been summoned to the director general's room and ordered to kill the investigation.

The flash of gold in Watanabe's lapel had been the Fatman's Club badge! They were classmates!

Aoki gazed across the icy, shadowy hall. The connection between Watanabe and Tamaki had tumbled in his head like an acrobat, somersaulted and landed upright, perfectly balanced. The superintendent was in the Fatman's pocket! Probably the yakuza's!

Wake up, his father had said!

Almost in a dream, he dropped the cigarette into a sand tray. A scenario was unrolling in his head: The Tokyo Citizens Bank's affairs with the yakuza had gone sour. In the eyes of the gangster bosses, Chairman Ito and Yamazaki of the MOF were to blame. Ex-governor Tamaki was the connection between the bank and the yakuza's business. The gangsters were watching Ito and Yamazaki; they had seen the duo's visit to this isolated region as a terrific opportunity to exact yakuza retribution. Sitting ducks. The Fatman, as head of the banking committee, had grabbed his opportunity to control the bank. It was the first and last time Ito and Yamazaki would sabotage the business of his gangster friends.

And Inspector Aoki. The unpredictable loaded gun; a future threat to the Fatman and his yakuza affiliations. Three birds with one stone! Watanabe, relentlessly patient, must've had the pair under long-term personal surveillance in relation to the Madam Ito case, his professional nemesis. *But that was no longer his boss's main game.* Aoki saw again Watanabe's every look, gesture, intonation at their last meeting . . . What a fool he'd been!

Aoki shook his head. The time frame to set up the mountain idyll had been really tight. *Never mind, it's been done.* The world at large might not know where Ito and Yamazaki had gone, but Watanabe knew.

Now, with absolute certainty, Aoki knew where he, and the bank chairman, stood—one step from the quicksand Yamazaki had stepped into.

Aoki walked out of the hall. *Who* was the yakuza operative? It had to be Saito—but a guy in his fifties? Though maybe he wasn't the knife man. The half-mad chef's face flashed back. Apart from going bankrupt, what else had he been up to in Osaka?

Aoki stood in the doorway, surveying the dark anteroom. The ragged icicles stabbing down from the eaves had melted to a third of their original size. The Madam Ito mystery had withdrawn from the limelight into the darkness, as had the missing sister and whatever the fascinating but impenetrable Kazu Hatano was up to. Cunningly, Saito had put the spotlight onto Ito's motive for revenge, and Aoki had been lining up the ex-husband and his daughters with their own such motives. The Go-player had been deliberately feeding the old mystery into his mind, entangling it with the current events to confuse him, until he could be eliminated. All the while Saito had been indulging his black-humored mentality beneath the facade.

Aoki hurried back to the hall and lit his way into the office. Kazu Hatano's fire had died to embers. With the flashlight he studied the old dark-wood desk. He'd seen her taking papers from it. It seemed to be the heart of the ryokan's administration, and maybe where she kept the guest register. He slid open one of the drawers: pens and pencils and all the accoutrements of record keeping and correspondence. He shut it, opened the next. No register. A stack of folders. He opened the top one, riffled through invoices for fish, meat, fruit and vegetables, propane, oil, telephone, electricity—

It was headed SENDAI SANATORIUM and addressed to Miss K. Hatano. He drew it out. His eyes raced over the detail. It was a statement of fees for a quarter's accommodation for a Madam Nagayama. Aoki's heart had begun to pound, his mouth had dried out, and he let out a long sigh. Was this the answer to the missing woman, or had he merely opened one small lacquered box in a cunningly fitted puzzle? But now he knew something that Kazu Hatano didn't know he knew. He gazed down at the invoice, memorizing the few details, then slipped it back in order and slid the drawer shut.

From the office door he stared out to the hall, again blinking quickly to moisten his eyes. He listened: just the sounds that were almost in his bloodstream. *Yet tonight, a new edge.*

The main thing he'd come to look for was the guest register. He'd had a hunch, and he needed to check who'd been in the Fatman's party last spring, but the book was nowhere in sight. He'd get hold of it later. The Madam Ito case might've stepped back behind the main action, but it still itched in his brain.

In the Camellia Room, he rubbed his hands vigorously to warm them. Why hadn't Saito sat quiet in the anteroom, playing his damned Go, until he was ready to make his move? Why risk playing a cop from Tokyo like a fish on a line? Aoki couldn't fathom this, or the undercurrent of derisive humor in the man.

He paced the room. The rocklike Shoba was on guard outside

Ito's room. Fervently, he wished he had his pistol, but he had his hands, just like Shoba. Hands against a knife? He must stay awake tonight, and super-alert. He prowled across the room, swinging his arms, then pulled up, frowning. Should he go and join forces with Shoba?

Chapter Eighteen

THAT MADE SENSE. YAMAZAKI HAD gone down, Ito and Aoki were the remaining targets, and together the banker's bodyguard and himself might stand a chance against the ferocious yakuza killer.

It struck him like a hammer: *Something bad was happening! Something he should be preventing.* In an instant dread was in his gut, his throat. *Ito's room.*

Aoki flung open the door to the corridor and hurried along it to the stairs, then turned into another corridor. The great freeze of the snowbound region roared in his head, and he shivered in the padded kimono as if it were a cotton vest. The light beam danced ahead of his feet. Amid the background "talk" from the ryokan, there was something different. He slowed, switched off the flashlight, and felt his way forward, his left hand brushing wooden walls, tracing over the papered doors.

A corner: the one from which he'd seen Shoba on guard outside the banker's door, ten paces away, an oil lamp close by. No light now. Another sound—human, moving away, *fast.*

Aoki jabbed at the button on the flashlight. *Hahhh!* Shoba was still seated on the chair. Blood was spouting from his neck, cascading over his shoulders and chest, pattering down onto the head. Aoki moved in. Shoba's eyes were half closed, the lips slightly apart. Spotlit by Aoki's flashlight, the brick-breaking hands were spread over the conical skull, as if to hold it secure on the blood-drenched lap.

Aoki swung the beam down the corridor until it hit a wall of darkness. *Ito!* Aoki's throat muscles felt like steel bands. The body-guard's blood was still jetting up like a fountain. The inspector moved past the dead man, slid open the door, and shot the light into the room.

The banker was on his side, leaning on an elbow, blinking at the light. *"Who? What is it?"* he cried.

"Aoki. Shoba is dead. Murdered." The fleshy face caught in the light was like parchment. Aoki swung back to the door.

"Aaaa . . . I heard something. Shoba moving."

Aoki hissed softly through his teeth. The only part of Shoba that had moved was his head. There was no hair to lift that by: the killer must've laid down the weapon and used both hands to dump it onto the lap and splay the guy's hands over it. *Why do that?* Blood must've sprayed the bastard's hands and clothing. A madman . . . *the samurai sword.*

A few seconds later and he'd have found Ito's corpse, too. Take a bet on that. Why hadn't the killer come back out of the darkness to kill them both? Aoki blinked hard with nerves. This was a pro, adept but cautious.

"Come with me," he snapped. He picked up a padded kimono and thrust it into Ito's hands. He didn't want the banker out of his sight. Ito froze in the doorway, staring at the corpse. In the flash-light's beams the birthmark was framed by the bloody spread fin-gers. The banker's mouth hung open; his chest was heaving, his breath wheezing. Aoki pulled at his arm and led him back to the stairs and up them. On the small landing, the samurai sword was still in its scabbard on the wall. Aoki looked at it grimly. Knives and cleavers aplenty in the kitchen. Sharp as razors. He'd decided where to go.

The oil level was low in the lamp outside Chef Hatano's room, but it still gave a feeble light to the corridor. Aoki paused outside the door, listening, but heard nothing. Ito stood back, his face obscure, his breathing now a faint sighing. A slight sound came from within. The chef was there. *Someone* was. Aoki reached for the door.

It was sliding open as if by its own volition. Aoki peered at the disheveled man in the doorway—every bit of him. He said, "Shoba is dead."

Hatano's eyes momentarily squeezed almost shut, then flicked past the detective to Ito. The tight mouth twitched. "*So.* I won't have to feed the greedy asshole anymore."

Aoki spat out, "Where've you been this past hour?"

Hatano hunched his shoulders, then reset them. "Why should I tell *you?* Shoba was pretty smart. He said you've got no authority, no badge." The sneering voice echoed in the corridor, in Aoki's brain. His anger boiled up—and the *fear.* Every muscle and nerve in him felt like a trip wire. *Watch it,* he warned himself, within an ace of grabbing the chef by his throat. He clamped his jaw tight.

Ito stood immobile, a dazed, dumb spectator.

The chef had decided something. He leaned forward. "Shoba dies and you come running *here!* Listen, I've been here all the time since nine forty-five. Have you got that?"

Aoki stared at the ex-husband of Madam Ito. This bastard seemed to've overlooked the meal he'd put together and taken to

Saito's room at 10:50 P.M.—another lie to circulate in this maze. He wasn't worrying about *how* Shoba'd left the world, either.

"Show me your hands."

"Get fucked."

Aoki grabbed them and pulled the chef out into the light. Clean as one of the kitchen knives. Still gripping his hands, he scrutinized the man's clothes. He dropped the hands in disgust. Hatano's visit to Saito's room? No. He'd keep the wraps on it; this bastard didn't know he knew about that yet. He pushed the man aside and went into the small room. There was nothing that looked out of place.

Aoki turned on the chef. "Okay, the cops'll be here before you can pick your teeth. Then we'll see about your fancy answers and look into your doubtless dirty past."

He turned his back on the wiry figure, the furious face, beckoned to Ito, and left. The man's gaze felt like it was boring between his shoulder blades. They climbed the stairs and stopped on the landing. Behind him Ito mumbled something, and he ignored it. Saito? What would he gain by interviewing the Go-player? He'd only get another theorizing filibuster with its undertone of contempt and black humor. There'd be no blood on that fellow, no weapon in evidence. Nonetheless, he led the banker to the northeast corner and stopped outside the Chrysanthemum Room. The sounds of heavy snoring came from within. Aoki's tongue flicked over his lips. Irresolute, he stared at the flower on the door; then, gesturing to Ito, he turned on his heel and headed for the office.

He strode through the ryokan. A yakuza was here, smuggled in the day Aoki arrived, or maybe the day before, emerging to do his brutal work, vanishing back into his lair, protected by a resident. He had no evidence on the chef, nothing on Saito beyond the Osaka man's briefing notes on himself and the missing woman. What he did have was an overwhelming gut feeling that they were both involved in the two murders.

As he ran his hand up the ice-cold bannister, the words of the Zen motto in Yamazaki's room chanted in his head: "If you meet a Buddha, kill him./If you meet a patriarch of the law, kill him." Chairman Ito, nicknamed Buddha, and Inspector Hideo Aoki, were the ones next in the killer's frame, aided and abetted by Superintendent Watanabe. No yakuza Aoki had ever dealt with or heard of had a taste for haiku or Zen mottoes, had ever crossed over into that rarefied world. But Saito! The fellow said plenty about the cultural life. They were his line, right enough, unless it was *all* fakery. He shook his head. He was numb with shock and weariness.

At 6:30 A.M., under Inspector Aoki's instructions, two squeamish housemen, whispering to each other, carried Shoba's quilt-swathed body down to the next level and laid it beside Yamazaki's in the Azalea Room. They'd woken up fast. Aoki led the way, carrying the head in a plastic laundry bag, yet again a body-parts courier.

The phone and electricity were still out, might never have existed at Kamakura Inn.

Returning to the upper levels, the banker close behind, Aoki found the cat sitting on a landing. It came to him, and he reached down to stroke it. A fragment of normality in this enclave of madness—though was that true? "What did *you* see last night, wandering one?" he murmured.

"What did you say?" Ito said suspiciously.

Aoki ignored the question.

In the office, Aoki read the new horror in Kazu Hatano's eyes. Nonetheless, her composure was extraordinary. Her ryokan had turned into a slaughterhouse and a morgue, and she was still functioning, but he saw that her composure had become fragile. The corpse had been wrapped up when she'd arrived at the Lily Room. Eyes wide, she'd stared at the great red splash on the door and wall behind where the late Shoba had been sitting. Aoki had stopped the maids from cleaning it away. A liar about her sister, and how much else? The freckles beneath her eyes seemed larger and darker. Fascinated, Aoki stared at her: no makeup, no time. He swallowed down his sudden emotion. "*Surely* the road'll be re-opened today?"

"My men say it may take until tonight. The phone and electricity could be back on at any time. It depends how high up the mountain the breaks are." Her voice was faint.

Aoki meshed his hands and squeezed hard on the fingers. It seemed ages since the snow had stopped. Last night he'd been in this room, and what he'd found out was waiting to be dealt with. He gazed at the desk, but the Fatman's visit here in the spring was the main item on his agenda. He turned to her. "Could I see your guest register for last spring, the Tamaki party?" She gave him a quick look and fetched it from a cupboard under the counter outside. Of course! She laid it on her desk and riffled pages, then abruptly presented it to the detective, her slim, pale hands moving efficiently; moving in him.

As if a trigger had been pulled, Superintendent Watanabe's name shot up from the page; the characters seemed to pulsate before Aoki's eyes. *Ahh.* Aoki looked up slowly, into her intense stare. The traffic of evil flowing in through her devil's gate must be beyond her most catastrophic fears. When would she speak what was on her mind? Not yet: probably not ever, to him. And Saito, doubtless, was still tucked up under his quilt, while the ryokan was drenched in blood and horror—and unanswered questions.

In the hall, the housemen had forced the door open, the shutters back, and were beginning to dig out. They were going at it with a will, glad to be done with carrying a headless corpse around and smelling the faint but intrusive odor of the other body. *Yeah,* Aoki thought. He watched for a moment, wincing at the incoming blasts of icy air, then lit a cigarette to steady his nerves and warm up his insides.

His boss's calculating looks and silences were now landmarks in their recent relations. A member of the Fatman's inner circle—a classmate! The knowledge was like a rock in Aoki's gut. *His* health and welfare! The Fatman's protection from investigation, prosecution, and then the perceived danger of revenge from an unstable and vengeful Aoki was what it had been about. Aoki shook his head, still not quite believing it. Most men with classmates who'd become famous made a big thing of their connection to that fame, but Watanabe was working down deeper. And the Fatman's Club was like a secret society, with members' identities sacrosanct. After the night Aoki saw him in the Ginza wearing the badge, he must've worried whether his junior officer had made a connection, or in due course would make it. It must've been festering away . . .

Why had he gone bad? The Fatman must have sucked him in with the classmate stuff, and money—and his permanently stalled promotion. Not hard to get the picture. Now Hideo Aoki was set up for the chop.

Aoki stubbed out the cigarette. He was believing it all. During his interview with Kazu Hatano, Ito had sat down on the bench that Shoba had briefly made his own. The banker had some talking to do. Aoki turned, but the bench was vacant.

"He has returned to his room, sir," a maid said.

Aoki hurried to Ito's room. What was the fool thinking of? He smelled the odor of murder in the corridor. Not many would have identified it, but he had his long experience. He glanced down: Blood was smeared on the sleeve of his kimono. He sighed with relief when Ito's voice bade him enter. The bank chairman stood at a radio, its aerial up, moving the tuner, receiving static. He glanced at Aoki, switched off the set, and turned to face the detective. Aoki thought, *He's doubtless picked up a lot more than I've heard.*

"What have you found?" The banker's face was haggard and his voice cracked.

Aoki studied him. The hands were shaking, and the eyes, above their dark pouches, were moist. Fear resonated in the room; the previous anger and contempt had been wiped away, and why wouldn't they be? The two guys closest to him here, slaughtered like animals. Aoki felt the same fear.

"I'm unable to tell you anything." Aoki paused, considering how to use the fear. "I'm working under bad conditions, no backup, no resources, no weapon, no *official* position. The police should be here tonight—latest, by morning. In the meantime you're in great danger. If I hadn't arrived at the moment I did—" He shrugged. "The best I can do is to try to keep you alive." He rubbed his mole with a thumb; he didn't intend to tell this man of his own danger. "If I knew why you're here, why Mr. Yamazaki was here, maybe that'd help."

The bank chairman gazed across the room at a point on the wall, his waxlike features recast into new fissures by his desperate concentration. Tea had been brought but remained untasted. The reddened eyes turned to the policeman, and he spoke in a harsh whisper. *"The yakuza."* Aoki waited. "Yamazaki and I came to the ryokan to mark the seventh anniversary of my wife's disappearance, to say prayers at her shrine, to discuss her case. It's become more troubling to me as each year passes. Yamazaki had no religion, but he came to accommodate me, and for another reason—we wished to discuss the bank's situation. To review action we proposed to take—"

Aoki's eyes jumped wide open. The banker had grabbed at his fleshy throat with both hands, was choking. Aoki leaped forward, but the spasm passed as quickly as it had come. The detective splashed tea into a cup and put it to the chairman's mouth. Ito drank it and broke into coughing.

Aoki stepped back, watched and waited. Ito swallowed hard and shook his head. His eyes were streaming; he wiped them and refocused on Aoki. "No doubt . . . you've heard the radio broadcasts. The bank's problems lie in various directions, but the catalyst of the present disaster is loans to certain corporations under yakuza control, some of which were introduced by Governor Yukio Tamaki. A name very familiar to you." He gasped in more air. "We've stopped all new lending to these companies. I personally canceled the loan for a project at Yokohama. I received threats. I'd decided to reveal to the media the full extent of the bank's yakuza connection—after a board meeting next week, regardless of how our directors voted." He'd become calmer. He stood now like a witness giving evidence, his small red hands laced tightly over his belly.

Buddha at bay, Aoki thought. His lips twisted sardonically, recalling the first interview with the banker, when the fellow had been sitting on all of this.

Anger flared on the banker's face. "My intentions were leaked, and Tamaki stepped in and sidelined me and the board." Bitterly he shook his head, then glared into the alcove. "Did he act to protect the bank's stakeholders, to protect the banking system? Forget it! *To protect himself and the yakuza loans.* He will find a way to patch up the bank, to keep those loans current, and even lend more!" He barked a sarcastic laugh. "The yakuza carry out their threats. Mr. Yamazaki received one, after a speech he made. *They are here.*"

Aoki's eyes narrowed. It was just the way he read it. "Who do you suspect?"

Ito spread his hands. "They're among the staff here."

"What about Saito?"

Ito's eyebrows lifted. Obviously, that hadn't occurred to him. "The Go-player?" he murmured. "A rich fellow, and that age? No."

Aoki was silent. Ito had only been planning to come clean because the bank had reached the end of the road, to fall on his sword, in an honorable way, as these men considered it. The game was over, the bank fucked; even Yamazaki's protection hadn't been effective any longer. He stepped forward. "Who were you dealing with on that Yokohama transaction? *Names.*"

"The executives are the front men. We never met the yakuza daimyo."

Aoki nodded. That would've suited both sides. "I heard you arguing with Mr. Yamazaki in his room. What was that about?"

The moist red eyes flicked at him with understanding. "I was going to offer a deal to Tamaki to keep his name out of my revelations— if he held his committee off the bank and gave us time to negotiate a merger. At least the bank might have survived. My own survival wouldn't have been possible." He stared at the floor. "Yamazaki didn't agree. Everything must be revealed, he said. If I didn't do it, he would."

Aoki grimaced, showing his disbelief at the devious MOF man's disregard of the consequences.

Ito grunted impatiently. "I told you he was afraid of nothing, and that was the truth. He knew he was finished—whatever was done. He planned to retire to Toyama prefecture, where he had a house, and he was confident the MOF would let him go." He paused. "That is the way it works. They don't want their dirty laundry aired any more than can be helped, and he knew plenty of other things." His tone had become obdurate and guarded.

Aoki kept his eyes level. Yamazaki—not afraid, but not that smart, either. These men had gotten in way over their heads.

"The yakuza," Ito spat out again.

"Why was Mr. Yamazaki mutilated?"

Ito closed his eyes and shook his head, as though unable to speak of this.

"Okay. I'll take you to the anteroom, and you must stay there. If you need to leave it, I'll accompany you. I'm counting on the police being here soon." The local cops didn't know what a mission they had ahead! "If they don't arrive by this evening, I'll keep watch outside your door tonight."

Ito looked down at the glowing charcoal in the kotatsu. "I am going to be brought down, but I'll take Tamaki with me." The overbearing voice was back. Aoki stared at the banker, stepped out of the room, and shut the door. He looked at the swath of blood on the wall. It resembled a giant brushstroke of calligraphy. What was the story on Yamazaki's mutilation? Why had one of his inner organs been removed and taken, when the other bits had been left on display? To throw dust in the eyes of the investigators? And was something similar intended for Ito? Himself?

Aoki turned colder, in body and spirit. Hell, he wished he had the pistol locked away in Watanabe's drawer in Tokyo. That made him think of something else. Going through his father's effects, he'd been startled to find a 1940s army revolver, .45 caliber. Examining it with professional interest, he doubted it'd ever been fired. His father had served in a clerical position in the army during the war, but for the gentle old man to have kept this relic? The old man's commission as a lieutenant and his discharge papers were in an envelope. He'd rewrapped the revolver in its protective covering and returned it to its place . . .

He nodded solemnly to himself. Ex-governor Tamaki and Superintendent Watanabe had now settled in deep runnels in his mind. They each had an appointment with him that they didn't know about.

"If I can make it through tonight," Aoki murmured.

Chapter Nineteen

AT 10:15 A.M. INSPECTOR AOKI escorted Chairman Ito, who was carrying a folder, to the anteroom. The fire was crackling away, but Ito chose to sit near the frost-rimed windows. Saito wasn't there, but the Go board remained in place. Aoki stared at it. The black stones had been removed and put into a deep bowl beside the one that contained the vanquished white ones. Aoki glanced at the two maids who were mopping the floorboards. After making their bows, they kept their eyes down, keeping the bloody horror at bay, he knew.

He turned and hurried back to the front hall. The housemen were still digging in the trench, their faces glowing red. He entered the office.

Kazu Hatano was there, having put paperwork aside, gazing into her own small fire. Aoki cleared his throat. "Is Mr. Saito in his room?"

She rose to her feet. "Yes, he doesn't wish to be disturbed. He's in meditation."

Aoki's eyes hardened. Meditation! Were old Zen mottoes, the historic Go match, and last night's events figuring? Hatano should be in the kitchen slicing up stuff for lunch. "Very well." He gazed at this beautiful woman, this enigma; she looked back with steady but troubled eyes.

She knew. More from a kind of current between them than from anything he read in her eyes, in the midst of this death and terror, she knew of his feelings. Silently he let out a breath, bowed, and left.

In the hall he pulled up and ran his hand through his spiky hair, getting himself together. He lit a cigarette. The maids would be working in the anteroom for a while, company for Ito. He turned and headed down the staircase. Outside the Azalea Room, which he now thought of as the morgue, tapers smoked in a tin of sand and incense suffused the air. He sniffed with distaste: a scent to conceal the smell of death. He took out his flashlight and slid open the door. The two bodies lay side by side. The laundry bag, in the shape of a soccer ball, had been correctly positioned against Shoba's shrouded corpse. A coverlet had been drawn over Yamazaki. Aoki lifted it. The face had shrunk, and the complexion had turned sallow; all traces of the MOF man's strong personality had vanished.

Aoki directed the flashlight at the incision on the abdomen. Yeah, the liver. Organs were routinely taken from executed prisoners in China for use in transplants, but that wasn't relevant here. The forensic guys were going to be doing some head-scratching with this one.

He didn't know why he'd come here again; perhaps, subconciously, he was fearful that the bodies would go up in smoke. Face expressionless, he went upstairs.

When Aoki returned to the anteroom, the banker had moved to the window and was peering above a snowbank at snow-drowned trees—maybe estimating how many more hours he'd be shielded from the world, or from death. Aoki studied the tense figure; hands behind his back, one within the other, Ito seemed to be drawing the freezing landscape into himself. He could have brought his radio, but he hadn't. The news was now a second-string preoccupation—or the radio's batteries had run down. The way he told it, he'd turned his back on the yakuza, but, for sure, this man knew that once you moved into their sphere no escape was possible; if you sought to draw a line, it'd be with your own blood.

Aoki went to the fire and warmed his hands. How far away was that snowplow, the linemen? He'd been looking for a weapon, and the samurai sword had been his first thought. If the outside world hadn't broken through by evening, he'd slip the blade out of its scabbard. The cover of darkness was needed to kill and get clear; they must be gambling that there'd be tonight to finish the job—if logic had any place in this madness.

Aoki's lighter flared, and he stuck a fresh cigarette between his lips. Saito or Hatano? But Saito *was* in his fifties, and Hatano was in residence when Ito and Yamazaki had arrived for their impromptu getaway; he couldn't have been put in place by the yakuza. Was it down to a random factor? Something that was way out of sight, that his thinking hadn't discovered—something like Kazu Hatano's devil's gate that couldn't be blocked by snow? Aoki's stomach had begun to ache. Forget that! Saito was in it up to his balls. He was playing the eccentric, Go-playing amateur criminologist to a *T*, reveling in his mysterious status, his black humor. But who'd actually done the knife work in each case? His earlier thoughts about an assassin being hidden here were as relevant as before. Grimly, his brow creased, Aoki tasted the tobacco, thinking, *A yakuza under Saito's instructions.*

He glanced across at the still rigid Ito. Whatever Kazu Hatano and her sister were up to was connected to the missing woman,

their mother—that was the way he read it. He couldn't see her figuring in the violence of her stepfather's situation or whatever her
half-mad father's agenda was.

After lunch, Kazu Hatano had nothing new to report. Her men had
dug out thirty feet from the main door, but it was a trench to
nowhere. The road remained embedded in an estimated ten or
twelve feet of snow. The detective and the banker had eaten lunch
at their separate tables. For a moment, Aoki had wondered whether
they should be putting this food in their mouths. Chef Hatano's disturbed face came up on his mental screen. According to him, loan
sharks and bankruptcy had pushed him over the edge, but Aoki's
vibes told him it was only part of the story.

Grim-faced, Aoki decided that doctored food wouldn't be
the way of it, and managed half a bowl of rice and drank a small
bottle of Sapporo Black Label beer; no Heineken in these mountains. He went to work with a toothpick, his eyes locked on the
banker.

At 4:00 P.M. the meager daylight was finished, and the maids hurried about filling the oil lamps, while shadows slippery from the
shine of lamplight reclaimed the rooms, alcoves, corridors, and
stairways. Ito had turned to the folder and become absorbed in the
papers it held. Saito hadn't appeared, and Aoki sent one of the maids
to find out if he was still in his room. He was sleeping, she said.
Sleep!

Ito got up, glanced at the detective, and went out carrying the
folder. Aoki followed. The small, dumpy man moved smoothly

down the corridor to the main hall and knocked on the office door. Aoki heard Kazu Hatano's voice respond, and Ito entered.

Aoki stood by the brazier, gazing at the closed door. What kind of conversation could those two have? This looked different from the banker's previous visits to complain about the phone. Noiselessly, Aoki crossed the hall and stood by the door, but he could hear only the faintest murmur of voices. They must be conversing almost in whispers. The ex-stepfather to the ex-stepdaughter, though was "ex" the fact? He went back to the brazier and gazed at the red charcoal, seeing her face in the glowing heart of the fire.

Ito took a bath at 5:30 P.M. while Aoki sat on a stool in the bathhouse and watched, wondering what the meeting had been about. The banker's face was closed with thought and resolute. The fear evident this morning appeared to have evaporated. Was the man willing himself to come through tonight, focused on getting back and settling his score with Tamaki? He'd arranged to dine at seven, seemed determined to keep up his routine. Aoki flexed against the stiffness in his shoulders. Did this man have a spare thought for the unfortunate Shoba? Aoki brooded on the wallowing figure in the stone bath. He hadn't once sighted Saito in the bathhouse; obviously he took his meals in his room, and his baths at eccentric hours. Apart from his appearances in the anteroom at the Go table, he'd been a virtual recluse at the ryokan.

What had evaporated in Aoki's case was his appetite. While two maids fussed around the solitary Ito in the dining room, Aoki went back to the office. The housemen had disappeared, and the doors and snow shutters were closed.

He knew that wanting to be close to this woman had drawn him

195

back here. He fancied that she'd been staring at the old-fashioned black phone. The office door was open, and he stood in it. She was seated at her desk wearing a kimono new to him: dark green, with a gold and amber pattern. It seemed to give off a mellow light. Her hair was immaculate and her face made up again; the freckles had done their vanishing trick. Drinking this in, he had a strong feeling that she'd steeled herself against future developments.

Aoki cleared his throat. "Please instruct the staff to retire immediately after dinner. No one should be out of his room after 9:00 P.M."

She nodded.

"As soon as he retires, I'm going to guard Mr. Ito's room. When you leave the office, please ensure his phone has an outside line switched through."

She gave him a quick look. "I'll have a brazier placed in the corridor." Her voice was low and husky. She pressed a bell, and when a maid appeared, she gave that instruction and one for a thermos of tea to be prepared.

"Very well," Aoki said. They exchanged a long look, and he turned to go. The lady at the sanatorium would have to wait. He had life and death on his plate, and three other things to check on before Ito was ready to leave the dining room.

Minutes later he'd reached the northeast corner and was outside the Chrysanthemum Room. Behind the paper wall, Saito's radio was playing music, and the man from Osaka coughed.

Aoki moved on, into the ryokan's subterranean region, and stood in the kitchen doorway, amid cooking smells and sizzling sounds. Four people were at work in the smoky room, preparing the last dishes of Ito's dinner. Hatano leaned arrogantly against a bench, and they stared at each other. Aoki left. He looked at his watch: 7:05 P.M.

At his next stop, the sword was no longer on the wall. Aoki stared at the empty scabbard and swore softly. It hadn't been used last night, so why tonight? Or had the killer anticipated his intention and moved to place the weapon beyond the reach of Hideo Aoki? An overpowering compulsion to check Saito's room came down on him again. If he burst in, would he find the Osaka man testing the edge of the samurai weapon?

Swiftly he descended the staircase, sliding his hand down the bannister. Each flight was lit with a single oil lamp, but many corridors were unlit. He flicked on his flashlight and lit his way into the one that led to the Chrysanthemum Room and hurried toward it. The flower seemed to rush out of the darkness at the light beam. The music was still playing. Without ceremony, he slid back the door.

The lighted room was empty; the bed wasn't made up on the tatami mat. Aoki let his breath out. Along the corridor, in the dark, a floorboard creaked. He swung the flashlight in that direction and gasped as it hit a white face. Saito! The man from Osaka was standing in an alcove staring toward him, must've been following him. Did he have super night vision? The thought scudded across Aoki's mind.

"What are you doing?" the policeman said roughly.

The low, harsh voice came. "What am I doing? Going to my room."

"From where?"

"From where I've been—the bath—and from communing with the restless spirits in these corridors. Spirits of those who have died violently and who will cause trouble unless appeased. Have you come upon the shrine in your own wanderings, Inspector?" Aoki held his flashlight on the long face, the glossy hair. Saito had raised a hand to shield his eyes. Spirits! The detective's jaw tightened.

"Please go to your room and remain there. Everyone is to keep to his room till morning."

Without another word, Saito brushed past and entered the Chrysanthemum Room. Aoki smelled the scent of sake on his kimono, the warmth of the big man's body after the bath.

The detective returned to the hall, and thence to the anteroom. It would be fruitless to ask anyone about the sword. He thought of going to the kitchen and seeing what he could pick up in the way of a weapon. Forget it! He had his black belt. Yet probably the deceased Shoba had had one, too. He stood in front of the fire waiting for the banker to leave the dining room.

At 8:45 P.M., when Aoki saw Ito back to his room, a brazier, its charcoal banked up and radiating heat, had been placed in the corridor near the black-lacquered hardbacked chair upon which Shoba had been seated. By the chair leg was a thermos flask. The only light was from an oil lamp positioned on a nearby chest.

"I will be here," Aoki said. "The phone will ring when the line is restored. It could be anytime now. As soon as it is, I'll speak to the police. I suggest you don't undress."

Ito was breathing evenly. He stood immobile in the dusk, his face mounds and shadows, the eyes dark holes. He'd wrapped a thick woolen scarf of indeterminate color around his neck. He nodded brusquely and entered the Lily Room. Aoki stared after him. No fear in those eyes now; his manner had transformed into obduracy and determination. Did he know something new? Aoki lit a cigarette and paced back and forth. The tobacco suffused his throat, and he coughed briefly. He heard someone passing on the stairs, probably a maid on a last task.

Shortly before 9:00 P.M. deep silence claimed the ryokan. His instructions seemed to have been put into effect. He swung his arms, loosened his shoulders. He'd put on the lightest of the padded kimonos to give himself more freedom of movement, and karate drills were running in his head. He remembered the words of his first instructor: "If an assailant with a bladed weapon comes at you, turn and run like hell; if you can't run, here are things you can do." He'd become professionally reliant on his pistol. Too reliant.

Four paces along the corridor, the great splash of blood across the door and wall had already turned a brownish color, and above it the white lily seemed to float in space. Aoki had that impression; he was no longer surprised at such thinking. Tomorrow, the ryokan would be back in the world, as far as it ever was, and tonight would be history. He hoped. He stopped his pacing. The sound of Ito's gentle snoring was coming through the fragile fusuma door. He shook his head in wonder.

Below freezing—it must be. Aoki's face stung, and his fingers had a chilblain tingle. The brazier was fighting a losing battle. He stood as close as possible to it. No way he'd sit down on that chair. It was near midnight. He jerked his head to one side, listening hard, always fucking listening . . . He fancied that the silence in the corridor had assumed a different quality. It was shrilling in his ears with the insistent intensity of cicadas on a summer night. Summer! A dream of paradise. Though this place was never *completely* silent.

He was scared and angry. Eyes straining, heart beating faster, he stared right, then left, into the shadows beyond the light from the lamp, but no danger declared itself.

At one o'clock, he took a mouthful of tea from the thermos. Its medicinal taste still in his mouth, he seemed to be entering a neutral space. The charcoal shifted, releasing an extra gust of warmth. Abruptly he sat down on the chair, sending the thermos cap rolling on the boards.

As furtive as a cat hunting in woodland, an insane spirit was feeling its way along the doors. Aoki could sense it, not hear it. His head, which had fallen down, snapped up and swiveled, straining to pick up movement, but he was confused. He jumped to his feet, his heart pounding afresh, loosening his arms. The corridor seemed to be swirling with fog. He blinked rapidly, trying to displace the fog in his head. That fucking tea!

Like a thrown knife a scream came out of the darkness. *The stairway.* His body had locked rigid. Immediately the scream's echo was fading away. A new shock: A female voice, pleading, desperate, came undulating through the corridors—but no words to understand. He was running in that direction before he knew it, slippers slapping down on the boards, but the voice was receding faster. Breathing hard, he pulled up on the landing, shaking his head again to clear it. The sound was still going away from him. *Being dragged away now.* Upstairs or down? Not another sound in the labyrinth. No responding cries of alarm and inquiry. Was he the only one who'd heard? *Impossible.* The sound had ceased, and the utter silence seemed a crazy sequel.

He realized what he'd done—been lured into doing. If he'd taken more than one mouthful of that tea . . . He wheeled and raced back to the Lily Room, flashlight jittering ahead, controlling his breathing, his effort. Old lessons kicked in: Never exhaust your-self in a pursuit; remain fit to fight. No lily in the flashlight beam. With the shock of a worst fear realized, Aoki saw that Ito's door had been slid wide open.

Chapter Twenty

THE QUILT HAD BEEN FLUNG back. The air in the Lily Room was disturbed, as if ripples from a stone thrown into a pond were still radiating. Aoki's throat was gripped by a steel band, but his feet moved fast and quiet over the boards.

Disturbed by the outcry, had the banker found Aoki missing and gone in search of the detective, or panicked and sought to hide himself? If he had a destination, it might be the anteroom. Aoki's heart was pounding in his chest.

The inspector lit his way along the corridors. All the oil lamps that he passed were out. He was sweating. The temperature had risen. More than drafts were wafting past him, he imagined. He grimaced in the darkness: That tea had come out of Hatano's kitchen.

In the entrance hall, eyes straining, he peered at the front doors. Bolted. Above his head the roof timbers creaked under the snow's weight as, being as quiet as he could, he hurried toward the anteroom. His flashlight flickered over a scroll of lake and mountains and shot into the anteroom, searching the corners, wavering over the seating groups. Nothing. The fire was out. Through the semimisted window he made out the stubs of the icicles and the snow glowing eerily. He listened and heard only the frozen mountains emitting the tortured roar that had become permanent inside his head.

In the corner of his eye—a slight movement. His hand and the flashlight beam whipped to the far edge of the big window. Something swinging there, a blurred shape. "Oh, shit!" He moved to the window, rubbed away the mist with his hand, and shone the light through the glass. The body twisted on a rope and turned with tantalizing slowness until the light played on the features; tiny yellow points burned in the open eyes.

Aoki's heart gave a gigantic thump. He was back in his small kitchen at Kamakura, another body suspended before his horrified eyes, his swooning mind. Microseconds ago he'd sucked in breath. He was biting his lower lip. He flicked the flashlight beam down, looking for blood, but the padded kimono appeared inviolate, as immaculate as when the banker had retired.

The only blood was wet on Aoki's cracked lips. He shifted the light again. The hands were loose at the small corpse's sides, the fingers now as fragile-looking as the icicles. On the floorboards near Aoki's feet were blobs of melting snow, and the door beside the window was ajar. He pointed his light downward through the window glass: footprints—but smudged in the fast-melting snow.

He swung around and rechecked the room, his nerves brittle as fuse wire. Why not the knife or cleaver again? Why all this trouble? Why not a bullet? Had the yakuza gone mad? This wasn't their way, more like the working out of a Kabuki plot. The thoughts tumbled in his mind, but this time no acrobat somersaulted and landed neatly on his feet.

Fuck! The flashlight made him a target. He flicked it off. The murdering bastards might still be nearby. Had to be two to string him up like that. Sensing something, cautiously he moved out into the room.

Ten paces away a shape rose up from the deep dark at the dining-room door and, as Aoki gasped in shock, came at him fast and fluid, steel glinting. Aoki sprang into a fighting stance—not thinking, doing. Dropping the flashlight, he vaulted sideways over a chest. The onrushing silhouette filled his vision, and a swishing sound went past his head simultaneous with a ferocious grunt. Knees bent to absorb the shock: Aoki had landed beside the table with the Go board. Doing *and* thinking now, his hand found the bowl of stones, plunged in, and came out with a handful as hard as steel ball bearings. The figure had veered to the center of the room, something above it—a sword!—held high and two-handed, its point describing small circles. For one wild instant, his eyes searing their sockets, Aoki thought of a force from the devil's gate, but the grunt had been as human as the sweat running off him. *"Come on, you bastard,"* he hissed across the space.

With all his strength Aoki hurled the handful of stones, and a pandemonium of clashes on steel, ricochets, and ripping of paper followed. The figure had paused but was coming again, relentless. Aoki seized another handful and, slamming his shoulders against the mantelpiece, balanced himself for a second throw. The figure checked, then whipped the sword down for a lunge just as the second volley went across the space between them. The shadow shrieked, reeled back, and in a flash seemed to be dematerializing before Aoki's eyes as the stones blasted through paper panels. Chest heaving, sweat streaming from his armpits, eyes aching, Aoki watched his front. *In the corridor to the main hall, the sound of fast-retreating steps.* He lurched forward and fell to his knees, fumbling for the flashlight, and his hand closed on razor-sharp steel. He cried out as it sliced into his fingers and palm.

A handkerchief wadded in his left hand, which also held the flashlight, the sword projected in his right, he moved along the corridor, fast, swollen with anger and bloodlust. He'd injured the bastard! In the main hall, he pulled up and listened. *Downstairs*—going deep into the ryokan. The wadded handkerchief was sodden, and blood pattered on the floor. He went down the stairs two at a time. At the bottom, he stopped again to listen: faint sounds from the heart of the building—from the direction of the courtyard and the shrine. He rushed on, the flashlight beam jumping along the corridors.

Ahead! In the darkness, the sound of slippered feet skimming over boards. He pressed forward, eyes and ears in overdrive. In the gallery beside the courtyard, he flicked the beam high, nearly caught something, sensed it plunge into space beyond the flashlight's range. He was breathing hard, still dripping blood; the shrine was to his right. Silence. Where to now? Should he descend to the next level, where Saito's room was? Or head for Hatano's?

The whining, twittering sound of startled birds.

Along the connecting passage, Aoki ran toward the sound. The floor was squealing now as though in agony. He reached the opposite corner and shot the flashlight down this gallery. The floor fell abruptly silent as the door at the end slid shut, then was screaming again as Aoki raced over it. Clumsy with the makeshift bandage, he grabbed the door handle, the sword at the ready, and wrenched it open.

A woman in kimono and obi stood transfixed by the light beam, her face extraordinarily white, the full dark hair piled high, an arm moving, and with it a small rubylike light. Then she was slipping to her left. "*Wait!*" Aoki hissed out of his shock. In a reflex, the flashlight jumped in his hand and fell. It crashed on the floor, and its light went out.

Aoki grabbed for the rolling tube, hearing to his right the soft fleeing movement. He had the flashlight, flicked the switch. Not working. He cursed, dropped it, and sprang through the doorway and went right, his left hand outstretched. His vision was changing; he could dimly make out things—in the angle of two timbers, a large triangular panel. He dropped the sword and pressed against it with both hands, and it swung inward. His fingers traced around the aperture. Crouching down, he squeezed through it, hastily drawing the sword after him.

Still crouching, his shoulders free, he felt himself in a large space. Staring hard, he straightened up. The thundering blow struck him on the top of the head. The discs of his spine were disconnected, rattling. Lights flashed before his eyes, became falling white stars. Then he fell and never felt the concussion, only the floorboards suddenly against his face, smooth as glass and icy. In his jarred brain, jittering disco lights showed white-stockinged feet, a small white hand reaching down, slender wrists floating like lilies in a breeze. Then it was black.

Chapter Twenty-One

CONSCIOUSNESS CAME BACK TO INSPECTOR Aoki in small stutters of
sensation. He was slumped in a chair. Behind his forehead there
was an immense throbbing. He gritted his teeth and fought to open
his eyelids, which were squeezed shut against cold daylight. He
turned his head and blurrily identified the main hall, then the kimonoed maids who were fluttering around him. In the back of his
head a phone was ringing; outside, crows were cawing urgently—or
were they inside his head, too? He blinked at his blood-smeared
left hand, then shut his eyes again.

A cold compress smacked onto his forehead. He realized Kazu
Hatano's face was close to his own. A glass was held to his lips, and
warm liquor plunged down in him. Pills were put into his mouth;
he swallowed them, and like a trolley car's displaced pole being set
back on the line, Aoki became reconnected to the world.

"Mr. Ito?" he croaked.

"Yes," she said, holding the compress in place.

"Where's Saito?"

"He has gone."

"Your father?"

❖

"Gone."

He edged his torso more erect on the chair, and dizziness spun in him. He gripped his head with both hands. How much could he trust these answers? He swallowed. "Gone! The phone?"

"It was reconnected at 5:30 A.M. We couldn't find you."

"I must make a call. Who found me?"

"A room maid coming on duty."

"Where?"

"Where you fell, in a room on the lower level."

"A secret room," Aoki growled. The vertebrae at the base of his neck were burning, and his neck muscles were locked rigid. He touched his scalp—stinging pain. His fingers traced a long cut, finding what must be coagulated blood. What had he been hit with?

Watching him, she shook her head sadly. He wanted to see that secret place in the light, but first he must make the long-delayed phone call. The women helped him to his feet and supported him into the office. It was 8:15 A.M. It took several minutes to track down the prefecture's chief of police. As he waited, one hand pressed to the compress, he thought, *The red scars on those white wrists—did I dream that?* Fragments of last night were coming back, though what part of it had actually happened, what had been hallucination? He remembered the tea and shuddered. Lucky for him he'd only taken one mouthful.

The electric lights flickered and came on; someone cried out and applauded. *Unbelievable,* Aoki thought.

The police would arrive within the hour. The local chief's voice had been deep and quivering, more so when he heard the identities of the deceased. From what they had been told by the taxi company, the police believed the two prominent men were at the ryokan, and they had been going to check it out as soon as the road was plowed. But dead! Aoki gave the chief Saito's and Hatano's descriptions.

Unsupported, Aoki went out to the hall. The orgiastic activity in his head was diminishing to briefer seizures. Beyond the glass doors, two housemen were at work widening the trench. The phone was ringing again. He winced. He'd been away from the streets too long. This smack on the head was a real drama—he'd heard the *crack* of his spinal column.

He was leaning on the counter when Kazu Hatano returned from whatever task she'd hurried away to attend to. He said, "How and when did Saito and your father leave?"

"Mr. Saito phoned for a taxi at about five fifty. It came within twenty minutes. Apparently the road was clear at about four thirty."

"They departed before you found Ito's body—and me?"

She hesitated. "Yes."

Aoki blinked, still clearing his vision. She looked tired and very frail, but with an effort he put his personal feelings aside. "How did he pay his bill?"

"With banknotes."

How else. "Call the taxi company and have the same driver come back, please."

Holding the compress in place, he walked slowly to the anteroom and stared out the window at Ito's corpse. A breeze lifted the banker's hair, giving an illusion of life. His white stockings were less than eighteen inches above the snow. Aoki opened the small door and stood close to the suspended body. The kimono was soaked with moisture from the dripping eaves. How had he been restrained? The hands weren't tied. Aoki deliberated on the puzzle. Of course, there'd been two of them. Then he saw the small stool upset in the snow and recognized what it was meant to mean.

209

Behind him a maid, eyes averted, hurried through the room with a swish-swishing of fabric.

Kazu Hatano came in. Her left hand was spread against her throat, but she did not avert her eyes. Steadfastly she stared at the body. Aoki took this in. Soon she was going to be put in the position of answering hard questions from the CIB. He noticed something, and a moment later held the damp folded sheet of paper that had been tucked into the corpse's sash.

Well then, let's go—
to the place where we tumble down
looking at snow!

Aoki looked up into her curious gaze. Just the kind of suicide note one would expect from a murderer who had regrets, or who knew the game was up—or who was tired of life and its problems. Putting it in his pocket, he shook his head, and grimaced from the stab of pain. *Don't* move your head.

The mind behind the note, and so much else that had happened, was as weird as you could encounter. No one would believe suicide. A joker was in action, and the plot of a Kabuki play continued to unfold. His father might have identified one that matched it.

Kazu Hatano's face was flushed now. Aoki's eyes kept going back to her. A glow of triumph? The women of this family were something, and especially this one. She continued to gaze unflinchingly at Ito's face, as though memorizing a life, until a maid came in.

"Excuse me," the proprietor said with a bow.

Aoki slowly crossed the room and sat where he'd faced Saito over that ill-starred Go match. Ill-starred in 1938 and during the past days. The bastard had been playing a chancy game, but how

210

he'd reveled in it, with his graphic account of the defeat of the old Master of Go, his versions of Madam Ito's disappearance and of Ito's and Yamazaki's bank troubles, his speculations about Ito's belated rush of shame at being cuckolded, and his act of revenge. Entangling the old missing-woman case in Aoki's mind to mask his murderous intentions! Much of it from that hoard of news clippings in his room . . . Playing a parallel match against the Tokyo detective, even massacring him at chess! Before he killed him!

As his father had warned, the killer instinct had been in Saito, as fluid as his commentary on the events in play.

Again Aoki put his head in his hands. In this room volleys of Go stones had whistled through the predawn air, and one, at least, had hit a target. He looked up at the ragged holes in the paper-screened wall.

Another maid had appeared, and a man stood behind her. The taxi driver had been coming up the hill again when his base radioed. He was the one who'd brought Aoki here four days ago. "Sir," he said, "I told you it was too late in the season." He was grinning nervously.

"Never mind that," Aoki said gruffly. "I'm a police officer. Where did you take the men this morning? The big man called Saito, and the chef, Hatano."

"To the station. They caught the seven fifteen to Sapporo."

"What did they say to you?"

"They never spoke."

"Describe the big man to me."

He did. It was Saito, all right. The taxi driver licked his lips. "The chef, I know him. His eye was bandaged. The women said nothing, either."

Aoki's eyes narrowed. *"What women?"*

The driver blinked. "One older, one younger, but they were so wrapped up, their faces covered with scarves, I couldn't make out much."

Aoki swung around and walked a few paces, wheeled, and came back. What in hell was going on? His head was throbbing again, fit to burst. "They took the train, too?"

"Yes, the chef and the women together, a different carriage from the big man."

Aoki glared at him. *Two women*. Kazu Hatano had come back, and he realized that she'd heard the last exchange. He nodded sharply to the man. "You can go, but don't leave the ryokan. Other police will want to talk to you." He turned and stared at her with fresh and despairing suspicion. "Two women. Why didn't you tell me that? Who were they?"

She lowered her eyes. She didn't appear rattled, merely deeply thoughtful. Despite his anger Aoki was struck by her calm beauty. He cleared his throat, impatient with himself. *"What is going on?"* She started to speak, then stopped. He licked his damaged lips and tasted brandy. He had to break into this, tip the scales his way.

"What is your connection to the Sendai Sanatorium?"

Her eyes leaped to his. Then her hands moved slowly from her sides in a gesture of resignation. She said softly, "The women were my mother and my sister."

So! Seven years of mystery and silence, swept aside with a gesture. Their eyes were locked together. Aoki felt he might fall into hers. He swallowed and, in a quieter voice, said, "Madam Ito and your sister—the geisha."

With a jolt, Aoki knew that he had another answer. Kazu Hatano hadn't come to the Camellia Room that night. His intimacy had been with the woman who'd fled. Her twin sister.

212

She nodded emphatically, and tears flicked onto the pale skin beneath her eyes—onto the dark freckles. Dazed with pain, dizziness, and weariness, Aoki couldn't work out where he was with this woman. With an effort, he said, "This is very serious. I very much regret it, but you'll have a lot of explaining to do to the police."

Aoki recalled with special clarity his wife's voice, and her message, when he'd first followed the corridor to this space at the ryokan's heart. *Some corridors lead to places of silence that bring true rest and induce insight.*

Going down the antique stairs, he felt the closeness of his wife and father. They were at his side. *Kazu Hatano.* Would his ghost-wife talk to him about her?

The daylight in the courtyard hurt his eyes. Several large rocks now protruded through the melting snow like black tongues.

His head lowered protectively, he stood in the room that he'd entered in darkness through the hinged panel. He stared at the ancient beam that he'd driven his skull up against; there was a splash of blood and some of his hair on the blackened wood.

She'd touched a button, and a ladder-stair was lowering itself from the wooden ceiling. Its join had fitted into the planked pattern above. Motioning to him, she ascended the ladder.

Aoki gazed at the space they entered. It was large, and the roof was roughly insulated. Two beds were spread on the floor and appeared to have been hastily left. Food and oil lamps were on a table. An old-fashioned Western-style bathroom was visible through a doorway.

A wisp of hair had escaped her coiffure. She turned to Aoki, her face businesslike, the tears brushed away to the past, her lips compressed. "For the last six years she has been in the sanatorium under a new identity. Those men had driven her mad, driven her to that desperate action at Tokyo Central station. But she still had enough of her old fire to plan and do that. To fight back against their cruelty and damage them—and she did!" She gave a bitter shrug. "But not enough damage. She was proud and strong, but also weak. She hadn't resisted Yamazaki's seduction. She'd been lured into her debasement, and accepted it for so long."

Aoki concentrated on each phrase. Thus far, to him, this woman had been a mystery, self-possessed and economical with the truth, if not a liar. Now she was opening up like a flower touched by sunlight.

"Her action at Tokyo Central station was a final effort before her total collapse, which she must've felt coming. Then she fled here, and we hid her. After twelve months, we were able to arrange for the sanatorium under the false identity."

Aoki nodded. All those old news clippings, their intriguing speculations, were now mainly incorrect footnotes to the facts. The police had searched this place, but mostly they'd been looking for a body in lakes or forests. Some of the ryokan's old servants must have known, but they'd kept silent. He brooded on the room. Madam Ito and her desperate act had had to be protected, her insanity and her dishonorable life with those men covered up—for her sake and for the sake of family honor. Except they hadn't been; the police and the media had spread the story in lurid detail across the nation.

His left hand rubbed over his cheekbone and found the mole. "The blood on the clothing in the locker was her blood group?"

"Two days before that, she cut her wrist for that purpose. She

214

bandaged herself. That is what I believe. She never speaks of it. She must have nearly died."

Aoki considered that piece of her madness, the second time she'd done that. "Why was she here now?"

"We bring her home once a year, at the anniversary. She is kept in this room, but sometimes at night when all are asleep she comes out to wander around, sometimes to cry out. My sister stays with her most of the time when she's here."

The screams, the pleading, the rambling tirade that had sent him running into the labyrinth, leaving Ito alone in his room— these were stark in Aoki's mind. Madam Ito on the loose! A random factor! But for that—in his confusion after that mouthful of drugged tea, he'd probably have been slaughtered at the door of the Lily Room like Shoba.

"The nightingale floor—"

"As you see, there's another way to this room. She used the gallery last night only because she was frightened and could get here more quickly."

"Your father knew she was at the sanatorium, sometimes here?"

She hesitated. "Yes. But they never met. They hadn't exchanged a single word since they parted."

Aoki broke his gaze away and paced across the room. "Where have they gone?"

"To a new place."

"Not back to the sanatorium?"

"No."

There was a note of defiance, but also something else in the in-clination of her head, the way her hands had moved. Entreaty? He thought so. She said, "It is an old, old case, which does not require solving. It is *not* connected with the murders here. It is our family business." Her hands had become joined. He could see the white of the delicate knuckles shining like bare bone. "What will you do?" A husky whisper.

He stared at those hands. "I'll have to think about it." He couldn't be sure what he would do yet. "Not connected? What about your father? What is his connection to Mr. Saito?"

She hesitated. "I can tell you nothing about that. My father is not a man who shares any part of himself." Her lips had tightened. "He knew Saito. I could tell that, also that he was shocked the night Mr. Saito arrived, then furious—and worried."

Aoki coughed. His chest hurt. They must've known each other in Osaka, but what hold did Saito have over the chef? If he knew the details of that, much would fall into place—especially as to how the yakuza fitted in. Osaka must be the link.

"When did Saito make his reservation?"

"The morning of the day he arrived."

"Out of the blue," Aoki muttered.

The story he was being told wasn't totally complete; she was telling him what she thought he would unravel, gambling that he'd let the affair of Madam Ito continue to dwell in the realm of unsolved cases. "The Mountain Beauty Mystery," as one paper had perpetuated it. She must've made a judgment on his humanity, on his character. Irritably, he reached for a cigarette.

Now there were more important matters that had to be dealt with.

Aoki went into the trench and emerged into full daylight. He stared at the white-covered mountains as though they'd just been created this morning, at the low clouds drifting past their peaks. The army of trees stood hip-deep in snow. A snowplow was clearing the forecourt, and the taxi driver stood nearby watching the work and smoking a small cigar.

Snow! But for the storm and the terrific dumping of it on these mountains imprisoning them all, events would've unfolded differently—though, was anything predictable in the convoluted situation he'd been sent into?

Two police cars and an ambulance drove cautiously down the slippery road, using sirens. The plaintive sounds went down the valley.

While he'd been waiting in the hall, he'd noticed an acrid, burned smell coming from downstairs. He'd gone down to the kitchen. Overnight, something had been burned to ashes in the big woodstove, and the kitchen maids could not account for it.

Aoki stood talking to the two respectful and curious detectives from the prefecture, who obviously knew of his celebrity. Tersely, he gave them the facts and provided more details of Saito and Hatano's departure. One went to his car to radio headquarters; then they went inside to view the bodies and talk some more. Aoki smoked incessantly throughout this. He wished that he'd brought more chocolate; he seemed to've developed a craving for it as strong as pregnant women's for ginger. An hour later, a message came through: No one resembling Saito had been seen at Hakodate. The chef and the two women had been sighted boarding a train for the south.

A van had arrived with the forensic team, who had sent for backup. The ryokan was now bustling with their activity. Three bodies in situ. Yamazaki's corpse was provoking a lot of terse comment among them; so was Shoba's. In contrast, Ito's was relatively run-of-the-mill. Aoki had been right: Yamazaki's corpse was minus its liver. When they told him that, Aoki nodded slowly, though he still didn't understand it.

The detectives had begun to question Kazu Hatano in the office, and Aoki had to get moving. He went to his room and changed, then packed his suitcase. The cat was in the doorway. He bent down to give it a final stroking. "Good-bye, Cat," he said. "Have a good life."

Thirty minutes later he paced the hall, pale and thoughtful. He must have looked like another man in the suit, except for his bandaged wounds, for she blinked at his appearance when she excused herself and came out of the office.

When he'd changed and packed, the five bonsai in their small ceramic pots were gone from the chest in the Camellia Room, but now Mori stood behind the proprietor, the cardboard box in her arms.

She came forward. "Here you are, sir. They've been watered, and the sick one is recovered."

Aoki nodded at her. "Thank you for looking after them—and me."

Aoki took his leave of Kazu Hatano. *Maybe I'll be back.* She walked with him to the police car. She bowed low, her bluish black hair shining against the snow-covered mountains. When her eyes met his, he detected the earlier question—entreaty—still there, but he couldn't give her an answer yet. However, maybe he had decided; he'd kept silent about the famous seven-year-old case when he'd briefed the two detectives. It'd cause him trouble if that came out—and it probably would. The local cops would be asking about those women, and one of the ryokan's staff in the know might inadvertently spill the beans. He shrugged. Of course, he could have been wrong about her look; really, he had no idea what it meant. Opening up like a flower? He shook his head at his earlier naïveté.

Saito and Superintendent Watanabe—he had a rendezvous with each of those dark and flawed guys, and nothing about that would be sure or certain. But it was ex-governor Tamaki who now dominated his future. Grim-faced, gazing across the mountains, Aoki swore to himself that the Fatman was going to be brought to justice. One way or another.

Journalists had arrived and were grouped near the entrance, corralled by two uniformed officers. They'd been watching Aoki and the ryokan's proprietor. "Who are you?" a man called out to Aoki, raising a camera. Ignoring the question, Aoki turned away quickly and climbed in beside the police driver, and they started off. The reporters would soon work that out, and he'd be back again in the fucking limelight. He twisted his head to look back at her, but they'd already gone around a bend, and there was nothing to see but the frozen landscape and the cloud-crowded, sliding sky.

Chapter Twenty-Two

AOKI ARRIVED AT AKITA ON the branch-line train just before midday, and fifteen minutes later boarded the bullet train for Tokyo. A soft rain fell as the train eased out of the small city. The detective caught the eye of a red-robed monk standing by the tracks beneath an umbrella and wondered at their different worlds. Soon the train reached high speed, and the poles beside the line were flicking past in a continuous blur.

A nationwide dragnet was out for Saito, Hatano, and the two women. He could hardly believe what had happened to him overnight, and now, as if by a stealthy hand, the ryokan was being drawn back into the past. In an hour's time, would he be doubting that it'd existed? He shook his head, causing a man sitting opposite to glance at him. However, he'd agreed to send a full report to the prefecture chief within twenty-four hours, and writing it down should set it in concrete.

As he sped south, his mind made a solid and deliberate shift to the gray, glass-encased TMP building he was headed for. To Watanabe. Cold-bloodedly, the superintendent had sent him to the ryokan—into the killing zone of yakuza assigned to murder Ito and

Yamazaki—a late addition to the program! Into the weird orbit of Saito and the crazy chef.

By now, Watanabe would've heard that he'd survived; would assume that he'd made the connections and reached disastrous conclusions—if they were brought out in the open. The superintendent would be sitting in his office waiting for Aoki, and he'd have a new plan.

Aoki moistened his lips and frowned at the swift-passing landscape. Should he bypass confronting the superintendent, take it straight to the director general? He recalled the DG's demeanor the day the investigation had been shut down: pragmatic yet embarrassed. Aoki shook his head vehemently. Probably the first stop after that would be the head doctors, and back into Watanabe's web. He had to personally deal with Watanabe. He could see no way around that. But how? He wiped moisture from his brow with a handkerchief. There was still too much he didn't know about the ryokan murders, about the journalist Kimura's. He stared along the carriage. It was vital that he put down what he *did* know, before Watanabe made his next move. Then, if he could get his revelations into the right hands, fast—maybe hands outside the department . . . Meanwhile, tonight, he'd have to play it as cool with Watanabe as the bastard had played it with him; keep the superintendent undecided about how much Hideo Aoki knew.

Carefully, he twisted his neck. The pain in his head had settled down to a dull ache. His left hand was bandaged and taped, the cut on his head smeared with ointment. At the station he'd inserted a coin in a vending machine, then sighed as an icy aluminum can dropped into his hand. He sipped the beer now and glanced at the paper he'd picked up at Akita: a gateway back into the real world. He read that the government was expected to announce the bank's fate tomorrow; that today police were hopeful of contacting its missing chairman and the MOF official. Aoki grimaced. *Tomorrow* there'd be blazing headlines on their murders. Beyond that, the Fatman's face cruised his mind, like a transparent moon in a noonday sky. His eye caught another item on the front page:

Prosecutor charged with taking bribes.
A senior prosecutor in the Osaka District Public Prosecutor's Office was indicted Thursday on bribery charges. It is alleged that the official accepted bribes from gangsters for information on investigations.

Aoki glanced over it and discarded the paper.

To Inspector Aoki, the Tokyo Metropolitan Police building housing his division of the CIB now presented itself as enemy territory, deadly dangerous for street criminals and rogue cops alike. He was sweating inside his overcoat as he rode the elevator to the superintendent's floor. It stopped briefly at his old floor, and across an acre of desks and heads he saw the glassed-in cubicle that had been his. Empty. He glimpsed detectives he knew; their faces looked older. He'd been vegetating nearly four months in his suspension, his troubles, but it seemed like a lifetime, and now, each passing moment, he was feeling lonelier and more exposed.

The elevator doors sprang open again as though challenging him to step out. His heart thudded as he did. A minute later he paused outside a door, steadying himself, sinking the anger, the hate, into deep concealment. He knocked, and the familiar voice bade him enter.

Aoki stepped into the room. Watanabe shot up behind his desk. "My *dear* colleague, welcome back. What a recuperation you've been having!" He came around the desk, his eyes staring into Aoki's. "Chairman Ito and Mr. Yamazaki—both dead! And you in the middle of it all!" He shook his head in wonder and smiled—a fleeting grimace. He took in Aoki's wounded head, the cracked lips dotted with dried blood, the bandaged left hand. "Well, well."

He must know I've worked it out, Aoki thought, eyeing the yellow silk tie like familiar scenery. *But maybe there's still a doubt in his mind that I've connected him to the Fatman. For sure, he'll be thinking: With the others dead, how am I still alive?* The superintendent had always been terse and aloof, even as he dispatched Aoki for the health cure; now he was absolutely comradely. Aoki nodded. "Yes, and the killer's still on the loose."

"Take your overcoat coat off and tell me all about it. The prefecture hasn't sent us much yet. What a case! By the way, congratulations. Your suspension's been lifted. You're back on duty, Inspector."

Aoki looked into the calculating eyes. The counterfeit concern for his health and future had fallen into the abyss, replaced by this false bonhomie. Eyes wide open, but otherwise expressionless, Aoki gazed at his boss. Here was the man who'd sent him to the ryokan like a lamb to the slaughter; to protect the Fatman. Luckily, he'd been out of sight, unconscious on the floor of that secret room, when Saito and Hatano had had to get out in a hurry to beat the local cops.

Face-to-face, instinctively he confirmed that the superintendent knew he'd been sprung. It was as certain as the next rice crop. The guy had no doubts. The mountain-ryokan plan to eliminate Aoki had failed, and Watanabe had to find another way. And it was really urgent now. The machinations that had caused Tokie's death had been at the behest of the Fatman and this bastard. Hatred burned in Aoki's heart, and fear, but he nodded and sat down like a reasonable man, a dutiful subordinate, back from the wars—in reality, a man who was buying time.

He lit a cigarette and looked across the desk at his boss as he described the three murders, sketched in Saito and Chef Hatano, and gave an abbreviated report of Ito's claims about the yakuza. He left out any mention of ex-governor Tamaki. He said nothing at all about the Madam Ito case. The lowdown on what had been his nemesis for seven years would've sent the superintendent into orbit! Even in the midst of whatever scheme he now had to dispose of Hideo Aoki.

The superintendent was sitting forward, his eyes sharp. "This Saito—have you a theory on his motive, on whether he acted for himself or for others? The yakuza?"

Aoki inspected the cigarette in his fingers and for a moment pondered his boss's disingenuousness. "Not at this stage. He's some kind of criminal, a very experienced type, very confident." He hadn't mentioned, either, the pile of news clippings he'd found in Saito's room—provided by the superintendent? Maybe not. He considered whether to say what had jumped into his mind, then did. "He's a skilled Go-player, some kind of master. It'd be surprising if he doesn't attend those big national competitions, isn't a member of one of the associations. Not under the name of Saito, of course." He paused. "Probably he's yakuza."

And probably the superintendent had no details on him, or on Hatano—their identities or anything else. That was yakuza business. Watanabe would just know that the job had been set up, and his part in it.

The superintendent hadn't moved his eyes from Aoki's. Calculating the odds, Aoki figured, reassessing where a guy with a damaged mind, who'd been in a mental institution, *could* take what he had. Whether he'd even get a hearing. Whether it was a risk that could be taken.

Aoki stubbed out his cigarette.

Watanabe was nodding slowly as if he'd decided something. He slid open a drawer. "I think the DG will want you to stay on the case. Here's your badge." He slid it across the desk. "And here's your gun." He weighed the holstered weapon in his hand, then pushed it toward Aoki.

Aoki pocketed the badge, slipped the pistol from the holster, and automatically checked its status. He removed the seven-shot magazine. It held no bullets.

The phone was in the superintendent's hand. "I'll find out when the DG can see us." He spoke and listened briefly. "Half an hour," he said, putting the phone back in the cradle as expertly as Aoki had handled the pistol.

The superintendent nodded at the weapon. "It's been too long. We've got time to go downstairs to the range. I'll check you out and sign you off." He was hissing softly through his teeth.

Immediately, Aoki knew what was going to happen.

The range was in a closed-off section of the basement. The sergeant-instructor normally put police through the periodic drills required by the regulations, something of a formality for an officer of Aoki's experience and proven marksmanship. The inspector's face had turned as hard as stone. *Nothing is normal about my life now,* he thought. *Or this occasion.*

"I'll take the opportunity to fire a bracket," the superintendent said. He gave a thin smile. "This is a new gun." He drew out a shiny bluish pistol, put on ear protectors, took up the firing stance, and gazed at the target down the range—a man's head and torso. "Six rounds each," he said. "We'll have a little bet. Ten thousand to the highest score."

The sergeant stood back watching with a dour expression, a small box of ammunition in hand.

Aoki's heart was beating faster, but he felt strong and alert, and his fingers around the butt of his own pistol were cool and nimble. *How is he going to do it? Or is it "they"?* But the sergeant had no weapon.

Rapidly the superintendent fired his bracket. They each removed the ear protectors; the air reverberated in hard waves in the concrete chamber. Two of the shots had hit outside the central zone. "Not bad, but I think my old gun's better." He turned to the sergeant. "Go and get my old one, will you? I want to try it again." He glanced down at the cleaning materials spread out on a bench. "While you're at it, I'll clean this one. Leave that box." He took the box of ammunition and carelessly shook rounds out onto the bench, sending them rolling. "Load up," he said to Aoki. "Six rounds only, mind you. This is for big money, but I know you are a very trustworthy fellow, and quite happy to lose your dough." He grimaced again.

But not my life, Aoki breathed.

When the sergeant had gone back into another room and they could hear the distant clash of unlocking, the superintendent, ignoring the cleaning materials, reloaded his magazine and reinserted it into the pistol. In Aoki's ears, the click sounded like a thunderclap.

Aoki had also carefully loaded. "Fire when you're ready," Watanabe said. *Any moment now,* Aoki thought. This was the *only* certain way out for the superintendent. He adjusted the ear protectors. His brain felt absolutely cool, his nerves steady. He adopted the stance and began to fire. *"One-two-three-four-five-six!"* the superintendent shouted. He peered down the range. "Not bad at all. Better than me."

Yes, I'm better than you, Aoki thought. He was standing in line with the target on the extreme right, five paces from his boss.

"Well, I owe you ten thousand." Watanabe raised his pistol and sighted it down the range. "This one is really not up to it, doesn't feel right in the hand." He shifted the barrel to sight quickly on a lightbulb, then to a sign on the brick wall prohibiting smoking; then with greatly increased speed he swung it to Aoki.

Aoki was dropping to his knees as Watanabe went into his last pivot, and the bullet passed a fraction above his head. At the same instant, he brought up his weapon and shot the superintendent through the heart with the seventh bullet in the magazine.

The sergeant came running back, horror flooding his face when he saw the debacle. Blood was welling up through the yellow tie. Aoki was getting up. His legs felt unreliable, and now his hands were numb. In a daze, he stared at his dying boss. *No one in my situation is totally trustworthy, and he should've known that better than most.* His daze was giving way to anger and helplessness. He'd taken a one-way road, with no turnoffs. Yet it had solved the problem he'd walked into headquarters with. Now he was in excrement of a different texture. Though it'd been self-defense, if anyone would believe him.

The DG's face was flushed as though with alcohol, and his hands were shaking. Calmly Aoki had explained what the superintendent had done in the firing range. They'd already found the bullet in the wall that had been behind Aoki's head. Detectives from the internal affairs department sat on either side of him. Of course, they'd taken away his pistol again.

The sergeant-instructor's shock had abated. Now he was dour and uneasy. He'd reported that when the last two shots had been fired, he was out of the room, but he knew the superintendent had fired first; he'd recognized his new weapon's distinct sound. Aoki had glanced at him with gratitude, regretting his earlier doubt.

"But why?" the DG said harshly. He hissed through his teeth. *"What is going on?* You'd better come clean, Inspector, and fast."

Aoki flexed his shoulders and tightened his lips, feeling as though he were about to step off a high building into thin air. "Sir, Superintendent Watanabe was in Governor Tamaki's pocket—also, I have little doubt, in the pocket of the yakuza. But maybe the last was indirect, the connection through Tamaki."

The director general fell back in his high-backed chair, incredulous. He was having trouble breathing. He twisted his head from side to side as if to get free of a tight collar. Aoki went on, respectful yet forceful: Revealing Watanabe's membership in the Fatman's Club and how he'd long concealed his classmate relationship with the politician; Tamaki's and the superintendent's fears that, despite the official abandonment of the investigation into the Fatman's corrupt activities, at some point, Aoki might take it up again—that, in his nerve-damaged state after his wife's suicide, he was unpredictable and might even come after the Fatman.

He lowered his eyes as he said the last. It was strange hearing his voice stating what was now rock-hard in his mind.

"The hell you would!" The DG's voice shook like his hands. "What evidence have you got—and why were *you* at that damned ryokan? *Why didn't I know about that?*" He was shouting, half up from his chair.

Aoki played his high card. "Because the superintendent insisted I go there. His story was that it was for my further rehabilitation. He made the reservation, got the train tickets." He brought out the piece of paper with Watanabe's handwritten travel details. The DG snatched it and scanned it. Again he sat back heavily, making his chair creak. His eyes turned thoughtful. Aoki surmised that he might be now considering the ryokan's link with the seven-year-old case of Madam Ito. Finally, he'd decided that his lips were sealed on that. He said, "Last spring Governor Tamaki and the superintendent visited the ryokan together—with the other classmate members of the Fatman's Club. There's proof of that."

The director general grimaced. He was studying Aoki's broad, balding forehead with its short, spiky hair, the nasty wound. What he was thinking was that despite his breakdown this fellow was a tough and competent officer. That had come to his notice during the Tamaki investigation. The superintendent had been playing with fire.

The senior police flanking Aoki sat stolid and silent, waiting for orders.

Aoki said, driving home a nail, "I was added to the yakuza death list. Tamaki, through his connections with them, and via the superintendent, had attached me to the gangsters' agenda for Ito and Yamazaki." He added, deadpan, "I imagine the yakuza are always happy to accommodate the ex-governor." The DG continued to gaze at him, then shook his head—whether in doubt at all or some of this, or in despair at the horrendous public relations implications, Aoki couldn't tell. He said, "When I turned up alive, Superintendent Watanabe had to do the job himself. He did try to kill me downstairs."

"Ito and Yamazaki," the DG said, twisting his neck afresh. "For those two, shit's going to come down on us from all quarters. *All quarters.* What about their killer—or killers? This Saito, this Hatano?" He already had his own ideas about Saito. A file on the man's identity had arrived on his desk within the last hour. Twelve possible names had been put before him, and this Saito under whatever name might not be among them.

Aoki hesitated. "He's a big fish in *that* pool. Obviously he's been around, but not out in the open. He might even be a daimyo who likes to keep his hand in at killing, to exact retribution." *Yes,* he thought, *that's part of the weirdness.* "The prominence of those two gentlemen might've been a magnet to him. I haven't got a line on his connection with Hatano." He shrugged. At this point, he didn't go into the weirdness—the tricky ingredients such as Zen mottoes and missing body parts, the setting and the drama of Kabuki. Maybe that would come out, maybe it wouldn't, when he wrote his report—none of it was straight in his head yet—or when the prefecture police wrote theirs, though the Hokkaido cops wouldn't find it an easy task extracting information from Kazu Hatano.

The director general's eyes clouded with doubt at the daimyo proposition. In his experience, a top-level yakuza, once he'd achieved that status, didn't step into a danger zone. He dropped his hands on the desk. Abruptly he raised them again and stared at the palms. Frowning heavily, he studied them, as though trying to read something there. They no longer shook. Aoki and the others watched him. The sweep hand on the wall clock completed a circuit and a half. The DG raised his eyes and put his hands flat on the desk.

"All right, Inspector, you're suspended from duty until our

colleagues here complete an investigation into this *accident.*" He looked hard at the two officers. "Two days, at most."

Aoki's face was expressionless. "Accident while cleaning his weapon" was probably how Watanabe would have played his demise; now, apparently, the superintendent was to be slotted into the victim role.

The DG waved them out. "Go home and write up a report on this debacle, and one on the events at this ryokan. Get them to me by noon tomorrow. I want you back on the case, Inspector Aoki. So stay available."

Aoki walked out of headquarters into cold air. The sweat in his armpits was beginning to dry. Two and a half hours ago, when he'd entered the building, he had no idea of what would happen. Now that tenuous future was the ironclad past. He paused to light a cigarette, setting down his suitcase and the cardboard carton. Traffic clogged the streets; a galaxy of lights blazed at his eyes, and music blasted his eardrums. Standing there, his eyes dull, he marveled at how Watanabe had established his "insanity," waiting for an opportunity to sink him. But the superintendent was the one who'd been sunk. It made him feel a little better about the world.

Aoki drew on the cigarette and remembered that he had an apartment to go to in Kamakura, which was a long way from the Kamakura Inn. "Okay. Let's go home," he said to Tokie's orphans.

Chapter Twenty-Three

THE NEXT DAY, AOKI SLOTTED himself back into the coffee shop–park–bar circuit. Had he ever left it? The ryokan and the events there had taken on the character of a dream, as he'd anticipated they might. Even Watanabe's crumpled body on the firing range floor was unreal to him. The pragmatic, competent cop he'd been for so many years seemed to have stepped off the edge of the planet.

Last night he'd fallen into a sleep of exhaustion. This morning he'd done a report on the superintendent's "accident" and sent it by messenger to the DG. He'd told it the way it was, so he didn't know what the internal affairs guys could do with it. The other report could wait.

A newspaper was tucked under his arm as he walked to the park. He'd glanced at the front page. BANK CHAIRMAN AND MOF OFFICIAL FOUND MURDERED. Old news.

It was too cold to sit in the park, so he went to the coffee shop and drank two cups of the Colombian blend. On his skin, the Tokyo air felt moist and gritty; even amid Kamakura's low hills and trees, the city's concrete-cladness encased his flesh and blood.

◆

Brazen. Unbeatable. Aoki gave the scene a jaundiced eye and turned his mind away.

The first thing he'd done when he got home last night was open a beer. Dizzy with fatigue, in his overcoat, he'd sat in the freezing kitchen drinking from the can and thinking everything over. Violent death had been a constant in his working life. When you put on your coat and went home at night, you didn't leave it behind; he never had. The recent mayhem was like a block of granite in his mind, yet he felt the ex-personalities of the dead, floating by as free as air currents.

Sipping coffee, he read the paper. The headline was predictable, the story short on detail; the police hadn't released much. His name wasn't mentioned—doubtless, the prefecture cops had received instructions, though it would come out in the end—but down a column his eye caught Tamaki's.

The Diet banking committee chairman, Yukio Tamaki, expressed regret at the "tragic deaths of Mr. Ito and Mr. Yamazaki, two men who had figured large in the financial world." The Diet member said the preliminary investigation into the affairs of the Tokyo Citizens Bank was completed, and his committee's report had been submitted to the government. He said the reports of the bank's yakuza connections had been exaggerated.

Aoki shook his head in mock wonder. Chairman Ito had been right: Tamaki was getting his spin onto the situation. He could see the Fatman's adept liar's face mouthing those phrases. Well, Ito wasn't worrying about it anymore.

At noon, Inspector Aoki left the coffee shop and went along the street to the bar, ate a bowl of nuts, drank a bottle of Heineken, and thought about what to do. He lit up a cigarette. Saito had read in him the paranoia about Tamaki. Apart from studying the news clippings on him, the Go-playing bastard had been peering into his brain like a neurosurgeon. Or was it his soul?

Aoki studied his left hand. He'd removed the soiled dressing. The cut was red but healing. No stitches . . . The DG needed time to deal with Watanabe' s demise, and Aoki calculated he had a day or two of freedom, though what did that mean in his twisted life?

The bar was deserted. He glanced around, then out through the plate-glass window to the street, looking for watchers. No one in view. That was one thing that'd changed. His eyes hardened. When queried by the press on whether there was a connection between the murders and the bank's disaster, Tamaki had said, "That is a question for the police." Aoki drew the paper to him again and stared at these words. But the print faded, to be replaced in his mind's eye by Saito's sardonic face at the Go board, cold, obsessive, and bent on a massacre. The mocking voice . . . Despite what had passed between them, the man's convoluted makeup and motives remained as obscure to Aoki as Mount Fuji on a pollution-saturated day.

Aoki gazed across the park. He looked over at the underemployed bartender. He stood up, shrugged himself into his overcoat, paid the bill, and left, walking fast.

His father had kept his small room immaculate. Aoki had only been in it once, when he looked through his father's things after he died, but he remembered the filed and annotated records.

He found the card quickly, a calendar for the previous year's schedule of major Go competitions. *October 26–30, Osaka.* The competitions must be held at a similar time each year. He slipped the card back into its file.

In the room's tiny alcove was a scroll of calligraphy. Aoki hadn't taken any notice of it before, but now such things had entered his life. Laboriously, he read:

I wondered and wondered when she would come.
And now we are together.
What thoughts need I have?
—RYOKAN

Aoki nodded his head slowly. He inspected his father's small family shrine mounted on the wall, looked at the photographs of his grandfather and great-grandfather, and went out to the living room and sat down.

Tokie and his father had followed him back from the ryokan. He felt them close. He glanced up at a scroll of his wife's calligraphy. Had she completed that early one morning, the sun warm on her face, while he was in the train going to the CIB in Tokyo?

Aoki gasped and broke into a flood of tears. After a while, he dried off his face with a handkerchief. "Ridiculous!" he told himself.

It's all right, Tokie said.

Of course it is, added his father.

They *were* back!

Aoki washed his face and ran his fingers through his sparse hair to neaten it. He stood there watching himself in the mirror, regaining control. He must get moving. Another idea had come to him. He fetched his overcoat, picked up his cell phone, which he'd recharged overnight—a further step back into the real world—let himself out of the flat, and took the train into the Ginza.

On the train his phone rang. He frowned with surprise and got it out. The director general said in his ear, "As of now, you're back on duty. Report to Superintendent Motono. He's heading up the team on the ryokan murders. And Inspector, keep your mouth shut about the shooting range. We're still working on that." The terse call terminated as abruptly as it had begun. Aoki slipped the phone into his pocket. Who would he tell?

From the station he made a call standing in a doorway in the concourse. He waited while they looked for the man and got him on the line.

An hour later Aoki arrived at the Marunouchi coffee shop and ordered a hamburger with french fries. He wolfed it down and was wiping his mouth with a paper napkin when a lanky, bespectacled man in a rumpled suit entered and looked around. Aoki stood up and beckoned. The man came over. They bowed to each other. It had been a couple of years since the journalist had interviewed Aoki about the big arson fraud. Since then Aoki's personal disasters had been in public view. Recognition of that was on the *Tokyo Shimbun* crime reporter's face as he sat down opposite the detective. Aoki thought he also read *poor Kimura* in his eyes. An ex-colleague. And: *How have you survived?* His name was Minami.

"I'm sorry about your wife, Inspector. You've been having it rough." He stared, unblinking, at the policeman.

Aoki nodded. "I'm back on duty," he said to clear that up. He thought, *If he knew I'd been at the Hokkaido ryokan, he'd be really sparking.* The waitress came, and they each ordered coffee. Aoki's eyes flicked around the room. "I'm trying to get a fix on the identity of a yakuza. A big fish, in his fifties, who keeps his hand in at enforcement. Gets a kick out of that. He likes knife work, and he's a Go-player. Maybe operates out of Osaka. I can't disclose the name I know him by, but it's false anyway."

Aoki watched Minami pour two packets of sugar into his black coffee. Twelve months ago Minami had written a series of articles on the yakuza. Aoki had gotten copies of them all then. He remembered that one of the pieces, referring to the nation's banking woes, had been headlined "The Yakuza Recession," the same phrase his classmate Shimamura had used. But Aoki hadn't gone near the journalist during the Fatman investigation; with the constraints they had, it'd been amazing that they'd put together a case against Tamaki at all.

"It's a guy I've come across, as I said, using a fictitious identity. I need to identify him, see where he fits into the gangster world, and into the case I'm running."

Minami nodded brusquely and stirred his cup. His glance said, *Which is?*

"This man's a highly unusual type." He described Saito's appearance. "Maybe he's a daimyo with a taste for keeping his hand in on enforcement for extra-special cases. A guy with power. Educated. He comes across as an expert on business and the economy." Aoki thought for a moment, then said, "He's quick with a haiku, as maybe he is with a knife. He compares our economy with the wild forests that once covered the country. Kind of a black humorist when he talks to you."

Minami frowned. Aoki watched the journalist's face. Was something stirring in his brain? "A Go-player," Minami murmured, still working on the sugar.

"I'd say of professional standard."

The journalist put down the spoon. "I've looked into a lot of the yakuza's dark alleys, but there's an infinity of 'em to look into. Nothing you've said connects with anything I know."

Aoki sat back. His left hand brushed his cheekbone, finding the mole. The journalist sipped the coffee and took in the detective's disappointment.

Aoki meshed his hands. How much could he say without risking Minami's picking up on the ryokan case? He decided. This hadn't been released to the media yet. "The liver's been cut out of a victim, and it's missing. A neat job. There was no chance of using it for a transplant—so why would anyone do that?"

The journalist's hand with the cup in it had frozen halfway to his lips. He was staring hard at the policeman. He put down the cup. "Now, that does ring a bell."

Aoki leaned forward. "Yes?"

"About three years ago, there was a piece in the *Osaka Shimbun*. Something bizarre. More than that. A refrigerator containing human body parts was found in a suburban apartment. The owner of the place, a single man who lived alone, had disappeared. Neighbors called the police, and they opened the fridge. The cops must've got a horrible shock. It held a human kidney and a liver. The theory was they'd stumbled on a supplier of aphrodisiac snacks to a super-exclusive clientele. A batch of really sick bastards. There'd been a case like it in Hong Kong in the seventies. This newspaperman, Nagai was his name, nosed around and came up with a follow-up piece, which posited one of the snackers was a top yakuza. It gave no names as to perpetrator or informant, but Nagai had a good reputation, and his sources had always been considered reliable."

Aoki swallowed, and the contents of his stomach shifted audibly. He was seeing the half-crazed anger on the face of Chef Hatano. "You said 'had.'"

Minami gave him a steady look. "Yeah, a week later Nagai was found dead, minus his sex organs and his liver."

Aoki stared at the journalist for a long moment. "And?"

"It was a dead end. Nagai's murder wasn't solved that I know of, nor was the supplier ever found. Bits of him might've been in that refrigerator."

But maybe not, Aoki thought. Had he heard about this case? It must be buried somewhere in the relentless flow of mayhem in his memory.

The journalist sipped his sugar-saturated brew. "Though Nagai's theory was that the supplier got scared and ran off."

Aoki stared into his coffee cup. How had the Osaka journalist linked that grim refrigerator with the yakuza? To one man? Did Osaka CIB still have an open file? Did they know more than had broken in the papers, but couldn't prove it?

"What about Governor Tamaki?" Minami asked, abruptly shifting ground. "Putting him in charge of the Diet banking committee was like letting the fox in with the ducks." He watched Aoki.

"Another case that's stone dead."

"Yeah, like my poor colleague Kimura." Minami shook his head sadly. "With him, it was a case of the Fatman snapping his fingers, and the yakuza going into action, wasn't it?"

Aoki didn't reply. Minami smiled. Aoki knew he was considering whether Aoki had found a connection between the mysterious man he was trying to identify and the equally shadowy figure in Nagai's article.

Aoki asked, "Is the big Go competition on in Osaka right now?"

"Yeah."

Ahh. Aoki swallowed coffee. Minami's eyes were trying to penetrate his brain, the way the reporter tried to see into everyone's. The detective looked away. Minami must be wondering what he was up to. Gutted by his bosses over the Tamaki investigation, suspended and under the care of head doctors, his wife a suicide, the journalist colleague who'd blown the whistle on the shelving of the Tamaki case murdered. What was going on *now?* Minami was the industrious, patient type. His suit and his hair might be rumpled, but his brain wasn't.

Their coffee cups had been refilled, and the journalist drained his, noisily sucking down the residue of sugar. He said, "If a story breaks, I hope you'll think of me first."

"I will," Aoki said. "And many thanks."

It was 1:32 P.M. when Aoki arrived at Tokyo Central station. He checked the departure time for the next bullet train to Osaka. Fifteen minutes. The Fatman's Club gold badge danced into his mind as he waited on the platform, followed by Minami's grotesque story about the Osaka journalist's murder. What were the connections to *all* the stuff in his head? Yamazaki's missing liver? It might be more significant than the excised genitalia, which had probably been Saito's ploy to point to Ito's jealous rage; a cuckold's cry from the heart. However, he'd gotten to know Ito better than that.

Going out through Tokyo suburbs, a picture of Chef Hatano slicing fish from the backbone came to him. Had the bastard gone into *that* horrendous sideline after his restaurant failed? Aoki's mouth tightened at the thought. The dragnet had failed to yield anything more on Saito, Hatano, and the two women who'd left the ryokan as he lay unconscious in the secret room.

Speeding south, it occurred to Aoki that all his moves since coming down from the mountains had the stamp of predestination. He lit a cigarette, took out the slim book he'd bought at a bookstore, and began to leaf through it. *The Master of Go.* Here and there, he picked up a move that Saito had replicated. The

1930s breathed from the pages, as past centuries had from the ryokan.

He put it aside and watched the evening lights appearing in the darkening landscape.

The bullet train slid into Osaka at 4:45 P.M. He asked for directions at the station's information desk. The clerk wrote them down. Aoki went out into the gray city, the gray air; another great Japanese urban-scape sprawling to all horizons, rebuilt after World War II, devoid of its prewar individuality, according to his father. The old man had come here for the Bunraku puppets. Aoki visualized him flitting through the streets to the historic theater, his mind immersed in the plots of the old plays. Surprising him, the title of one jumped into his mind: *Love and Suicide.*

He sniffed. Odor of sewage. It was much worse in summer.

He'd turned his cell phone off. Superintendent Motono was on the back burner.

Osaka police headquarters loomed up in a blaze of lights. The taxi dropped Aoki at the door, and he entered the building. Police and others were coming and going in the main foyer. Over the years, Aoki had dealt with officers here, but standing at the desk, his badge in hand, he found out that his contacts had been transferred away or retired. He was directed to the third floor, and ten minutes later, he was sitting in a cubicle with a young detective who showed no surprise at this Tokyo colleague's request. The three-year-old case was brought up on a screen. "Dead end," Minami had said, and this status was confirmed.

The young policeman shrugged. "Nothing done on it for over a year." A rash of NO SMOKING signs had invaded the building, so

Aoki was suffering. No one who'd worked on the case was available. Aoki brooded on his cigarette-less hands. Old cases did come out of the woodwork, did get a new life, did get solved. Take Madam Ito's, though the police computers weren't going to show that, if it rested with him.

"What about the file?" Aoki asked. "And the one on Nagai's murder?"

They arrived in twenty minutes, and Aoki was left alone with the two dossiers.

They were in living color: red meat fresh from the butcher's block. Expressionless, he examined the graphic photographs of the refrigerator's contents. *Devil's smorgasbord.* That thought came, and with it *the devil's gate,* and he heard the lilting, husky accents of Kazu Hatano's voice. His memory seemed attuned now to voices from the past.

He searched for a photo of the missing refrigerator owner, Okura. None. No background on the guy at all except what his neighbors had known, and that was hardly anything, which probably meant "Okura" was a false identity. He checked; they had prints from the apartment.

Then he was looking at the serious face of the *Osaka Shimbun* reporter, Nagai. A risk-taker, but his face didn't show it. Had Nagai worried that this might be his final assignment?

He opened the murder file and flicked through the pages. A suspected gangster hit; no suspects; cross-references to the other file on the desk. He sighed and went back to that, turning to the progress summaries of the investigating detectives. Accustomed to such files, he worked quickly. He found nothing on the journalist's source for the body-parts/yakuza piece. Either Nagai hadn't committed this to writing, or it'd been lost or destroyed. There was a batch of yellowing newspaper clippings. He scanned them. No clues there—

It was folded in three, and he almost missed it: dated 1998, from an obscure northern magazine. He began to read it, and in a moment it had his complete attention. He finished and sat back, thinking about the former colonel of the Japanese Imperial Army by the name of Oto, who'd been tried for vivisection and cannibalism at the Tokyo War Crimes Trials after the war, and acquitted. Several witnesses hadn't lasted the distance. Colonel Oto had died in 1998, which had clearly prompted the piece.

Aoki gazed out at the cold city lights. What had brought this to Nagai's attention, and how did it connect to the Osaka case and the unnamed yakuza identity? Had the 1998 piece on this Oto presented a new angle for the Osaka reporter on the body-parts case? Though he hadn't used it in his article, maybe he'd intended to. Somehow, maybe it'd opened up the top yakuza's identity—sent him probing in a fatal direction. Whatever, when the original material he must've had disappeared this was overlooked.

Aoki stared down at the file. It seemed truncated, like a serial story missing the last installment. That feeling had come over him. Inside the back cover were printed boxes that recorded where the file had been, who'd signed for it, and the dates in and out. Idly he glanced at the last box.

He blinked. The last place it'd been was the Osaka district prosecutor's office. June 4, 1999. A name had swum up at him. He frowned. What was this? The next moment he had it: It was the name of the senior prosecutor he'd read about in yesterday's paper, indicted for taking bribes from gangsters.

Aoki whistled. *That guy!* If it'd gone to the DPO there must've been a prosecution brief—or some communication, maybe from

the police, seeking guidance. Or the DPO—this corrupt official—
had called for it. June 4, 1999. Nagai's article on the body parts and
the unidentified Yakuza daiymo's involvement had been published
on May 15.

Aoki looked at his watch. He'd been lost in the arcane and nasty
case for two hours. He'd noted that a detective named Ishi had run
the body-parts investigation early on. Ishi might know about that
last transit the file had made. He closed the dossiers. He had to get
out and have a smoke.

The young detective stood in the doorway. "How'd it go, Inspector?"

Aoki's eyes narrowed. "Nagai's article pointed to the yakuza, to
one unnamed top gangster, but there's nothing in the investigation
reports that ties that in. Or in *his* murder investigation."

The Osaka detective's face was blank. He had this week's
headaches on his plate. Aoki sipped water from a paper cup. He
didn't want to let it go. "I think I might have a new angle. Is Assistant Inspector Ishi still around?"

The Osaka detective winced. "Died last year. Stomach cancer."

Aoki's eyes drifted away to the slitlike window. Framed in it,
lights flowed away into darkness in curving patterns like bright yellow wheat thrown out of a bucket. The computer hadn't revealed
any comparable crimes. No more refrigerators. *If* Okura was
Hatano, had he fled to the mountains when Nagai's *Osaka Shimbun*
piece came out? Or when the reporter had been murdered? The
case stank of disappearance and collateral death. Maybe the perpetrators, the gourmets, were still out there in this Osaka night, snack-
ing away. No. Instinct told him that the special dining had been
very occasional—for obvious reasons.

Rendezvous at Kamakura Inn

Aoki rose and patted his pockets. "Thanks. I've got your name card. I might be in touch."

In the main foyer he checked his cell phone. Two messages: An irritated Superintendent Motono demanded his presence at headquarters, and Minami's cautious voice said, "When I got back I looked up the archives. Nagai had the job of covering Go competitions nationwide for the *Osaka Shimbun*. He was a good player himself." A slight pause. "I've heard from police contacts re this Hokkaido ryokan case that the MOF guy's body had the liver and certain appendages removed. You haven't been taking a hot-spring health cure by any chance, have you, Inspector?"

Aoki gazed across the foyer without seeing it. Go seemed to be hovering over his life. He shook his shoulders and grunted, "Huh! Health cure!" But then, maybe in a way it was that. For sure, his mind had traveled into new territory; that was one of the few indisputable facts in his convoluted world.

The competition venue was a short taxi ride away. Gazing at lights and traffic, Aoki let his mind range over recent events and into the future. Probably this move would be futile. Common sense said that Saito would've gone to ground or transferred to another identity. Yet, instinctively, Aoki knew that Saito was an individual with a fatalistic attitude toward his existence; not much would stand in the way of his obsession with Go, with anything. He loved danger. Aoki was sure of that. Doubtless he was a fugu-fish eater, too, eating the flesh a fraction away from the venomous liver—making his lips and tongue burn and tingle . . .

This was a premier competition in the nation. The man was

245

addicted to the game, supremely arrogant, and probably considered himself untouchable, so maybe the odds weren't so loaded against his turning up here.

Saito and Hatano had murdered Ito and Yamazaki—and the bodyguard, Shoba. Now, maybe, the bastards were fitting into this Osaka body-parts case. Gently, he touched the cut on his head. Hatano's prints would be all over the ryokan, and Okura's were on file.

But even if he could be found, how to flush Saito out from under the wing of the yakuza? If they could track down Hatano, maybe that'd be a way through that warped and macabre bastard's defenses. Little fish to catch the big one. In his career, Aoki had never encountered a problem anywhere near as hard as this.

A traffic light laid a bar of red into the taxi's interior, and the driver's white gloves shone against the steering wheel. A sweet lily fragrance suffused the cab. Aoki's head fell forward. He jerked his body upright. He'd been drifting into a dream. "A person must follow his star, especially into the unknown"—his father. Yeah! Saito was a way station on the route to the Fatman. Ex-governor Tamaki was the ultimate destination. His hatred for Tamaki had been suppressed by the madness at the ryokan, but now it was back, pulsating in his mind, and he was wide awake.

A huge, unprepossessing building, with a giant banner proclaiming the sponsor's name looped across its front, confronted Aoki. Men, many in traditional dress, moved in the street, coming and going. Aoki stood on the pavement, watching. Then he went through the doors into a vast hall.

The hum of a thousand voices enfolded him, resonating high up in the cavernous space. Men sat at Go tables or nearby, observing the

matches in progress; others moved around. A week ago Aoki
would've been astonished at the sight. Now his heart sank at the
task. In their uniform traditional clothing, individuals were a homo-
geneous mass. The competition was in its third day, and many of
the tables had become vacant as contestants were eliminated.
About a hundred tables were still in play: the high-grade players. If
he was here, Saito must be in that group.

Aoki, his face hard, hissed softly through his teeth. What now? At
one side of the hall there was a low gallery, only about ten feet above
the heads of the players. A few of the spectators were sitting there. It
was a place to look down on the tables without being conspicuous.

He found the stairway, and minutes later he was seated in the
gallery's second row, scanning the tables below. The farthest occupied ones were about ten yards from his position. Saito was tall, but
sitting down, that distinction was lost. Methodically Aoki's eyes
moved over each table, each person. The players were in profile to
him. He was looking for the long head, the abundant brushed-back
hair with its blue sheen, the big shoulders. After five minutes, no
such individual met his careful scrutiny, but the tables were close
together, and he wasn't sure that he hadn't missed one. He blinked,
moistening his eyes. He repeated the process. Nothing. He sat back
in his chair. If Saito was here, he wasn't at one of the tables.

"But what are the odds that he *would* be here?" he asked himself with renewed doubt. The fellow could be in Paris or New York,
or anywhere the yakuza had a bolt-hole, or he could be back home,
deep in his real identity and existence.

Shaded electric lights brightly illuminated each match. Below
him, the embattled formations of stones glittered. Grimly, again he
remembered how handfuls had whistled viciously through the anteroom's darkness. Should he go down and walk through the crowds

of observers? The organizers would have a list of the participants, but Saito—his Saito—wouldn't be here under that name.

In the corner of his eye—*a golden flash*. He swung his head around. Again the winking flash. A man at a table, only six paces or so out into the hall, had turned to speak to someone behind him; had turned toward Aoki. The insistent flash had come from a badge on the front of his cloak.

Aoki's breath choked in his throat. His heart seemed to stop. Saito! The luxuriant brushed-back hair was gone—this man had a sparse dark thatch streaking over yellowed skin—but seen from the front, the long, saturnine face was unmistakable to Aoki. He was smiling his sardonic smile as he listened to the man behind him.

Aoki thrust forward. Caught by the movement, Saito's eyes lifted to the gallery and met the detective's. Aoki couldn't detect the facial reaction, though the Go-player's gaze remained steady. Now he was speaking to a second man behind him, out of the corner of his mouth.

Aoki left his seat, ran up the gallery stairs to the corridor at the rear, and raced along it. He'd almost reached the stairs to the main floor when two men in suits rushed up them. They were in their thirties, well built, well dressed, looking tough and competent. Their suits were of identical cut; one was blue, one dark gray. They came to a halt, blocking the detective's way. Aoki pulled up, his eyes narrowed. No trademark tattoos or missing fingers in evidence, but they were yakuza.

"Mr. Aoki?" one inquired. He'd put his hand in his pocket.

Aoki nodded. "And you?"

Gray-suit smiled condescendingly. "Mr. Saito would like to speak to you."

"Then we're on the same wavelength," Aoki said tersely, and started to move past them.

"Just a minute," blue-suit said, stepping forward. "Excuse, please." He ran his hands expertly over Aoki, especially checking for an ankle holster. "Hmm," he said.

The suits escorted him to their boss. "Clean," blue-suit said.

Saito stood in the center of a small room at the side of the hall, his big hands locked together across his belly, a slight smile on his face. "Inspector Aoki, congratulations!"

Aoki stared at him. The hairpiece Saito had worn at the ryokan had been state-of-the-art. He had less hair than Aoki, and what there was was cut to a stubble. Several large brown marks showed on his cranium. "I thought I'd seen the last of you. However, Go was a link between us at the ryokan, wasn't it? And, after all, you're a top detective."

The room had a bare wood floor and was unfurnished except for a couple of hard-backed chairs.

"So. You're yakuza," Aoki said.

Saito tilted his head, raised his eyebrows. "What makes you think that?" His harsh voice echoed in the empty wooden space. Aoki jerked his head at the two suits, who were standing with their backs to the door.

Saito smiled. "Everyone has bodyguards these days, from corporate chiefs to top government bureaucrats."

With a small shock, Aoki realized that the gold badge wasn't the Fatman's Club's. It might've been a Go club badge; he couldn't recognize any distinguishing feature. He raised his eyes from it to Saito's face. "I'd like you to answer some questions."

The man who was possibly from Osaka, who was certainly in Osaka right now, nodded. "Why not? But are you still suspended,

Inspector? You're not carrying a weapon. *So,* an *unofficial* visit?"

Aoki ignored the question; his distrustful expression didn't change, but his eyelids flickered. " 'If you meet a Buddha, kill him. If you meet a patriarch of the law, kill him.' " He spoke with cold aggression.

Saito's eyes narrowed. After a moment, he said, "Yes?"

"Your little motto for Ito and Yamazaki—and perhaps myself?"

Saito laughed. "Motto? But you're still alive."

"Things didn't go as programmed."

Saito moved his shoulders in a slight flexing movement and thought for a moment. "I'm involved in this interesting case at the ryokan, am I? Under suspicion?" He shook his head ruefully and gazed down at the boards. "Why did I leave before the arrival of the police?" He looked up at the detective's face. "It was *possible* to leave; it was *time* to leave. Have you considered that one might not wish to be caught up in that kind of sensation, for what I'd call legitimate reasons?"

Aoki stared at the half-amused face, trying to read it, to analyze the brain processes. The mask of the joker? All that he could make out was arrogance, and a bizarre agenda exuding from the big man like a hot breath from a furnace. Nothing that he said could be trusted.

"I enjoyed our conversations. I hoped I was being of assistance to you, showing you just where the fault lines were, so to speak. Crimes of passion, crimes of revenge—my interest in them is quite genuine."

Aoki stared into his eyes. A great game-player, and still playing. A competitor, and a cynical, tantalizing, contemptuous murderer, maybe the one who'd dined off the parts in that refrigerator.

It came at him in a rush. That fatal night, under the plate cover, had Hatano been taking Yamazaki's liver to this man? He drew in a long breath. He had the bastard's number, but not enough evidence to nail him. Would he get out of here alive, even? Now Aoki felt sweat running in his armpits. At the ryokan this yakuza boss had imparted his comments to the hick cop with avuncular contempt. Power, and killing people with impunity, bred such superiority. Aoki's mouth tightened until its corners tingled.

Saito, the gleam of mirth in his eye, said, "In this morning's paper I see *someone's* dug up the interesting fact that Miss Hatano and her sister are the sole beneficiaries of Mr. Ito's estate . . . Ah, you don't know that. I wonder why that banker would leave a fortune to a stepdaughter who hated him? Guilty conscience? Atonement? Or maybe it was just an old will he never got around to changing."

At a loss, Aoki rubbed his jaw with his hand. More fucking smoke being laid down! He was being led in circles. Saito spread his hands in the air. "Try to look more at the big picture. Open up your mind."

In a voice barely under control, Aoki said, "Ito and Yamazaki were corporate and human garbage, but *no one* deserves to die like they did."

The tall man smiled down on the detective. "You're a simple kind of fellow, Aoki, which has its points—"

"*Cut the crap.* It might take a while, but we're going to get you." Aoki realized he'd snarled like an animal. The yakuza, any place, any time, could chomp up and spit out the likes of him. Choking on his emotions and his impotence, he stood there. It was fortunate they'd taken away his gun.

Saito's smile broadened. "And I suppose you think you'll reopen the investigation into ex-governor Tamaki, or maybe do something on your own account." He shook his head in mock sorrow. "Inspector, get in touch with the realities in our nation."

"More crap," Aoki hissed.

Saito laughed indulgently. The hubbub of the Go hall rose up in the silence between them.

Aoki said, "I know about your perverted diet. Chopped liver, lightly fried, is it? With Chef Hatano's delicate touch, and a special sauce?" This time Aoki forced control on his voice, kept it level. "Something to make normal men vomit their guts, something to share with another pervert—Colonel Oto." Aoki threw in the last bit recklessly.

Saito had become absolutely still. The humor had dropped from his face like a discarded mask. He was as deadly as the winter-entombed mountains where they'd met. "Good-bye, Inspector. Don't try to find me again." The new voice was as razor-sharp and as final as a blade slicing a throat. Gray-suit had put his right hand in his pocket and was gazing at his boss.

Aoki turned his back and walked out of the room.

His heart was pounding and his limbs were trembling with anger as he pushed his way between gray-robed bodies, not seeing the academic faces preoccupied with arcane formations of small round stones, but in a few moments he was calming down. He went to the administration desk and showed his badge to an elderly man. "Table number 44," he said. "The very tall competitor, who is he, please?"

The official consulted a list. "That is Mr. Yamamoto, from Kobe. He's an amateur of the seventh grade." He peered up at Aoki.

"Do you know him well?"

"He comes here each year. I believe he's a merchant."

"What is his address in Kobe?" The man consulted a thick folder and pursed his lips. "Would you write it down for me, please?" The man wrote it on the back of his own name card.

Aoki walked a few paces from the desk, then returned to it. "Do you have records of matches played at past competitions?"

The man nodded and placed a volume before the detective. Aoki found the results for 1998 and ran his finger down a column. His finger stopped. He nodded to himself, gave his thanks to the official, and left the building.

Aoki stood in the cold street. Yamamoto had played Nagai in a quarterfinal, and beaten him. He inhaled, took chilled car exhaust fumes deep down into his lungs, and coughed. Nagai had lost match, life, and body parts; it'd been a case of winner take all. Neither Saito nor Yamamoto was the Go-player's right name, and the Kobe address would be fake, so where did he go now?

Thirty yards along the pavement to his left, three men had come out another door and were walking toward a limousine parked at the curb. Saito's tall figure was between the two bodyguards, his head bobbing above theirs. Aoki gazed after them as they hurriedly got in the car and drove off. It'd happened in seconds, and though he started forward, he couldn't get the license plate number.

In hazy yellow blobs, the big-city sodium lights floated away down a wide avenue, and now he gazed in that direction.

Saito had failed to kill him at the ryokan. He'd had luck on his side—the dual incidents involving Madam Ito, first drawing him away from the banker's door, and then, later, into the secret room had taken him out of range. Hatano had made a mess of it in the anteroom, and Saito had run out of time. For Saito the priorities had been Chairman Ito and Yamazaki. Aoki had been added to the list at the behest of the Fatman and Watanabe. Even so, with his hench-man in tow, why not tonight? The broad avenue gave no answer.

In his mind, the world of Go had died out. The unfinished busi-ness behind him with Saito was relegated to a waiting room. He *was* calming down. He'd found Saito once; maybe he'd be that lucky again.

Aoki shuddered. In his brain, the Fatman, grinning and un-scathed, had stepped forward from *his* impregnable world. The man who had brought disaster to Aoki, whose power had killed Tokie; the player in this dark sequence of events most deserving of retribution, who, against all the odds, must be brought to justice. Aoki's eyes glowed in the Osaka gloom. He had a good idea where he might find him. It was Friday night.

Chapter Twenty-Four

THE BEST MOMENTS IN OSAKA were those at departure. Aoki had always loathed this city, and more so now. The bullet train picked up speed until it was purring through the night. Aoki sat weary, stiff, and hurting, but alert. Saito's world had been left behind. Ahead, in Tokyo, waited that of the Fatman, ex-governor Tamaki. Before his eyes, he had this flowing, dark, tumbled landscape into which humanity had shoehorned so much infrastructure, so much of its history, and, as he saw now, so much of its culture. He lit a cigarette and gazed at it wide-eyed.

At 11:15 P.M. they arrived at Tokyo Central station. Passing the lockers, he had an image of Madam Ito moving up the thronged concourse with her damaged wrists, her damaged mind, and her parcel of bloodstained clothing.

He took the suburban train to Kamakura.

The apartment was steeped in its silence. A small space of iced air; he still hadn't turned on the heating. He didn't feel as if he wanted to resume residence. Tokie's scrolls hung on the walls, memorials to the poems she'd loved. He put on water to heat for coffee, then went into the bathroom and splashed his face. He gasped at the icy shock. In the living room, a message light winked on the phone. He pressed a button. "This is Superintendent Motono. Where are you, Inspector Aoki? I need to confer with you urgently. Phone me. Now."

Aoki shrugged. For the second time that day, he entered his father's room. The locker seemed to await his hands. He took the sealskin pouch and lifted out the revolver. It was clammy, and he carried it to the kitchen and wiped it off with a rag. The old man had drowned it in oil when he put it away—sixty years ago? Many of his father's writer-heroes had committed suicide, Kawabata and Akutagawa, and some who weren't his heroes, like Mishima. From his outsider's place, with his detective's mind, Aoki had listened to him on this. As a young patrolman, he'd cut down suicides from trees on Mount Fuji. He wondered if his father had kept the gun with suicide in mind. When old age became insupportable? It was a distinct possibility.

Aoki broke open the revolver's chamber. Five years ago he'd taken a course at a prefecture academy where they'd been shooting .45s, and he'd helped himself to a few rounds. He found them among the paraphernalia in his desk drawer: three stubby, brass-rimmed rounds. Five years—would the charges still be sound? He shrugged. He went back to the kitchen and fed the rounds into three of the six chambers. Again an atmosphere of predestination washed through him. He put the revolver into his overcoat pocket.

This isn't the way, you know, his father said.

I don't know, said his wife. *It just might be.* A point of difference between those two! He sipped coffee. He had to step out of their world now, into his own.

Aoki hadn't eaten since the hamburger and felt empty. At Central station, he glanced at his watch, then went to a tempura bar, where he sat on a stool and ordered two crisp-battered prawns, one eggplant, and rice. He washed the meal down with tea. One of his night-owl snacks. Ten minutes later, he caught the train.

The Fatman was a creature of habit. In the seventeen-month investigation he'd run, Aoki had at times thought he knew as much about the ex-governor's surface life as the Diet member did himself; just as he knew about much of his covert criminality, assembled in the sealed records at headquarters, presuming they hadn't walked.

Each Friday night, Tamaki had gone to his parents' house to spend the night alone, sending his driver and bodyguard home. He'd never missed once. The old house with its traditional garden, rooted in Zen, obviously cast a strong influence over the Fatman. Aoki had wondered about the sentimentality this implied. Was it an escape to the past, to a cleaner life? A respite from the dirt in his political and business lives? He'd decided that the evil bastard wouldn't be capable of such a notion; it was merely the Fatman in another mysterious dimension.

Now, maybe, it gave him his chance.

The night he'd come out here after Tokie's death, had he had this confrontation in mind? He couldn't remember; he'd been in too much of a daze to know what he'd been doing. There'd been a cop on his tail then, and was his mind any clearer tonight? He wanted the man in court, exposed, and put away as a common felon. Yet the fact was that he was untouchable. Realistically, bringing him to justice seemed to have a snowball's chance in hell, now that the political power brokers had killed the investigation. So was he just easing his honest cop's conscience with the justice bit? The only way with Tamaki was a bullet, and it was the only way that would ease the pain in his heart about Tokie. Yet maybe he could force him to come clean—get it all out into the press, through Minami . . .

The police kiosk was lit up, vague figures moving in its lighted interior. Aoki went in the opposite direction, as he had on the last visit, and walked up the dark street beneath old maple trees, whose branches were nearly skeletal against a sky strangely clear for late fall. A breeze sighed. A stand of bamboo whispered back. Nature was being its enigmatic self. He walked silently, the .45 a heavy drag in his pocket.

The house took shape in the darkness. How many Friday nights had he and colleagues watched here in vain for clandestine visitors, for a new element in Tamaki's variegated agenda to surface? Another world from his luxury high-rise apartment in Roppongi, strung with security gadgetry. But no one had come; no new element had surfaced.

Aoki blinked. The two stone lanterns at the gate were lit. The Fatman, or someone, was here. The house had a narrow frontage but went back a long way in a series of rooms to the garden. The hall was hard-packed earth, as were the passages. An elderly maidservant was usually in residence; once, when she went shopping, Aoki had looked the unlocked place over, roaming through the rooms, looking for papers. He'd found none. The woman had never been here Friday nights.

Maybe the bastard came to plot the political strategy for his faction; to steer it to ascendancy, and himself to the prime ministership. They said he'd quit the Diet to run as a prefectural governor when it seemed his chance at prime minister had gone. The prospect had revived, and he'd reentered the Diet. Full circle; the Fatman being his convoluted self.

Aoki stood next to a tree trunk. No voices, no music, only the breeze. He waited. It didn't seem so cold here; the mature trees hemmed the houses in, their big roots prowling under the mossy ground. With the dense vegetation, the neighboring properties seemed more remote than they were. He opened his overcoat and transferred the .45 to his belt. Careful of his footing on the mossy stones, he entered the tiny front garden, slid back the door, and stepped into the hall.

There was light deep in the house. Softly he walked the dusky passage, pausing at each threshold to check each dark room. He was moving past artifacts of old family life, of historical Japan. His heart was cold, his breaths short and controlled. The light ahead was drawing him like a moth. Grimly, he thought, *A deadly moth.*

The living room was deserted. For a sickening moment Aoki thought he'd come into a trap. Then he noticed that the door to the garden was open. He took a deeper breath and edged through it.

The garden was only about twenty yards long but had an illusion of spaciousness. The dark figure stood ten paces away, in profile, gazing up through the trees at the sky, hands folded on a great belly: a gross silhouette communing with the night, absorbing a big harvest moon.

Aoki thought, *Or considering Superintendent Watanabe's surprising exit? He would've heard of it.*

Aoki's eyes smarted with strain. He moved forward, and his shoe hit a rock. The uplifted face swung around and saw the intruder against the light of the room. *"What the hell! What—"* He moved with surprising speed and commitment across the space between them. Aoki's hand raced to his belt. Tamaki pulled up, shoulders thrust forward, his face peering at the intruder. *"You!"* he snarled. *"What's the meaning of this?"*

Aoki's hand was inside his opened overcoat. He gazed at the

wheezing, overbearing figure. "The meaning? I can understand you'd be surprised to see me, Governor. Though you must've heard I survived the ryokan."

"*What?* Get out, you're babbling like a madman!" Tamaki moved again, to pass the madman and get to the phone. Smoothly Aoki brought out the big revolver and stuck its long barrel into the huge gut. The Fatman leaped back, letting out a hiss, then became still again. The light from the room gleamed on his eyeballs.

"Keep *very* still," Aoki said. "I'm going to put some questions to you—"

"*Finished.*" The word sprang from the thick lips. "You imbecile, you fucking imbecile! You don't have the faintest fucking idea who or what you're up against." The big plump fingers opened and closed in the night air.

"Like you."

The ex-governor gasped. "You! You think *you* can arrest *me?* You'll be crushed! A fool for a second time. You must have a brain to survive, Inspector." Loaded with contempt and anger, shoulders hunched, he peered at the detective. Aoki stared back at the face a yard from his own. Naked power was pouring from the politician, flowing in sweat from his brow; clearly it was beyond his comprehension that a single bullet could take it all away. He'd survived too often, and too much. Aoki's brain was sorting out the options.

"*What are these fucking questions?*" A gush of breath, ripe with brandy.

"Who killed Eichi Kimura? Cut out his eyes, cut off his tongue, his ears?"

Tamaki gestured angrily. "Ha! Nothing to do with me."

Aoki lowered the gun's barrel from the man's chest and trained it on his private parts. Audibly, he drew back the hammer.

"*Maybe* it was the yakuza," Tamaki said in a harsh whisper that finished in a quaver of fear.

New note, Aoki thought. His brain seemed to be clicking away like clockwork. "I'll count to five," he said. "Then you get the first one in the balls."

"*All right.* It was Watanabe's idea. Kimura was a troublemaker, a muckraker who had to be stopped, for the good of the party."

"For the good of the *party* . . . Who did it?"

"How in hell do I know? One of Watanabe's contacts." The lies spread across the serene garden's aura like a stain of factory pollution in a clear night sky.

"*And* I only shot Watanabe in the heart!"

"*Shit,*" Tamaki breathed.

"Who instructed Saito to finish me off at the ryokan?"

"*Who the hell is Saito?*" Fear and anger and genuine-sounding surprise were in his voice.

Aoki thought, *It figures.* The Fatman would never've known the name of the assassin, and "Saito" was a transient identity anyway. Tamaki was truthful about one thing, though; in the cool serenity of this garden, he was. Nothing would ever be brought home against him. It'd be hard enough even if witnesses had seen him personally standing over Kimura's body, a bloodstained knife in hand. Swiftly the witnesses would've disappeared: paid off, frightened off, or killed. Probably he'd have gotten rid of his classmate Watanabe in the end. The superintendent had known too much.

Aoki's eyes were burning now from his unblinking vigilance. Even if he forced Tamaki to write down and sign a confession, duress would be claimed, and believed, and Hideo Aoki, the damaged, half-insane cop with psychiatric-ward time to prove it, following his bitter, misguided vendetta, would be sedated and dragged off to the oblivion of a sanatorium. If he made it that far!

This is the rocklike truth of the matter, Aoki, he thought bitterly. The situation was precisely what he'd already known it to be.

Tamaki's heavy breathing was filling the garden. As if sensing the detective's indecision, he said, "Listen, Aoki, I can understand the shock of your wife's death. Allowances can be made—"

In a surge of pain, Aoki thought his heart was going to burst. This scum alive, and his wife dead! "I can't stand your life," he snarled, his mind in a bloody haze, and pulled the trigger.

The click of the misfire made an inoffensive sound. Tamaki swayed back, then broke into a shocked laugh. "Shit! Your tricks don't frighten me, you nobody cop—" He grabbed for the gun. They wrestled for it, swaying backward and forward. Tamaki was surprisingly strong. Aoki drove his head up into the contorted, hard-breathing face. *Crunch!* Tamaki screamed and reeled away, blood streaming from his nose. Aoki had been forced back onto a sand garden. He pulled the trigger again, and the explosion cracked against the rocks and reverberated away into the night. The Fatman shuddered, and blood spurted from the hole in his kimono. For a moment he kept his feet, then crashed down on his side. At Aoki's feet, great gut heaving, he exhaled a long bubbling breath. Beneath his robe the thick legs kicked spasmodically, once, twice, then were rigid.

"What was that?" Behind a bamboo fence, someone called.

Aoki pocketed the revolver and went quietly and quickly out through the house. No one had rushed into the street. Swiftly he retraced his steps. The cut on his head had reopened, and he dabbed up blood with his handkerchief. A big mistake. The magnitude of what he'd done remained to be dealt with. Right now he felt he'd completed a Herculean task, broken out into a big space. He went, a shadow along the street.

Inspector Aoki was home in two hours. He'd walked to a station one stop nearer Tokyo Central. On the way he'd wiped off any prints and dropped the revolver down a deep storm drain. If it was ever found, it'd be a dead end. The American firebombs had wiped out half of Tokyo in 1945; he was confident no records would exist showing whom it'd been issued to sixty years ago.

He had a freezing shower, then sat in the living room without turning on the light. Despite the violence of his feelings, he'd never visualized himself at this point. Now, it seemed to have been destined for such a closure. Programmed, like Saito's last moves in the 1938 Go match.

When he'd shot Watanabe, he'd taken a one-way highway— then the DG, for his own reasons, had given him an escape route. There could be no escape from what he'd done tonight.

But he'd join Superintendent Motono's team tomorrow. The Fatman would be front-page news by then. The ex-governor's enemies were legion, and Aoki would speculate as much as anyone else about that. He held a towel to the reopened wound on his head. He'd left his blood in the Fatman's garden, maybe on his corpse. Probably the die was cast now for Hideo Aoki. However, he must get some sleep and have a clear head for tomorrow. He'd play out his cards to the bitter end.

He half-expected to hear their voices in his sleep, but he sensed they'd finally gone. He sat up in the dark. They'd been lingering in a halfway house, getting him through his grief and guilt and the breakdown, showing him that other world. Now they'd passed on. To where? His father had believed in an afterlife of the spirit; Tokie'd never said. He felt a warm sensation and, listening intently, as sometimes he heard a distant break of jazz, heard the notes of an Osaka samisen.

Chapter Twenty-Five

INSPECTOR AOKI WAS AWAKE AT six. He felt refreshed and calm. There was no food in the apartment, so he drank the last of the Colombian coffee and smoked a cigarette while he listened to the news on the radio. Nothing about Tamaki. Was the ex-governor's body still lying undiscovered in his garden? Before seven he walked to the station, bought a hamburger and ate it slowly, seated at a bar. Probably the cut on his head should've been stitched the first time. This morning he'd crudely applied Band-Aids to it. As he ate, nerves began to shoot in him. "But, after all," he told himself, "what is going to happen, will."

On the platform, he looked at the front pages of two papers. Nothing there, either. Overnight, the yakuza had visited a mobster in the hospital, sans flowers, and put half a dozen bullets into him as he lay in bed. A couple of gangs settling a dispute, the police hypothesized. "It was like a yakuza movie," a shocked fifty-five-year-old male patient told the reporters.

Aoki grimaced. *Just like my life.* He discarded the papers.

He arrived at headquarters at 8:30 A.M. and reported to Superintendent Motono. A squat, gray-headed man in his midfifties, the senior detective blinked and raised his eyebrows. Minimal bows were exchanged. They'd never worked together before.

"Why didn't you respond to my calls?" Motono's voice was even, but his eyes had narrowed as if he were peering into a smoky room.

"I had urgent matters to follow up when I got back from Hokkaido."

"Which took you to see colleagues in Osaka."

Aoki nodded. Someone from Osaka had been on the phone. He'd expected it.

"We'll go into that in a moment. Have you heard the news?"

Aoki stared at his superior. "What news?"

"Yukio Tamaki's been found murdered—forty-five minutes ago."

Aoki widened his eyes. "Shit! How? Where?"

The superintendent was still peering at him in that way. "Shot. At his family house in Hakone. Your old adversary, Inspector Aoki." Motono moved a sheet of paper on his desk. Superintendent Watanabe's untimely end would be sizzling away in the TMP building like an overcooked steak. Aoki knew that. *That* was the expression on Motono's face, but doubtless the DG had decreed a blackout. Now they had the Fatman, another interesting sector of this inspector's past.

"Well, Tamaki's not our worry. Superintendent Shimazu and his team have been assigned. Let's talk about *our* worry, and I trust I'll hear it all, including what happened on your trip to Osaka."

For half an hour, Aoki described the three murders at the ryokan; he talked at length about Saito and his wide-ranging dialogues but said nothing concerning the denouement of the Madam

Ito mystery, though, of course, the old case came up as he described his interaction with Saito. Then he told Motono what he'd found out about the Osaka body-parts case and the journalist Nagai's murder. He omitted the district prosecutor and Colonel Oto from the Imperial Army. He needed to look further into those angles. Finally, he covered the confrontation at the Go competition.

Motono interrupted with a few questions but mainly kept quiet, his eyes either on Aoki's face or on the sheet of paper in front of him. He looked as if he were considering the career of Inspector Aoki equally with the triple murders and the rest of it.

Aoki sat back, at last lit a cigarette, and lowered his gaze to the desk surface. The room was overheated, and his body felt moist. Motono was almost as Sphinx-like as Watanabe had been, yet he gave off more human vibes.

"Human-offal eating, Go matches, and Zen mottoes? Hmm, a fellow of extra-special tastes—and a mystery man," the superintendent said, impassive. "But that chef, Hatano, no longer is."

Aoki's eyes flicked up.

"Forensics found a match with the prints taken at the ryokan in the central records. They're the same as those in that specialty butcher's flat in Osaka. As you say, the fellow calling himself Okura, who disappeared at the time of Nagai's murder."

"Ahh . . ." Aoki released breath in a long sigh. There it was. Motono had been looking into the Osaka body-parts case this morning. He'd given no sign of it when Aoki reported on his visit to Osaka police headquarters. Aoki said, "What about the prints in Saito's room at the ryokan?"

"No match there."

"What else have they found?"

"The obvious things. They're looking into hairs and fibers and blood." He paused. "And the whereabouts of Yamazaki's missing part. Also the whereabouts of that sister and the other woman. The prefecture report is a series of questions, yet they talked to you, Inspector, didn't they?" He studied the cut on Aoki's head.

Aoki was silent.

"Very well, I want you to go and brief *our* team. Then get your report down on paper. The DG's demanding it. I'm making you my deputy on this one. I want you to go after this Saito and this Hatano, or whatever their names are. I want you to report to me twice a day, A.M. and P.M., and if I find your cell phone switched off—"

He stared meaningfully at Aoki, then reached into a drawer for the service pistol and pushed it across the desk. *It's being passed around like a hot coal,* Aoki thought.

He left Motono's office and went downstairs. Where could he restart with Saito? The Kobe address would be a fake. And Hatano? As for cold-as-mutton Tamaki, when would they question Aoki himself about his past with the Fatman, about his movements last night? They surely would. That was certainly on Motono's mind, as it would be on Superintendent Shimazu's.

He gazed at his hands. The yakuza's Yokohama deal had apparently been the catalyst that'd sealed Chairman Ito's fate. Maybe that was where to start.

Aoki gave twenty-odd detectives the same briefing he'd given the superintendent; they already had their assignments. Then he went to a desk and began to write his report. As he typed it out, the ryokan came alive again in his mind. When he was about half done he phoned the young detective in Osaka and asked a question about the Osaka district prosecutor who'd been arrested three days ago. The cop called back in twenty minutes. Aoki nodded to himself when he heard what he had to say.

At 11:10 A.M. the internal phone rang, and Superintendent Motono said, "Never rains but it pours. We've found Hatano—or a fellow of that name, who answers the description—on a slab at the central morgue. He was filled with bullets last night at Shibuya Hospital. A yakuza hit. He'd just had an eye operation. They're printing the corpse, but *you* get out to the morgue and identify him. I'm sending men to the hospital."

Aoki sat, gazing across the busy room. Could it really be the angry, fish-slitting bastard? The news item he'd read coming in on the train flashed back. He slipped the disk of his report into his pocket, put on his overcoat, and went on his way.

Hatano, all right. The chef's face was stamped with the anger of his last moment—though the guy's face had never showed anything except an evil temper. Aoki counted six bullet wounds on the naked corpse. The left eye was surgically bandaged. Go stones were as lethal off the board as on it! The attendant slid the tray back into the wall; the autopsy was to be done at 1:00 P.M.

In his overcoat, a cigarette stuck between his lips, Aoki paced the room. Had Saito—he couldn't think of him as Yamamoto, his Osaka Go-competition identity—had the chef, with his dangerous knowledge, taken out? Blasted full of holes in a hospital bed? That would've tickled Saito's crazy funnybone. Sans flowers, all right. Had he put his damned wig back on and done the job himself? The last thought came without a trace of humor.

Aoki gave the central morgue's room a long stare. He might've sealed the chef's fate when he revealed to Saito that he knew of his grotesque culinary obsession, of Colonel Oto—*if* that was his obsession, and *if* there was a connection with the dead colonel. He shrugged. Whatever the reason, Hatano deserved his fate. Aoki turned on his heel and left. He'd go to the hospital and see what they'd turned up on the killing.

He was heading for the subway when his cell phone rang. He answered it on the move and pulled up. For a second he couldn't believe the voice he was hearing. "Where are you?" he gasped. Instantly he was breathing hard.

They were fifty yards away, in the coffee shop next to the public health building that accommodated the morgue. Almost in a dream, he retraced his steps. He entered through the revolving door. The dream evaporated, and excitement was pulsing in him.

Kazu Hatano and her twin sister rose from their table as one, bowing. Spellbound, Aoki stared at them, then belatedly responded. His eyes were wide, and the skin of his face felt tight. His left hand had gone to the mole on his cheekbone. They had on street clothes. Coats and hats. Each different, but to Aoki the faces were identical. Sad and worried faces. He pulled out a chair. This was a shock—and a wonder.

Kazu Hatano was on the left; now he could see that. The stamp of the manager-proprietor gave her an air of authority. Her sister, who'd been in his arms, was soft and self-effacing. Kazu Hatano smiled, a brief shadow of a smile, doubtless at the expression on his face. "We've come here to attend to the formalities for our father. You know about that?" Aoki nodded quickly. "And we wish to talk to you." She hesitated. "The time's come for that."

The familiar voice with its mountain accent seemed to be filling Aoki's head.

She looked down at the handbag in her lap, then brought out a paper-clipped sheaf of papers and put them into his hand. "This is a copy of a document our father made two days ago, relating to his connections with Mr. Saito. The man you know by that name." Aoki continued to stare into her eyes. "He intended to send it to Mr. Saito—telling him that if anything happened to him, the original would be put into the hands of the police. Unfortunately, before this could be done—"

Aoki's mind had moved into gear. The chef had had bad timing throughout.

"Our father has done terrible things." Her voice had dropped. "Things we could never have imagined, that can't be forgiven. Much of it forced upon him by Mr. Saito." She paused; this was an ordeal. "*Too* much. We can't discuss it." The freckles were covered up this morning, but as if he had X-ray vision Aoki could see each one of them. Her eyes showed her pain; nonetheless, they were unwavering. "We could only bear to read a part of it."

Aoki nodded, glanced through the four sheets of paper, then nodded again. He folded the document in two and put it in his breast pocket.

She said, "My father asked me to find a lawyer. To accompany him to the interview." *What an experience for her, for the lawyer,* Aoki thought. "The original is in a safe place and can be provided. My phone number is here."

The sister wasn't going to speak, that was plain. Aoki couldn't stop himself staring at her beautiful red-painted lips. The face was inscrutable behind makeup, having thoughts he couldn't even guess at.

Kazu Hatano placed a small sheet of green paper before him. "Mr. Saito may be found here. Under *this* name."

Aoki stared down at the Aoyama address. Oto! His mouth fell open. That name. His true identity? The one at rock bottom for him to slot back into? He looked up at her. "How did they find your father?"

Huskily, she said, "He wasn't an intelligent man. We believe he may have telephoned Mr. Saito from the hospital. That his call was traced."

Aoki nodded slowly. Saito wouldn't have wasted any time. He wondered how much the prefecture detectives had found out from her. He'd see the report . . . According to Saito, these women were the beneficiaries of Ito's will. Had that been the reason for the banker's visit to her office on the eve of his death?

She said, "Inspector Aoki, you've been good to me, to our family. We . . . I will never forget it." She bowed deeply.

They hurried away to make the funeral arrangements. The body would be released in three days, Kazu Hatano had said, as if discussing the laundry schedule at the ryokan. Family duty. No sentiment—except for the deep dishonor.

When they'd gone, Aoki ordered black coffee and thought about the two women. What a wonder! He was still under their spell. He stared into the coffee when it came. At the ryokan the physicality of Kazu Hatano, the sight, sound, and scent of her, had consumed him. For him, something had begun. Briefly, he'd thought of a future, tenuous, but a possibility.

There wasn't one now. He was under suspicion, and his blood was on the Fatman, and in his garden. He no longer heard his wife, but, if that time hadn't passed, he thought that she might have told him, *I'm so sorry, Hideo.*

Eventually, his mind released these thoughts and went on into territory just as tricky. He glanced at the sheet of green paper and shook his head. Oto! This Go-playing yakuza boss who'd called himself Saito, this director of a large construction group, would know who'd killed ex-governor Tamaki; he had looked into Inspector Hideo Aoki and, expertly, had read what his ultimate intentions for the Fatman would be. It hadn't been the bastard's intention that he'd survive to do *anything*. But he had survived. If Oto/Saito were arrested, Aoki had no doubt that he'd point the finger straight at him—as the Fatman's killer.

Perspiration had sprung out on the detective's brow. He lit a cigarette and absorbed the tobacco taste. He touched the Band-Aided wound. Whichever way he turned, he was fucked. Immediately he stubbed out the cigarette. He'd go to Aoyama and have a look at the twelfth floor of this building; then maybe he could get his thinking straight. He left the coffee shop, stepping into a misty noon.

En route to the Aoyama address, his cell phone rang. "What's the result?" Superintendent Motono asked.

"It's him, all right. Hatano the chef, six holes in the corpse. I'm going to the hospital to interview the witnesses."

"Superintendent Shimazu wants to talk to you, Inspector. He's out at Hakone. Be in his office at 6:00 P.M. They've found shoe prints in Tamaki's sand garden, and blood that isn't his on his kimono. It's routine. Nothing a DNA test and a look at your shoes won't sort out. It was a .45—one shot in the chest."

Feeling cold in his heart, Aoki said, "A .45, eh? It'd take that caliber to stop the Fatman." He put his phone away. The chill was spreading in him. There'd been a trace of irony in Motono's voice. Events were taking over, and his thinking was suddenly much straighter about his future. At a kiosk he picked up a chocolate bar, and ate it as he went.

The building was a stubby, modern glass box, its top six floors taken up by the construction group. The twelfth floor, the note said. It was the highest. Concentrating hard, Aoki decided that at this stage he wanted to see without being seen. He rode the elevator to the sixth floor. It was the main reception area.

The receptionist rose and bowed, and Aoki produced the name card of the Go administrator at Osaka. He'd thought of something. "Is Mr. Yamamoto available, please? I met him at the Go competition in Osaka, and as I'm visiting Tokyo I wish to pay my respects."

The girl looked puzzled. "We have no Mr. Yamamoto here, sir."

Aoki threw his hands up in despair. "There were so many people at the competition. I must've got his name confused with someone else."

Her pretty brow showed concentration. "Our Director *Oto* was in Osaka last week."

Aoki smiled tightly. "*That's* the name."

"Please see his private secretary on the twelfth floor."

Aoki reentered the elevator. He sighed with relief when the door opened at the twelfth floor to show a lobby divided from the executive suite by a glass wall and a security door. Behind the glass, at her desk, another secretary glanced up as he appeared. Ignoring the security door, he strolled to a sofa as though killing time, sat down, picked up a newspaper, and began to read it. Peeking over the top of the paper, he could see down a wide passage flanked with chrome containers of shiny-leafed plants. Glass-walled offices opened onto the passage.

Moments later, a well-groomed woman of about thirty walked the length of the passage, hips undulating, carrying papers, going away from Aoki. And there he was, in the blue suit, fifteen paces away, stepping out of a room to talk to the woman. Unmistakable. Saito of the mountain ryokan, minus the hair, Yamamoto of the Osaka Go competition, Oto of this doubtless yakuza-owned construction company with a big problem in a Yokohama project, and probably daimyo of one of the major gangs in Japan. He had his back to Aoki. Swiftly the detective got up and, keeping his own back to the executive suite, crossed to the elevator. The few seconds it took to ascend to the floor seemed like minutes. As he went through its door, his eye caught the sweep of the security camera, and he swore softly. High up in a corner. He hadn't seen it.

In the traffic-saturated street, he grimaced. Maybe he hadn't been spotted, but in a place like that that was hard to believe.

He took the 3:15 P.M. train out to Kamakura, thinking it all over, and went to the bar where he'd spent so much time in recent months. One thing, Oto wasn't going anywhere right now, unless he put on that false hair and came after Hideo Aoki! He ordered a Heineken and slowly read Hatano's affidavit. The chef's stark, semiliterate story brought into focus the one he'd been compiling in his head. He'd been on the right track. Saito and Hatano went back to 1990, when the Go-player became a patron of the Osaka One restaurant. The eatery had crashed because of Hatano's drug habit. Aoki shook his head; he'd missed that, though the signs were there.

Saito had tracked down the bankrupt chef in his seedy Osaka apartment. The drug addict was startled to find out that Saito and an aged uncle, a former officer in the imperial army, were into much more exotic fare than he'd served at Osaka One. It was a question of health and vigor, long life and sexual prowess—*and* Saito's taste for the grotesque. Money talked, and a few times a year special supplies arrived for Hatano's refrigerator, brought by a shadowy gangster the morning of the periodic dinners that Hatano prepared and served at an obscure inn. Saito used his Osaka identity, Yamamoto, for his dealings with the chef.

It had also been a question of history. The colonel had developed a taste for this dining in wartime China and inducted his nephew into it. That was what Hatano understood. Then the old man died.

Aoki sipped beer and read on. Into the picture came the journalist Nagai, who'd met Saito across the Go table. Hatano didn't know how Nagai had gotten his information, but in a matter of days Nagai had written his pieces and been eliminated by Saito. Saito had dined solo on the journalist's liver. Hatano had had enough and fled to the family's ryokan at the other end of Japan. It had been a safe haven until the past had caught up with everyone.

Aoki ordered another bottle of beer and moved on to Kamakura Inn. Each had had a shock, finding the other there. The meeting had an interesting potential for Saito, an unpleasant one for Hatano. Aoki looked up and stared across the bar. It wasn't such an amazing coincidence. Saito had come to the ryokan in pursuit of Ito and Yamazaki, who were there because of Madam Ito—as was the chef. They'd all been in a kind of dance of common destination, incestuous connection, fate. And the devil had been calling the tune!

The chef hadn't known about the underpinning of Saito's vendetta with the Tokyo finance chiefs, just as they hadn't known of Saito's connection to the Yokohama company they'd pulled the plug on. Aoki stared out at the shadowy park. It was clear now. Ito and Yamazaki hadn't come up against the daimyo. Probably even Governor Tamaki hadn't known this daimyo under any name. Sure as hell, the Fatman had his connections to the yakuza, but it was a labyrinth, and Saito, a big fish, had been too deep in it, even for the Fatman. But *he* knew them all.

Aoki drank more beer and continued reading. Saito'd soon brought Hatano into that picture, including the outcome proposed for the Tokyo cop. He was now committed to putting Hatano to good use, and Hatano hadn't had a say in it; his Osaka activities hung over his head like a sword. "We'll do it tonight, and then leave immediately," Saito had said, but the snowstorm had terminated that plan.

Saito had killed Yamazaki, and the chef had done the carving up. Saito had decapitated the bodyguard, Shoba. They'd both taken care of Ito. Hatano had gone after Aoki with the sword in the anteroom while Saito slipped away. Saito's kimono had been liberally sprayed with Shoba's blood, and the chef had burned it in the big stove. On the flight from the ryokan, Hatano had dumped the two women and shadowed Saito back to Tokyo. Why? The chef was silent on his reasons, but it was rat-cunning in action. An investment in his future safety. He must've had a lot of luck in pulling it off.

But a fatal move, Aoki thought. His visit to the twelfth floor of the Aoyama building had the same potential.

The story was sordid and bizarre, but it had the ring of truth. He put the papers aside, poured another beer, and gazed at it for fifteen minutes without tasting it.

He wasn't going to make that 6:00 P.M. appointment with Superintendent Shimazu. He was going home to do some work on the computer, and now he'd have to move fast. He stood up, put on his coat, and left the bar. He'd worked out what lay ahead for Hideo Aoki. Now that he looked back, a path like this had been laid out from the day Tokie had died.

He headed for his apartment across the park. It was getting darker and colder. The park habitués had disappeared. Aoki swept his eyes around, searching for figures, movement. A breeze brushed at his sparse hair. In the middle distance, a piece of white paper blew in fits and starts across a graveled area. Nothing else. But he knew he should be alert. His street cop's vibes were pinging. He loosened the pistol in its holster, and the burred metal butt felt like the surest thing in his life, and in his future.

According to the chef, Saito had carried a pistol at the ryokan, but only knife work would do—and a piece of rope. Aoki tasted his healing lips. It was a craziness in the case, in Saito, that he still hadn't come to grips with, maybe never would.

At the door to his building he stepped into the foyer and, hidden from the street, watched. Again nothing, but his street smarts were still giving him a warning.

He'd made two big mistakes: The misfire had caused him to leave his footprints and his blood in Tamaki's garden; and tonight he'd exposed himself to that security camera.

He worked on his old word processor for an hour, adding to the report he'd done at headquarters, and then put in the four pages of Hatano's affidavit. Finally, he added his suspicions about the arrested prosecutor from the Osaka district office: his link to the 1999 body-parts case and the journalist Nagai's murder. The young Osaka detective had reported that the prosecutor had gone to pieces and was singing about his latest activities. Aoki was convinced that he had a song to sing about Saito and the Nagai case, too. He added the daimyo's name and address almost as a throwaway postscript. *Oto!* Then he gave Kazu Hatano's phone number. He was reluctant to do it, but they'd need to talk to her, and they'd need the original of the affidavit.

He made another disk.

No coffee left. Just a few liquor bottles, and he poured a shot of Suntory whiskey into a glass and drained it down for warmth. He sat with his memories in the chilly room. For years, Tokie had gently reminded him of his promise that they should, at least once in their lives, take the night walk up Mount Fuji to greet the dawn of a new day. In this season he didn't know how far he'd get up the mountain, but that was what he was going to do tonight. He glanced at his watch: 7:15. He'd missed his appointment, and Shimazu and his men would be looking for him.

Aoki went to his room and put on thick rubber-soled walking shoes, then the cable-stitch sweater she'd knitted. He transferred his pistol in its holster to his belt. He'd prepared two envelopes for the disks. They bore a miscellany of postage stamps he'd taken from a tin. He put on his overcoat and left the flat, leaving the lights on. He wouldn't be coming back. In the portico, he stared at the bonsai plants. They'd survived their trip to the mountains; he could do nothing more for them now.

The streets of Kamakura were windswept. People were mainly inside bars and restaurants; just a sprinkling in the streets, innocent citizens going about their business. Ones who weren't innocent were there, too, but out of sight. He felt it even stronger. He walked fast and reached the station in ten minutes. He turned a corner onto the concourse, quickly slipped the two envelopes into a mailbox, then bought a ticket from a machine and went onto the platform.

Five minutes to wait. Twenty or so persons waiting. Aoki sat on a bench and stared at a chrome-framed vending machine. The colorful cans and bottles were in pristine rows, waiting for coins. How many times had he stared at these gleaming refreshment machines? All his life he'd used them, would rank as a gold-class customer if such existed. He watched a youngish, shaved-skull monk in a red robe, with steel-framed glasses, feed in coins and retrieve a can, then turn away flipping it expertly in his hand. A vending-machine-savvy monk.

He'd waited on this bench with Tokie. He remembered once she'd laid her hand on his arm, a gesture of affection, an attempt at communication. He'd deliberately ignored it, committed to his street world, his street thoughts, his tough persona. She'd flitted through his life like a painted butterfly on a screen or a fan. He'd never once held her hand. Well, he would tonight, as they climbed Mount Fuji.

His eyes kept moving. The train was coming. Aoki took a seat where he could see the entire carriage. At Central station he'd take another train, then a taxi to the base of Mount Fuji, where he'd start their walk.

He gazed out the window at the dense suburbs, and without warning, the picture of Saito began to emerge. Fragments came slipping toward him fast, twisting and jerking, as though under pressure, to be slotted into his mind's eye like pieces into a colored glass window. Like Go stones onto a board. In twenty years of dealing with criminals, he thought he'd seen it all. The pathologically violent, the devious and corrupt, and the rest of it, but Saito had transcended it all. He was the arch-criminal, the user of Kazu Hatano's devil's gate. A psycho who played the grimmest games of all, who relished blood and brutality and everything right out to the limits of existence. A joker to whom haiku and Zen mottoes on scrolls were black-edged embroidery.

Inspector Aoki gazed at the Tokyo night and let it wash over him like an incoming tide. In this trade, in this life, there was always deeper and darker, waiting to be found out. Compared to this fiend, the Fatman had been almost an apprentice.

The train arrived at Tokyo Central station at 8:47 P.M. He wasn't thinking about anything now except their walk. He fed in coins and extracted a ticket from another machine. Fifteen minutes to wait. He bought a paper cup of coffee from a dispenser and stood sipping it with his back to the wall near the kiosk, watching the concourse. Salarymen starting their homeward trek passed in review, most of them glum, a few red-faced and boisterous. The Tokyo life: a daily three or four hours of deadly earnest commuting, maybe relieved by a manga comic, or evening alcohol. Life . . . ?

Inspector Aoki drained the cup, crumpled it, and dropped it in a trash can. Ten minutes to wait. He walked across the concourse to the men's room, entered, and urinated against porcelain. The train journey would take about one hour.

He turned and found a large man in his path, motionless, staring at him with great concentration.

"Ahh!" Aoki went for his belt, but the snub-nosed automatic was already in the man's hand. The punch in the chest turned Aoki halfway around, and as he fell the sound of the shot exploded with deafening force in the white-tiled space. He was on his back, his pistol still in his belt. He tried to lever himself up on an elbow, trying to reach it, but couldn't. The big man was moving toward him, the automatic extended, reaiming.

All feeling was flowing out fast through Aoki's extremities; his eyes were blurring. Mount Fuji was in the mist. In that mist the red-gowned monk was launched in the air, a human missile heading for the man who was still sighting his gun on Aoki. Then a red robe was flying and a suit was being propelled into the gurgling urinals.

Chapter Twenty=Six

FOR THE SECOND TIME THAT fall, Aoki reentered his life. This time he found himself in the intensive care unit of Shibuya Hospital, though that detail only became fully apparent to him the next day. A nurse, a blur of white face and white gown, told him he was going to be fine. He seemed to remember her voice talking to him in a misty past. Five days he'd been here, she said.

The next day, he was moved from the ICU to a private room. Later, the nurse from the ICU came down to see him there. "You should know," she said, "that Miss Kazu Hatano was here each day. She sat by your bed for the time permitted."

Aoki felt that he was adrift in a boat on a lake, like the fishermen painted on the scroll in the ryokan's corridor outside the anteroom, and only dreamily took in what she said.

He was properly awake the following day, and recent events began to come back. The shooting was the first: the guy with the gun, the red-gowned monk. Then the Aoyama building; exposing himself to the security camera had been careless. What was going on with Saito-Oto? He'd sent one of the disks to the director general, the other to the journalist Minami—five days ago? He lifted his head from the pillow to look out the window at a misty sky—as if to check that days still passed . . .

Then ex-governor Tamaki, in his moonlit garden, stepped forward. Aoki dropped his head back on the pillow. By now, they'd have checked out the DNA from the Fatman's garden; he guessed there would've been enough of his blood on the floor of the station urinal to run a hundred tests. He gazed across the room at a picture that resembled the one at the mental clinic.

Aoki slept till evening, when he was awakened by a nurse who was taking his blood pressure. "You've got colleagues coming to see you tomorrow afternoon," she said. "Perhaps they're coming to give you a medal?"

Aoki was puzzled, wondering what she knew, but he kept silent. *They'll be coming to read me my rights,* he thought. He didn't sleep that night until they brought him a pill; then he went under.

The next day he was fatalistic yet nervous. At 3:00 P.M. Superintendent Shimazu put his head in the door. "Ah," he said, and stood aside. Director General Omori walked in and strode to the bedside. Superintendent Motono followed him in.

"How are you feeling, Inspector?" the DG asked.

Aoki tried to sit up. "Much better."

"Much better than some others we know about," Shimazu said with a touch of humor, pulling up a chair for the DG.

Aoki looked nonplussed.

The DG sat down. "You don't know?" he said, frowning.

"He's been in the ICU, unconscious, sir," Shimazu said, in case it had slipped the CIB chief's memory.

"Hmmm . . . The daimyo, Oto, alias Saito, et cetera, and two of his men were shot dead on Tuesday night when we attempted to arrest them at Aoyama."

"One of my men was wounded," Shimazu said. "Not serious."

Aoki blinked a few times at the news. He'd need time to think about this.

The DG cleared his throat. "It was extremely irregular to send that disk to the newspaperman Minami." His voice held a condemnatory tone, though in recent days, since the situation had unfolded, he'd quieted down and his blood pressure had improved. In the uneasy silence, the DG gazed at some mystery in his mind. They all understood that Aoki had not intended to survive that night.

What are they waiting for? Aoki wondered.

The DG placed his hairy hands, palms down, on the bed's white cover. "The daimyo's death and the information from Hatano have cleared up the ryokan murders case—and Hatano's. We're assembling the evidence. Also the Osaka journalist's—linked to the body-parts case. That prosecutor has tied it up nicely."

Shimazu said, "Doubtless the reporter Kimura's death is connected, but unfortunately there are no real leads on that." Superintendent Motono hadn't said a word.

Aoki moved his eyes over the three policemen, waiting.

The DG cleared his throat again. "Governor Tamaki's murderer is still at large," he said, as if it were totally unrelated to anything else that had been said. Aoki had put nothing about the Fatman's death in his report on the disk. Omori shook his head. "Superintendent Watanabe's tragic accident has shocked us all." He got up suddenly. "All right, we'll expect you back on duty as soon as possible." He nodded at Aoki. At the door he halted and turned his head, but not his solid torso. "For once, I can feel happy about monks," he said to them all, then left.

Shimazu frowned at the picture on the wall and rubbed his chin, as though he were carefully assembling phrases in his mind. He turned to the man in the bed. "Inspector, certain parties were quite happy to see Governor Tamaki exit the scene. Those parties don't see any advantage in raking over his past activities." He shrugged. "Of course, his murder will be fully investigated, but I have to say that we don't have any promising leads."

Amazement was sweeping through Aoki. He glanced at Superintendent Motono, who didn't look happy. Aoki could see on his face his dislike of solutions based on expediency and lies, which flushed questions of morality down the toilet. Obviously the DG hadn't wanted to be present for this part of the visit.

Then they were gone, too.

The next afternoon most of his old team came out as a group. Assistant Inspector Nishi made a short speech. "Someone finished the job for us with Tamaki," he said. "Good luck to the guy." They'd brought out issues of the *Tokyo Shimbun* in which Minami had broken the story of the ryokan murders and the Osaka case. Aoki's photograph and Saito's were together on the front page. The DG was prominently mentioned for his personal involvement in the cases.

Aoki was thinking better now. The government didn't want the kind of anarchy exposed that saw a police officer taking out a prominent politician. But there'd be a price to pay. Lying there in the long healing nights, he knew that. Shimazu had been careful not to say it, but from now on a number of people would have their eye on him. He'd be a marked man, and you could never know when the politicians might come knocking on his door, with some little commission in mind.

Five days later, Inspector Aoki went home. He was to return to duty shortly, and in the meantime he took his father's short walks to the temple and spent some time at the bar. He read a headline saying that the Tokyo Citizens Bank had been merged with another city bank. Day by day, the aching of the wound near his heart was fading.

He'd thought a great deal about that last night when he was heading for the slopes of Mount Fuji. Providence, or fate, had intervened in the form of the yakuza and the red-robed monk. The monk had come to see him at the hospital. From behind his steel-rimmed glasses he'd looked Aoki over, as though he owned him. He stayed only a short while and hardly spoke; a Zen karate instructor, Aoki had found out from a police colleague.

Tokie's bonsai plants had survived. His old uncle had reappeared, like the semi-ghost he was, to serve him in another emergency. The small clipped plants were healthy, although, in tune with their bigger brothers and sisters, they'd dropped their leaves.

One morning the doorbell rang. It was a messenger with a wicker basket. "What is this?" Aoki asked the man.

"It's a cat, sir."

To Aoki's astonishment, it was.

The tabby cat walked calmly out of the container and rubbed against his legs. Aoki bent down to stroke her. Here was a flesh-and-blood message from the ryokan. From Kazu Hatano, he knew instantly, but how to interpret it? "Well, you're a detective, aren't you?" he muttered. Even as he said that, he remembered that each day she'd been at his bedside in the ICU while he was unconscious—hadn't the nurse said?

Aoki felt a spreading lightness in his heart.

"Okay, Cat," he said, "let's take a look around. I don't think there are any mice here, but in summer there are nice fat frogs in the pond."

Author's Note

My grateful acknowledgment to Yasunari Kawabata's *The Master of Go*, from which I have drawn some facts and information on the famous Go match played in 1938.